**This was a man who** ~~wouldn't hurt her. Every~~ **bone in her body sensed this. He would die before raising a hand to strike her.**

Perhaps even die fighting to keep her safe from others who did. Cooper Johnson was a Navy SEAL who had sacrificed much for his country, and his code of honor extended far beyond his military service.

In the end, he broke the kiss, drawing in a deep sigh, the blue of his gaze darkened. Trembling, Meg stared up at him, licking her lips.

He pressed a finger against her wet mouth.

"Don't do that. Makes me want to kiss you all over again."

"What's stopping you?"

A rueful grin touched his own mouth. Cooper tugged at the jeans that obviously felt too tight. "A certain something that's urging me to do more than kiss you."

\* \* \*

**We hope you enjoyed this exciting installment in the SOS Agency miniseries!**

\* \* \*

**If you're on Twitter, tell us what you think of Harlequin Romantic Suspense! #harlequinromsuspense**

Dear Reader,

Who doesn't want a sexy cowboy Navy SEAL to come riding into her life to save her from the villain?

Meg Taylor doesn't.

Meg is a wealthy, but penniless, woman on the run from an abusive ex-husband who controls all her money. Meg wants justice, but the last thing she wants is hunky Navy SEAL Cooper to protect her.

Cooper Johnson is on leave from the Navy and takes Meg in as a favor to Jarrett Adler, whose SOS underground railroad promises Meg safe shelter. The troubled beauty shatters all his barriers and threatens the one thing he fears most—losing his heart.

Domestic abuse is a crime that is too often hidden in the shadows of real life. Many women are afraid to leave their abusive partners. In past travels for my day job, I've met poor women who were battered and abused by their husbands, and I've worked with nongovernmental organizations that aid these victims. When the survivors have the means to leave their abusive homes and start a new life, their transformation is a wonderful thing to behold. They blossom like sunflowers, always looking upward at the light, instead of at the darkness of their past.

Meg and Cooper were two characters I enjoyed creating: a heroine and hero who deserve their happy ending. I hope you enjoy their love story— one of courage and loyalty, and learning to have faith in each other.

Happy reading!

*Bonnie Vanak*

# SHIELDED BY THE COWBOY SEAL

—

**Bonnie Vanak**

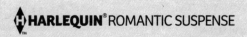

HARLEQUIN® ROMANTIC SUSPENSE

Recycling programs
for this product may
not exist in your area.

ISBN-13: 978-0-373-40200-7

Shielded by the Cowboy SEAL

Copyright © 2017 by Bonnie Vanak

**HARLEQUIN**®
www.Harlequin.com

**Printed in U.S.A.**

*New York Times* and *USA TODAY* bestselling author **Bonnie Vanak** is passionate about romance novels and telling stories. A former newspaper reporter, she worked as a journalist for a large international charity for several years, traveling to countries such as Haiti to report on the sufferings of the poor. Bonnie lives in Florida with her husband, Frank, and is a member of Romance Writers of America. She loves to hear from readers. She can be reached through her website, bonnievanak.com.

### Books by Bonnie Vanak

### Harlequin Romantic Suspense

#### SOS Agency
*Navy SEAL Seduction*
*Shielded by the Cowboy SEAL*

### Harlequin Nocturne

#### Phoenix Force
*The Shadow Wolf*
*The Covert Wolf*
*Phantom Wolf*
*Demon Wolf*

*The Empath*
*Enemy Lover*
*Immortal Wolf*

In memory of Lora Celmer-Donato,
who couldn't escape.

# Chapter 1

The late-autumn snowstorm promised to be a killer and her car was dead.

Fat flakes swirled lazily in the wind outside the battered 2010 sedan. A curtain of darkness had fallen, turning the pretty country road ink black. She should have checked the battery before leaving Florida. Certainly it would have saved her from being stranded here on a lonely stretch of New Hampshire road.

Meg August—no, she was Meg Taylor now; the "August" part of her life was back in Palm Beach with her soon-to-be ex-husband—tried the engine again. Nothing. She turned and looked at her traveling companion. "Well, Sophie, looks like we are up a particular creek without a paddle or a life raft."

*Woof!*

Snug inside her pink-and-black Louis Vuitton dog purse, Sophie licked her hand. Shivering, Meg patted the dog's head. She'd stopped to let Sophie out for a rest break and the car had died. The icy rain had turned to snow, but not before soaking her blue suede jacket. Perfect for chilly nights in south Florida. Not so perfect for this.

Meg removed the wet jacket and tossed it onto the backseat. Clad only in a thin yellow sweater and black linen trousers, she kept shivering. She went to rub her arms and winced.

Her left arm still felt tender. Prescott's fists had landed there two weeks ago, shortly after she confronted him about her discovery that he'd shipped out defective body gear manufactured by Combat Gear Inc., the company she'd founded to provide quality, low-cost body armor to US soldiers and law enforcement personnel. Not only did he authorize the shipments months ago, but he'd filed the incorporation papers for Combat Gear Inc. with her first and middle initials, Margaret Elizabeth, and her maiden name, Franklin, as the CEO.

She was the one responsible for any deaths resulting from use of those vests. She had to make this terrible wrong right.

Prescott disagreed. When she'd threatened to call the authorities, he beat her. The bruises were myriad rainbow colors instead of black. She could silently endure his growing rages.

But she would not stand for others getting hurt because of her product.

She'd called her former college roommate, Lacey Adler. Asking for help was the hardest thing she'd had to do since burying her grandmother a week ago. Lacey told her about her charity that helped women flee their abusive husbands.

She'd asked for a safe house in New England, and Lacey had given her directions to a remote farmhouse in New Hampshire. Cooper Johnson, a Navy SEAL friend of Lacey's husband, Jarrett, agreed to give her shelter through Project SOS Securities, his security firm.

Cooper would give her a place to stay with Sophie as long as she needed. She'd be safe. Coop, as he was called, was great with dogs.

Meg hated relying on strangers. But she needed a hiding place until she could obtain the proof that Prescott knew the body gear was defective.

If Prescott didn't find and kill her, the New England storm surely would.

Now, they were parked alongside a dark road, no one in sight. She glanced down at her fashionable clothing. Perfect for leaving Palm Beach and avoiding suspicion from any of her neighbors.

Not so perfect for braving the chilly temperatures of the north. She tried turning the ignition again. Nothing.

After putting Sophie on the backseat, Meg climbed over the console and joined her. She reached for her grandmother's antique quilt, her most precious possession, and wrapped it around them both. Sophie wagged her tail and licked Meg's face, as if to offer reassurance.

Shivering, she curled up next to Sophie, the cold spiking her body like steel nails, and said a little prayer for some kind stranger to find them.

And not her soon-to-be ex-husband.

Cooper "Coop" Johnson rubbed the shoulders of the quivering mare. "Easy, girl," he murmured.

Betsy was going on thirty, and had a mild case of colic. Colic had already killed one horse on the Sunnyside Farm, and he wasn't about to see his baby sister's favorite mare succumb to it. He walked her around the barn, mindful of her arthritis, rubbing her down, hoping the heavy blanket would help.

Jarrett, his former squad leader from the teams, had asked him to give refuge to a woman in trouble. Coop agreed because he would do anything for his ex-boss, but family came first these days. He'd taken leave from the Navy to help his mom run the bed and breakfast while her sister's family visited relatives in Oregon. Mid-November was the slow time, so his aunt, uncle and their three sons decided to combine a family wedding with a much-needed vacation while Coop helped out with the farm and inn.

They'd closed the inn after his oldest sister, Brie, had died. Fiona, his mother, had reopened it two months ago, but with the approaching winter, only a few guests had registered. Keeping horses was expensive. Summer boarders helped pay for food and overhead. Those boarders had packed away their mounts into shiny trailers and headed south.

Probably to Florida, where it was warm.

Or Palm Beach, where it was warm and wealthy, where his assignment was supposedly traveling from.

Meg. He didn't know anything about her, other than the photo Jarrett sent and the fact that she lived in wealthy Palm Beach and she needed a place to stay while her divorce was being finalized.

No one would take her in because her dog was vicious and bit people.

Jarrett said Meg's money was all tied up until the divorce and she couldn't afford a pet-friendly hotel. Coop doubted she was in trouble. The photo Jarrett sent showed a brunette woman who looked like a beauty queen dripping in diamonds. But it wasn't his place to judge, just give her shelter.

All Jarrett had told him was that Meg had a dog that Coop needed to train. He refused to share anything else out of respect for Meg, who was supposed to arrive six hours ago.

Maybe she had to stop somewhere to buy the dog a prime rib dinner.

Coop stopped walking Betsy and placed her in the stall. "Good girl," he crooned.

His sister had had a way with animals, and could always make Betsy better.

Betsy nosed around, looking for the carrot Brie had always placed there as a treat. Coop's throat tightened. He stroked her withers.

"I'm sorry, sweetheart. You can't eat yet, not until you get over this colic."

Betsy whinnied.

"I know," he whispered, laying his head against the horse. "I miss her, too. But I promise, I'm going to do everything she would have to get you well again."

Giving her a final pat, he headed outside, pulling up the collar of his faded sheepskin jacket. Dark storm clouds had blotted out the moon, and the night had turned wicked cold.

Inside the house, he went into the private family living room and found his mom sitting by the fireplace in the rocker Brie had always liked to use when she was home. Fiona glanced up, lines furrowing her brow.

"How's Betsy?" she asked.

"Better." Not exactly a lie, but he wasn't going to worry his mom any more than necessary. "Horses are all fed, bedded down. They'll be fine. And the guests?"

"They left a while ago. They wanted to get a head start away from the storm. I refunded the rest of their stay."

Cooper wanted to protest, but his mother's warning look stayed him. "Why?" he asked.

"Return business is important, Cooper. I didn't want them to think we put our guests' safety last and money first."

It sounded like a wonderful principle, but it wouldn't pay the bills. They were okay for now, but the first payment on the refinance of the farm was due soon.

Not to mention the costs of burying Brie…

He rubbed at the tightness in his chest. Sabrina was only

twenty-six when a stray bullet pierced her body armor. She'd been responding to a routine domestic disturbance call with her partner. The husband shot them both, but Brie's partner wore the standard departmental body armor.

He lived.

Brie died.

Cooper had purchased the armor especially for his baby sis when she started working as a beat cop in dangerous areas of the city. He didn't want her having the standard body armor the department issued. He wanted the best.

Now Brie lay six feet under, and Combat Gear Inc., the company that produced the defective gear, kept rolling in profits. He would hire a lawyer to sue, but the company's owner, M. E. Franklin, probably had enough money to purchase a cruise ship filled with attorneys. Coop had googled his name, but found nothing. He seemed a total mystery.

All he'd found so far was that the bulletproof vests were invented by Randall Jacobs, vice president of Combat Gear Inc. Coop had done a little more checking and found out the man owned a posh summer home on a lake near here. Once he got over some of his grief, maybe he'd pay the man a visit.

He studied his mother, worried about the purple shadows beneath her eyes. Today had been a tough day. Federal authorities had opened an investigation at last into Brie's death after someone tipped them off about the faulty bulletproof vests. He'd sent the family lawyer to give a statement to the Feds and the media.

Dredging up Brie's death had opened old wounds. For all of them.

Fiona's warm brown gaze sharpened as she looked up at the antique clock on the fireplace mantel. "Isn't your guest overdue? I made up the cottage with fresh linens and blankets, and stacked firewood."

Coop stiffened. "I thought she could stay at the inn."

"She has a vicious dog. Better if she stays in the cottage." His mother gave him a knowing look. "With you."

Uh-oh. He recognized that spark in her eye. "No. Maybe for the night, but, ah, no. I can find a place for the dog." He flexed his hands in their worn leather gloves. The cottage behind the barn, with a fabulous view of the White Mountains, had been Brie's retreat.

"Brie would approve of a woman in trouble staying there," Fiona said in her gentle way. "You can't keep that house as a memorial to your sister, Cooper. You have to let go sometime."

"It hasn't even been six months." He went to the fireplace to warm his chilled body. "And I'm not sure how much trouble this Meg is in. She lives in Palm Beach and she's rich. She looks like a spoiled beauty queen."

"Don't judge. Your friend Jarrett vouched for her. Isn't that enough?"

Guilt pinched him. Coop turned around with a sigh and squinted at the now-darkened skies. "I'll try calling the number he gave me for her cell phone."

But after dialing it, it kept ringing. Fat flakes of snow began to fall as he paced the porch. Coop pocketed his cell and went inside.

"I'd better go look for her."

"Call me when you find her." Fiona always worried ever since Brie's death.

"Of course."

Gathering several blankets, he tugged his wool Stetson low over his brow, pulled up his collar and went outside. A blast of icy air slammed into him, sending a chill snaking down his spine. Cooper climbed into the Ford pickup and started the engine.

Damn nasty night to be outside. Maybe the princess

had decided to sightsee and didn't have the foresight, or the courtesy, to phone and let him know she'd be delayed. But as he drove through the increasing snowflakes, worry niggled him.

Coop knew his irritation masked a greater emotion—grief. It was far easier to give way to anger than to examine the winking light of deep grief that had gripped him since they'd lowered Brie into the ground. He'd refused to cry, held back the tidal wave of sorrow so he could stay strong for his family.

Focus. It was what had gotten him through missions with the team and brought him home alive time after time. He squinted as the truck's headlights barely pierced the thick gloom of snow.

*If she's decided to hole up in some ritzy hotel and I'm out here for nothing, I'll really be pissed.*

But the same tingle that skated down his spine grew stronger. Gut instinct. Had saved his butt a time or two before on missions, so he never ignored it.

Instead of continuing down the main road, he turned off the side road that was a shortcut leading to the farm. Jarrett had given Meg directions, a disposable cell phone that couldn't be tracked, and the fastest way to get to the farm. If Meg used this road and her car had broken down by chance, she'd be doomed because only locals used the shortcut.

And most locals were smart enough to be snug at home, curled up by the fire with mugs of hot chocolate, not riding around in a late-autumn blizzard.

He drove for two miles and was nearly ready to give up when he spotted an older model white sedan parked by the roadside. It looked deserted, but the tingle down his spine intensified.

Cooper parked behind the car and got out. A blast of icy

wind slammed into him, slicing his cheeks like tiny darting needles. Damn, that was cold! The snow had stopped and turned to freezing rain. Driving on these roads was gonna be hell, but the truck was steady and he knew this turf.

His sole concern focused now on the occupant of the car. Using his Maglite flashlight he always carried in the truck, he shone light into the car.

A slender woman and a dog lay on the backseat curled up beneath a quilt. Neither responded as he opened the door. The dome light overhead didn't even turn on.

Damn it! Cooper was glad she'd had the sense not to lock the car doors. He checked her vitals. Alive, but groggy, suffering from the early stages of hypothermia. He gathered her into his arms. His heart raced. She was so tiny and fragile. Storms blew in fast in this region, and what started out as a sunny day could quickly turn into bone-chilling temperatures.

He surveyed the fashionable, ankle-length black suede boots, thin trousers and light sweater. Dressed for a cocktail party, not the northern climate.

The woman, barely conscious, moaned as he picked her up and placed her into the back cab of his truck. Coop covered her with the thick wool blankets, slammed the door shut with the heater running, and returned to the sedan.

A small brown-and-white dog lay on the seat, looking half dead. Its fur was clipped short in a puppy cut and its eyes were closed.

A sparkling rhinestone collar with a heart pendant ringed its fat little neck. Next to it was a fancy-looking dog purse with a gold monogram that looked expensive enough to feed his horses for the next three months.

Despite the freezing rain dripping down his neck, Coop stopped and stared. "This is the vicious killer? I had stuffed animals more ferocious."

Sheesh.

He gathered the dog into his arms and raced to the truck, placing the dog gently on the seat next to Meg. Then he made a quick call to Fiona, assuring his mother he'd found Meg and would return home shortly.

Coop cranked up the heat to full blast, then climbed into the backseat. He removed his jacket and wrapped the dog in it until it resembled a furry burrito.

Had to get this wet clothing off Meg. With a murmured apology, he removed her damp sweater, trying to avoid looking at her breasts, but it was tough. She had lovely breasts, full and generous, and a lacy red bra that was mouthwatering.

Focus.

As he went to drape her in a blanket, he saw enormous yellow and blue bruises on her arm.

Cooper went still. Rage boiled inside him. He gently touched one and heard her moan. Cooper pulled her upper body into his lap and tucked her hands between his thighs, knowing that area held the most warmth.

Yeah, it was doing wonders for his groin, but he'd survive.

Her eyes fluttered open. Green as the Caribbean he loved for scuba diving. Confusion flickered in her irises, then she blinked and panic set in. She tried to pull her hands from between his thighs.

"No," she whispered. "No, please don't make me do that. Please don't hurt me anymore."

Jaw tightening, he forced her hands to remain between his legs. "It's okay," he soothed. "I'm not going to hurt you. You're safe now, but you're in danger of getting hypothermia."

Had to get her back to the cottage, get her warm before the storm got worse. Cooper gently disentangled himself from Meg. The little dog looked up, whined. She'd feel safer with the dog in her arms. As Cooper reached out for the dog, the animal growled.

And promptly bit his hand.

# Chapter 2

Such delicious warmth.

Meg slowly opened her eyes. She'd been back at the car, Sophie curled beside her, wondering how they would survive the storm and not freeze to death. The cold had pierced her bones like icy knives.

And then she'd closed her eyes, trying to keep her dog warm by holding Sophie tight. The nightmare had been too real. Sophie, kicked out of the house by her husband, wandering the streets during a south Florida cold snap. Curling up in a doorway to stay warm, whimpering and afraid, confused as to why her owners had abandoned her...

She drove, as she had in the past when it really happened, searching the streets for her beloved dog. But this time during the nightmare, a handsome stranger picked Sophie into his arms and scowled at Meg, as if blaming her for Sophie's condition.

Now as she stirred, she became aware of lying in a warm bed, blankets piled atop her. A lamp glowed softly on a nightstand.

Meg realized she wore only panties and a bra.

And in addition to being half-naked, there was a hard male body next to her, also half-naked. Panic swept through her. She startled and moved away, but a strong, muscled arm hooked around her waist.

"Relax," a deep male voice said. "You're not going anywhere."

The voice was strange, tinged with amusement and a New England accent. The body belonging to that accent was hardened with thick muscle, not soft with fat like Prescott's. She became aware of the scent of him, all cedar and spicy aftershave, a pleasing masculine smell, not the fancy and expensive cologne disguising the vodka Prescott had consumed far too much lately.

"Get away from me," she mumbled. "Why are you doing this?

"No one dies on my watch, Princess, and you were entering hypothermia. Body heat is the best way of keeping warm. I daresay your little dog knows this, otherwise she'd be nipping at my toes instead of snuggled beneath them."

He added, with a wry sound, "And if you got frostbite, the local doc would have to amputate those pretty pink toes of yours."

She had to get out of here, but oh, the warmth beneath the blankets and the firm, muscled body beside her gave off heat like a blast furnace.

Meg blinked hard, trying to summon precious energy. "Her name is Sophie."

"Should have called her Ouchie."

Meg's mushy brain couldn't register the joke, until she lifted her head and saw her rescuer hold up his hand where a half moon marked the skin. "Bit clean through my glove."

"Oh no! I'm so sorry." Mortified, she struggled to sit up, more concerned about her dog biting a total stranger who had saved them from death than her lack of clothing.

He pushed her down. "Easy now. You need to stay under these covers a while longer."

"My dog…"

"No worries," he said easily. "I trust she's had her shots, and I've had mine, so you needn't worry about your fur-ball getting a disease."

Meg realized he was joking. The tension gripping her sore, tight muscles eased a little. She peered upward to get a closer look at him. A thick shock of wavy dark brown hair was cropped short. He had an intense gaze, thin cheek-bones and a wide mouth. Handsome, with a hint of Irish blood in those ice-blue eyes.

A dusting of black hair covered his muscled chest. Washboard abs rippled beneath smooth, tanned skin. He was mouthwatering, a prime example of masculinity. Meg stared, still struggling with the unreality that this man had rescued her from the cold and warmed her with his body.

"You're Cooper Johnson?"

"The one and only," he drawled. "Your host over the next several days."

She pulled the blankets up to cover her breasts, well aware her lacy red bra provided thin covering in the chill, and her nipples had turned rigid.

From the cold. Not the pull of attraction toward this handsome stranger. It didn't matter if her libido sat up and started shimmying.

All she had to do was think of what Prescott would do if he found her, and her heated blood turned to ice.

"Where's Sophie?"

Cooper lifted the bottom of the blankets. Snuggled at his feet, wedged partly beneath the covers, her dog snoozed. Relief filled Meg. She tossed back the covers, climbed down the length of the bed and gathered her dog into her arms, checking her over anxiously.

"She seems okay." Meg drew in a deep breath as the awakening Sophie licked her face.

Sheer male interest flared on Cooper's face. He rearranged the blankets around his waist. Realizing he must have had a bull's-eye glimpse of her rear end, Meg flushed. She clutched the dog just a little too tightly, and Sophie squirmed.

The interest faded as his expression shuttered. He scratched the bristles on his hard jaw. "You feeling okay now, Princess?"

At her nod, he flung back the blankets, displaying a pair of long, muscled legs. A dusting of hair didn't hide a wicked-looking scar on his left thigh. Her fascinated gaze traveled upward to the black Jockeys he wore…

And the very large bulge beneath them showing a blatant male reaction.

Seems as if Cooper Johnson was equally attracted to her.

Not that she'd do anything about it. Not in her lifetime.

His mouth curved into a knowing smile as he reached down to the floor, retrieved a pair of jeans. Cooper slid into them and stood, buckling the belt.

"Had to get you warm. Can't help the consequences. I'm a guy, and you're a very attractive woman."

He shoved a hand through his thick hair and the move flexed the biceps of his right arm. A tattoo of a snake writhed with the motion as well. Sailors got inked, from what she knew. And he was a Navy SEAL.

Not regular Army, like her brother had been.

SEALs were tough, Lacey had told her, but their missions and lives were shrouded in secrecy. She wondered what happened to him that he was here now with her.

It wasn't her business. She released Sophie and held out her hand. "Thank you for rescuing us, Mr. Johnson. And my name is Meg."

Surprise flickered across his face as he sat on the bed. "Cooper."

His grip was firm, but not crushing, and he quickly released her hand. Then as he started to reach for her, Sophie growled.

Meg gripped her dog. As his gaze landed on her bruised arm, she flinched.

Cooper's gaze narrowed as he muttered a low oath. "Is that what your husband did to you? Jarrett said you were in trouble, but he didn't give details."

"Ex-husband. Soon, anyway. I keep calling him my ex because I've x-ed him out of my life." Meg felt her flush deepen, this time from shame. "It wasn't that bad, this time."

"This time is the last time," he said in a low, deep voice that sent a shiver racing down her spine.

His expression turned intent. Totally concentrated and fierce, as if someone had flipped a switch inside him. She shivered. One would not want to cross him.

"I'm sure you have a story to tell me. Like why you're driving. Why didn't you take Jarrett's offer of a bus ticket here?"

Keen, assessing. Little would escape this man.

"Too slow. I needed my own wheels. And I knew my ex would be able to trace my car, so I bought an older model for cash for the drive here from Palm Beach."

Two nights in cheap motels, trying to sleep, fearing to shut her eyes in case Prescott had sent someone after her...

"Why did you buy such a lemon?"

Meg struggled with her pride. How ironic that she was once the heiress of Taylor Sporting Goods, one of the country's largest producers of sports equipment, and she didn't have a penny.

"I know it sounds implausible, but it's all I could afford.

My ex controlled all the money in our household, and all my accounts."

She'd managed to save a little money and hide it. And she didn't dare use her easily traceable credit cards.

Silence fell between them as he gave a pointed look to the diamond encased in an old-fashioned gold setting hanging from her neck. Meg fingered the necklace. "This was my grandmother's. I suppose you deserve an explanation, since you're kind enough to give me a place to stay."

He rubbed the sexy dusting of dark bristles on his chin. "Let's wait until you're ready. Know this, Meg. We've had dogs on the farm before and mostly they stay outside. Your dog…"

At this pause, she tensed, ready for him to tell her he didn't tolerate dogs who bit and he was going to toss Sophie outside, no matter that it was freezing. Prescott surely would have.

"She's safe here, just as you are. I don't tolerate abuse. Anyone who hits women, children or animals—" his hard blue gaze flickered to Sophie "—even animals who growl at them, will be strictly dealt with. You can relax. No one will get you here."

Relief swept through her. "You're not going to make Sophie stay outside?"

He lifted a dark brow. "In this storm? Relax, she'll stay here with you. I only want one question answered."

She tensed.

"Your last name. Need to know that in case anyone comes asking."

His words sent a shiver of fear sliding through her again. Prescott knew people. Lots of people across the country. "Meg… Caldwell," she said, giving her brother's first name.

Cooper nodded. "Good. I'll let my mom know. She runs the bed and breakfast at our farmhouse."

Doubt filled her. "Is it really safe here? My ex has a lot of money and influence."

"And I have a nine-millimeter and plenty of ammo."

His reassurances should have made her feel safe, but they only made her aware of what kind of danger she placed this man and his family in. She couldn't stay long. Just long enough to recover, figure out a plan and then move on.

Then Meg remembered her suitcase and all her most precious belongings were in the car. She had to retrieve them, snowstorm or no snowstorm. Anyone could find her things and know who they belonged to. One call to Prescott and he'd be here in the corporate jet. Her chest hurt and her heart constricted painfully and she found it hard to breathe.

"My things… I have to get my luggage. The quilt in the car, it's an heirloom."

As her voice rose, he remained calm. Steady. Not ruffled one bit at the hysteria in her voice. "Easy, Princess." He pointed to the closet. "Everything from the car is in there. This is your room for the night. I put your cell in the kitchen on a charger. Your car is dead. I'll have Mike, the local tow truck driver, haul it to his shop and fix it."

"Thank you." She released a deep breath. "If I had someplace else to go, I would have. I don't plan to stay."

That deep blue gaze burned into her. "What about your family?"

Familiar hurt squeezed a tight knot in her chest. "I don't have any. My father died in a car crash shortly after my parents' divorce."

"And your mother?"

She gave a bitter laugh. "She went to Europe to be with her lover after Dad's funeral. I haven't seen her since."

"No brothers, sisters, aunts, uncles?" Cooper gave her a disbelieving look.

"One brother. He was killed in Iraq shortly after he enlisted in the Army."

"I'm sorry." His tone softened. "What unit?"

"Does it matter? He's dead." Meg's chest tightened, making it hard to breathe. Caldwell's reckless disregard for safety while in combat was the reason she wanted to manufacture body armor for soldiers. She thought of her older brother's bright, cheerful grin and how he'd always let her tag along, always promised to be there to keep her safe and happy because their parents didn't care about them...

Caldwell broke that promise the day he enlisted.

"No aunts or uncles?"

"No. I was raised by my grandmother, and her funeral was a week ago." She lifted her chin and gave him the impervious stare used when it was necessary to keep others at bay. "Are you finished with the interrogation yet?"

He gazed around the bedroom. "You and my sister are about the same size. I got you clean, warm clothing from the upstairs guest room in case you didn't pack any winter clothing in your suitcase. You might want to consider wearing it. It'll keep you warm more than those trousers. Feel free to borrow anything else of hers while you are here. Get dressed and meet me in the kitchen. Mom made a pot of stew. It's on the stove."

Her mouth watered at the mention of hot food. The ice inside her melted a little. "It sounds delicious. Thank you. And please, thank your sister for me as well, for lending me her clothing."

Cooper tensed as if someone had shoved a rod down his back. With a nod, he left the room, making her wonder what she had said that made him shut down like that.

What Cooper Johnson felt was none of her concern.

And Meg knew she didn't dare tell him or his family the full truth. Guilt pinched her. He was better off not knowing he'd given shelter to a possible killer.

She needed to regroup and plan and get out of here.

Before Prescott found her, and she endangered anyone else.

# Chapter 3

The princess, no, her name was Meg, was certainly pretty. With those big eyes, the tumbling curls spilling down her curvy backside, generous breasts and wide hips, she was stunning. Coop had always preferred curvy women, and Meg fit the bill.

But she was an assignment for Project SOS, not a potential date. At least she'd had the courtesy to thank him for pulling her rear end out of trouble.

And it was a very nice rear end. He'd gotten a sample as she'd crawled down the bed to get her dog. A thin triangle of red silk stretched across her pretty bottom, the kind of bottom a man could cup and squeeze as he drove deep inside her in the dark of night.

Forget it. She was clearly traumatized and the last thing Meg needed was him panting all over her as if she were steak and he hadn't eaten in a month.

*Well, it has been a few months since you had sex*, his libido cheerfully reminded him.

*Get used to celibacy. We have a job to do.*

He stirred the pot of stew his mom had made, glancing out the window at the darkened skies. The snow was really coming down now, blowing in the fierce wind. He hoped

Betsy was doing okay. Normally he'd spend the night with her in the barn, checking on her. Maybe once he got the beauty queen settled, he'd head there.

She sure was a beauty queen, too. Those big green eyes, perfect cheekbones and lush mouth made for kissing...

Hearing footsteps, Coop spooned out a generous portion of stew into a bowl and set it on the kitchen table upon a hand-sewn place mat, where a spoon rested. Meg entered the kitchen, the dog on her heels. She carried a can of dog food and a monogrammed dog dish and went to the can opener on the counter.

As the opener whirred and clicked, Sophie whined and pawed at Meg.

"Down, Sophie," he said mildly.

The dog sat on her haunches, looked up at Coop and growled again. He shot the furball an amused look as he found a spoon for Meg to dish out the dog food.

"Well, hello to you as well. Don't worry, I'm not going to steal your chow. Mom's stew is much better. But if you're staying here, you will learn manners."

After setting the bowl of dog food on the floor, Meg slid into the seat with an appreciative sigh. "Thank you. This looks delicious."

As he started out of the kitchen, she blinked. "Aren't you eating? I hate to eat alone."

Sighing, he fetched another bowl. Ever since his leave, he kept up with PT, but watched his calories, mindful of his weight. Two dinners tonight. But he'd work it off tomorrow.

He joined her at the table. "It's not filet mignon, but it'll fill you up on a cold night, Princess."

She frowned. "You don't like using my name? Why do you keep calling me 'Princess'?"

Cooper blinked. "You look straight out of the pictures

I've seen of beauty queens. And I give nicknames to every-one. I do on the teams and around here."

"Oh? And what did they call you?"

He considered. "Usually Coop. Farm Boy, too, because I grew up on a farm. Sometimes Beast because I get real ornery when I get hungry."

As they ate, she kept stealing glances at him, maybe wondering if he'd rocket off into a temper because of his beast rep. Knowing she had been abused, he hastened to add, "I may get mean, but that's only around the guys. You'll see."

"I won't be around here long enough to find out," she told him. "This is temporary."

"Doesn't matter if it is, you're going to need new cloth-ing if all you packed are clothes fit for Palm Beach. Like those fancy boots you were wearing." He shook his head. "Totally inappropriate for New England weather."

"Those are my eight-hundred-dollar Jimmy Choos. They're suede," she shot back.

"Jimmy's shoes? Who's Jimmy?"

"Jimmy Choo," she said very slowly, as if conversing with someone with the mental capacity of a three-year-old. "He's a famous designer."

He knew this, knew all about expensive shoes because an ex-girlfriend raved about them. "So you like wearing shoes with a guy's name on them? Your Jimmy's shoes aren't fit for snow and slush and mud. They're worth about ten dollars now at a yard sale."

"What's a yadh?"

"Yard." He spoke slowly. "My accent is coming out. Happens when I get tired. Better get you to a store to-morrow to fetch you some real boots."

"Real boots?" Meg frowned. "What do you wear around here?"

He stuck out his foot. "Tractor Supply. Steel toe."

Meg stared, a look of incredulity on her pretty face. "You expect me to wear Tractor Supply? I expect you'll next want me in Farmer John overalls and a chambray work shirt?"

More like out of them, wearing nothing but skin. He swallowed hard at the mental image. And a pair of red suede pumps with stiletto heels. Coop imagined her wearing those only for him with the crimson panties and bra. Hoo-yah.

He assumed his best poker face to hide his thoughts and adjusted his jeans.

"Jeans will do just fine. We don't put our hired hands to work in fancy yoga pants. You'll need something that will wash out real good after you muck out the stalls." He cocked his head. "You did come here to work in the stables. That's what Jarrett said."

"I, er, no, I…"

Laughing, he waved a hand. "I'm teasing."

"Thanks," she said through gritted teeth. "Not. Lacey didn't tell me you were such fine entertainment."

He sat back, enjoying the glare. Made her eyes all sparkle like Fourth of July. "Got you to stop thinking about it."

"Thinking about what?" Meg dug into her stew and ate a spoonful.

All seriousness now, he glanced down at her dog. "What you're running from."

She didn't look at him. "I didn't pack much. There was no time, and I couldn't risk my ex-husband seeing my warm clothing gone. He'd guess that I fled north."

Wise move. "I'd have done the same. Tomorrow we'll go into town, get you dressed for this weather."

A faint pink flushed her cheeks. "I'll be okay with what I have. I can't afford to pay for it right now…"

Knowing how that admission must have dented her

pride, he softened his voice. "No worries. Part of SOS's services. Jarrett will foot the bill."

The dog gulped down her food and finished, then sat by Meg's side, growling at him. Cooper pointed his soup spoon at Sophie.

"Hey, watch it, mutt, or you won't get dessert."

Meg's mouth curled into the first real smile he'd seen from her. She was so pretty, her mouth all rosebud red, her cheeks flushed.

"Sophie is not a mutt. She is a purebred shih tzu."

"A shih-what?"

"Shih tzu."

"Sounds like something I suffered downrange in Iraq that the medic had to treat with antibiotics," he muttered.

Coop stared in frank bewilderment at the growling mop of fur. Any temporary bond created when he'd rescued the dog had been broken, as evidenced by the bared fangs.

"Sure has a sharp set of teeth for such a little thing."

Guilt flashed across Meg's face. "She's very protective and loyal. Unfortunately, she hates men."

"Selective," he murmured. "Or did she learn from her owner?"

Her big green eyes narrowed in apparent anger. "She learned it from my ex-husband, who tried to starve her to make her mean."

Coop looked at the dog. "You had it rough, huh? Guess I can't blame you for biting me if you thought I was a threat to your mom here."

Meg blinked. "Most people think I'm exaggerating about my ex. He's very well respected in the community. He's on the board of several charities and he's known for his contributions to society."

"That doesn't mean he's not a jerk. What people show in public can be very different from their private lives."

"You believe me?"

She sounded incredulous, as if she'd stated her ex was a little green alien instead of a bastard. Cooper carefully set down his spoon. "I believe the dog. Dogs, like horses, learn to be mean when they're treated badly. It's self-defense."

Judging from the bruises Meg sported and the suspicious looks she cast him, the princess had been treated the same.

"Let me try something." He picked up a piece of meat from his stew and held it out to Sophie. "Look, Sophie. Good stuff."

More growling. Cooper avoided looking straight at the dog. Looking head-on at the canine would indicate aggression. "It's okay. Come on."

Sophie trotted forward, snatched the meat from his outstretched fingers and pranced backward, as if afraid he'd suddenly hit her.

Cooper leaned back, well away from the dog as she ate the meat.

"Good girl," he crooned.

Sophie sat back and licked her nose.

"Lacey told me you're good with dogs. You're a Navy SEAL and Jarrett was your leader. Did you work much with dogs when you were deployed?"

Grief pinched him as he thought of Max. He stiffened. "I'd rather not talk about me. Let's get you and the furball settled for the night."

It took a few minutes for the tour. Meg gripped the dog as he showed them the master bedroom upstairs and the bathroom with the old-fashioned claw-foot bathtub. The guest room where she'd sleep was downstairs next to another bathroom. He stood in the living room, wondering if she'd noticed how worn the plaid sofa was, with bits of fabric fraying at the armrest, or how the chair by the fireplace sagged a little too much.

Beneath the northern window overlooking the barn was a small table and two chairs. Brie had found the set at an antiques fair in Maine. He remembered that day so clearly it hurt. He'd taken her for an outing before one of his deployments, and they'd eaten hot dogs at a stand. It was a crisp, cool May day with pink and purple pansies and petunias starting to bloom, and she'd seen that little table with a long scratch down the middle and declared it needed a little TLC and would fit perfectly beneath the window.

He'd sanded, buffed and stained it, and she'd hugged him so tight he could barely breathe.

Soon after, she announced she was going to work in the inner city where she could do more good in protecting women and children. He'd tried to talk her out of it, but Brie was stubborn. So he'd purchased a new bulletproof vest his brother Derek said was the best. Combat Gear Inc.'s vests were lighter and more flexible, allowing Brie to get out of a tight space quicker.

He knew all about getting out of tight spaces.

She'd thanked him over and over when she'd tried on the vest, marveling at how thin and sturdy it seemed. He'd hung up the phone that day, relieved his little sister would be safe.

That body armor had proven faulty when Brie was killed. If he ever found M. E. Franklin, the man whose name was on the corporate documents… His jaw tightened as Coop shook the cobweb of memories from his mind. Had to focus on the present, and Meg, who kept staring at him as if he were an ogre.

"You look really angry," she whispered.

"Sorry. Just woolgathering. This place used to be my sister's."

"Does she mind if I stay here a few days? I don't plan on being here long."

Meg wasn't going to settle here for a while. She probably

saw how shabby everything was and figured this wasn't the Hilton. He wouldn't force it. "She's dead," he muttered.

Ignoring her apology, he focused on building a fire. As the flames caught and flickered, he thought of how homey and cozy the cottage was. Brie had teased him about how he should use it for a tryst with a sexy brunette.

Funny how the princess fit the description. Her body, yeah, just his type, but not the personality. He preferred country girls who loved riding horses, didn't mind baling hay and enjoyed dancing at the local honky-tonk.

Not wealthy women who carried dogs in designer purses.

After piling wood into the fireplace and igniting it, he dusted off his hands. "There's plenty of food in the pantry. Thermostat's on the wall behind the sofa if you get cold. Power may go out in this storm, but the heater is gas so you'll be set. I'll leave candles and a flashlight on the hall table."

Meg sat on the sofa, eyes huge and round as she clutched her dog. "You're leaving us alone here?"

Damn if she didn't look lost and forlorn, like a stray puppy. He stood and cleared his throat. "I have to spend the night with Betsy."

Her expression fell. "I understand. I'm sure your girlfriend wouldn't like you to stay here with us."

Cooper grinned. "Betsy's not my girlfriend. She's a horse with colic."

Meg's eyes widened, and then a lovely smile graced her full lips. She gave a little laugh. "Oh! I thought…"

Admiring the pink flush on her china-doll cheeks, he pointed to the window. "I was going to spend the night in the barn, checking up on her. But I'll come back here later, make sure you're okay."

"You really do care about your animals."

His throat went tight. "Yeah, and ole Bets is special. She belonged to my sister."

He didn't want to launch into an explanation, but Meg nodded and a soft expression filled her face. "Of course. I understand. The animals come first. Because they can't defend themselves. Your sister would do the same, I'm sure."

Cooper rubbed a hand across his flannel shirt, suddenly uncomfortable. He hated talking about Brie. Any time her name was mentioned, it sent fresh grief through him, and he had to fight hard to maintain his composure.

"I'll leave my cell number if you need anything. Barn's not far."

"My cell phone couldn't get a signal, probably because it's an inexpensive throwaway phone. Otherwise I would have called you."

"Ah. That's why you never called. I waited and waited. Hate it when a woman says she'll call and never does."

He liked her smile, wished she would relax. But he saw in her eyes the same trauma he'd seen overseas in women who had suffered much.

For a minute he imagined what this must be like for her—homeless, on the run, at the mercy of a stranger. A big stranger. She was so tiny and frail-looking, yet he suspected within hid a core of steel. It took courage to pack up and leave everything you knew. He couldn't imagine doing it....

"When did your husband beat you?"

At first she didn't answer, and the pink of her cheeks warned he'd stepped over an invisible line. Coop suspected she was ashamed of the incident and what happened to her.

He gentled his voice. "I only want to know if you need medical attention. If you don't want to talk about it, tell me."

Meg's head bobbed in a jerky nod, and she looked away.

"He wasn't that bad this time. But the time I ran off last year, before my grandmother got sick, that was very bad. I was in the hospital for a week. When I returned home, Sophie was gone. I found her in a shelter known for euthanizing dogs."

Cooper wanted to find her husband and show him exactly what he thought of men who beat women and animals. He'd had plenty of experience in dealing with those types and didn't tolerate them well.

Drawing in a deep breath, she picked up Sophie and hugged her until the dog whined. He started toward her, but Meg flinched.

It would take time for her to trust him. Sighing, he took the pad and pen by the old-fashioned rotary phone hanging on the kitchen wall and scribbled his cell. "Service out here is sporadic, but I installed special equipment to boost the signal. I'm going to call your cell to make sure it works."

After he dialed the number, the cell phone he'd plugged in at the counter began to chirp. Nodding, he hung up the phone.

"Everything's okay."

"I wish I could believe you."

"No one knows you're here," he assured her. "Only Jarrett and Lacey, and they wouldn't tell a soul. You're safe. And no one has the phone number of this cottage except my mom and me. Tomorrow we'll move you up to the main inn."

Wishing he could make her believe him, he snatched up his jacket from a peg by the door, along with his Stetson, and tugged on his gloves.

Cooper paused at the kitchen door. "Remember, you need anything, just call me. You'll be fine."

The dog looked at him and growled.

"You too, furball."

Then he winked at Meg, opened the door, went onto the sunporch and into the storm.

When Cooper left, she peered outside, watching him struggle against the howling wind. Meg rubbed her arms, shivering from nerves, not the cold. Certainly it was warm enough here. But she hated being alone in this cottage. And how did she know he wouldn't turn her over to Prescott? Judging from the faded, worn furnishings, Cooper didn't have much money. Money could influence people, even those with the best intentions.

She'd seen it before too many times. But Lacey trusted him. And she trusted Lacey. It would suffice for now.

Not for long. Prescott would find her eventually.

The only person she could trust besides Lacey was Randall Jacobs, the longtime family friend who worked for the company. Randall had invented the fiber they used for racquetball paddles and Meg got the idea to incorporate it into flexible body armor.

After Randall discovered the material was too unstable to stop bullets, he pleaded to halt production. Prescott ignored his entreaties. So Randall hid copies of Prescott's internal confidential documents ordering the shipment of the defective vests to Boston.

He'd told Meg he would give her those documents for her to turn over to federal authorities, and then give himself protection under the federal whistleblower act.

She picked up the cell phone and checked the charge. She'd texted Randall while on the road. He had this number and promised to call by tonight to arrange to meet her at his family's summer house in a nearby town. What if something happened? Could someone trace this phone back to her? She'd been so careful.

Where could Randall have hidden those documents?

Sophie trotted on her heels into the living room after Meg washed the bowls and cleaned up. Sitting before the fire, she stared at the flickering flames.

Leaving Sophie to doze before the fire, she went into the bedroom and fetched her grandmother's quilt. Meg wrapped it around herself and curled onto the sofa.

"I miss you, Gran," she whispered. "Why did you have to leave me?"

Letticia Taylor had been a healthy seventy-year-old until a few months ago, when she began to sicken. She died in the hospital two weeks ago, Meg stroking her chilled blue-veined hand.

Prescott attended the funeral, and a few days later, they went to the family attorney in Boston. Bert Baxter informed Meg that Gran had left everything to Prescott. Everything.

She was literally cashless and powerless.

The sexy Cooper with his crooked grin and burning blue eyes assured her this cottage was safe. He would protect her.

*No one can really protect me.*

She hadn't been safe all those times before when she'd tried to escape Prescott, and she had no real confidence Cooper Johnson could deliver on his promise.

Meg turned on the television in the living room. It was an older model, and nothing compared to the wide-screen HDTV in her mansion.

She channel surfed, restless, until landing on a news channel. And then she stiffened as she recognized the familiar surroundings. It was a news report from Florida, with several police cars surrounding a BMW she knew... for she had been there the day he'd bragged about getting that "sweet" car.

*No, please no.*

The television news reporter was talking.

"Murder in Palm Beach! The body of Palm Beach millionaire Randall Jacobs was found this morning inside his car in a public park near a playground. There are no suspects at the time and police are investigating…"

Meg snapped off the remote and stared at the blank screen. Wind pushed at the windows, howling to get inside.

Her chest hurt and her throat tightened. "Randall, oh God, I'm so sorry," she whispered.

Randall Jacobs, the only man she trusted, the only one who had the evidence to convict her husband and send him to jail, far out of reach, was dead.

# Chapter 4

It didn't matter if Cooper Johnson had a room filled with weapons. She wasn't safe here. Prescott had murdered Randall. She knew it.

Wrapping her arms around herself, Meg paced the living room, thinking hard.

She went into the kitchen and unplugged her cell phone from the charger.

The light blinked, indicating a voice mail. She dialed it and listened, her blood turning to ice.

Randall.

"Meg, they're after me." A small, gruff laugh, filled with terror. "Should never have stayed in this game, but I got greedy. I'm sorry. I'm so damn sorry for what I did."

Sounds of a train going by in the background. Randall's voice became more frantic and he spoke in a rush.

"Meg, I don't have much time and I can't be certain this phone isn't bugged. Prescott's in deeper than I thought. It's not him you have to worry about…it's his new friends with deep pockets, and they're planning something big. Be careful. The documents and cash for you to live on are hidden. Remember 43.961281 and -71.058542. There's also a backup microchip close to your heart. Watch yourself, Meggie."

Hands trembling, she shut off the phone. Meg jotted the numbers down on a nearby pad. Then she looked at the cell phone. Police were investigating and would trace the phone number back to her.

Pulling open drawers, she pawed through their contents until she found an old-fashioned meat tenderizer. Perfect. Meg removed the battery from the cell phone and then set the phone on the floor and smashed it. Then she took the shards and placed them in a plastic bag to dispose of later.

It was a prepaid cell phone with a new SIM card that she'd paid for in cash. The police could call the number and use the phone to track her down. Randall's call came three hours ago. Enough time for them to start checking out his phone calls.

The numbers played over in her head: 43.961281 and -71.058542. Tears burned her throat. Randall had lived a lavish lifestyle, jet-setting and spending money extravagantly, but he was a good man at heart, wanting to do the right thing.

And now he was dead because of it.

She went to the fireplace and warmed her ice-cold hands. All she had as clues were the numbers and a vague message about her heart.

What did those numbers mean?

A loud crash sounded outside, making her jump. Sophie barked and scrambled to her feet. Meg's blood turned to ice. Immobilized with fear, she stared in the direction of the kitchen.

Right outside the sunporch.

Turning off all the lights, wishing she could bank the fire as well to plunge the room into total darkness, Meg took a deep breath. Gathering all her courage, she peered out the living room window that paralleled the sunporch. Fat snowflakes swirled in the storm, making it difficult to see, despite the dim glow of the porch light. Tree branches scraped against the side of the house like nails against a chalkboard.

The crash was probably the wind knocking over one of the clay planters on the steps. It made no sense that Prescott had found her, unless he'd traced her to Jarrett and Lacey...

Meg ran to the fireplace and seized the poker, carrying it like a weapon. She found the coat Cooper had left for her, hanging on a peg in the sunroom. Sophie trotted behind her, but she motioned for the dog to stay quiet.

Taking a deep breath, she opened the door. If something was lurking outside, she wasn't going to hide in here, cowering in fear.

She was so tired of being afraid all the time.

Snow pelted her face, danced around in the air as she stepped onto the landing. The tiny light outside did little to illuminate the gloom. Wind whipped at her hair, sending tiny stinging needles into her skin.

Meg held up the fireplace poker, ready to swing at an unknown assailant. But no one was outside. The clay pot, containing only dirt, had been knocked over and lay in shards on the snowy ground. Nothing. Just the pot, knocked over by the wind. Still she stood there for a minute, listening to the wind howl and the trees moan under the storm, cold snaking down her spine.

A deeper cold she knew would never leave, not until she'd freed herself permanently from Prescott's clutches.

Finally, the cold became too much to bear and she returned inside.

Meg set down the poker on the kitchen table. Using the kitchen phone, she dialed the toll-free number Lacey had given her.

Her former sorority sister answered on the first ring. "SOS."

"Lacey, it's Meg. I made it here, but I'm not staying." She spoke in a rush, worried the connection would get cut off.

"Meg! We were worried about you." Her friend's relief was obvious. "Stay there with Cooper. You're in a safe house now. We need you to stay put until we can find another place to move you."

*Move me. Like I'm furniture, only the moving meant putting more people at risk.* Her throat tightened. She'd already played havoc with too many lives and endangered good people. It had to end now.

Fingering the diamond around her neck, she thought of the cash it would bring if she pawned it. Enough to find another place to run and hide, until she could figure out the numbers Randall had left her.

She hated pawning her grandmother's jewel, but Gran would understand. Meg's hand trembled as she gripped the phone. "No. I have a little money. I'll find a place on my own. Thank you, but I can't risk it."

"Meg, please, I know you're scared, but Cooper is the best…"

"You don't know my ex. He's ruthless and has enough money to make anyone vanish. You both aren't safe. If he finds out you helped me… I can't risk your lives, Lacey."

"Nothing's going to happen to us, Meg," Lacey told her. "Jarrett takes every precaution when it comes to our underground railroad of aiding women in distress. Coop's going to give you a new ID, new passport, driver's license…but it will take a little time."

"I don't have time. It won't matter." She gripped the phone and thought of Randall, and his cheerful, round face, now frozen in death. "Cooper Johnson can't help me. He has his hands full here."

"Cooper is a professional soldier and he'll make sure you're safe. He's okay, Meg. Trust him," Lacey told her.

"I can't stay here. And you and Jarrett and Fleur are in danger, because if Prescott finds you..."

A crackling over the phone and mumbling in the background.

"He's not going to touch Lace, or Fleur, and if he gets within one hundred miles of our house, I'll be on him, Meg. Stay with Coop." The deep, rumbling tones of former Navy SEAL Lt. Jarrett Adler sounded confident and assured.

But she could not take chances.

"Watch yourselves." Meg hung up the phone, then she went to the window, worried about the storm. No time to go out in this mess. She had no car, and for now, she was stuck.

Stuck in a cottage with someone outside. She lifted the checked curtain at the kitchen window and peered out into the darkness again.

Was someone out there now, watching her every move?

Fear soured in her stomach. The barn couldn't be far. She suddenly couldn't stand to be alone anymore. She found Sophie's leash and hooked her up and took the key to the front door off the peg in the kitchen.

"Come on, Sophie. We're going to find Cooper."

"Easy, girl."

Coop finished walking Betsy around the barn, cursing the storm that kept the mare inside. Then he rubbed down Betsy once more for the night. He lifted the latch on the stall door and locked it behind him. In the stall next to Betsy's, Adela poked her head out and looked at him suspiciously.

"Hey, Adela," he murmured. He went to the minifridge where he kept carrots and apples and medication for the animals, and fished out a red apple. Coop unlatched her stall door and stepped inside.

But Adela backed away, laying her ears back.

Still wouldn't take food from his hand. He needed to work with her more, needed time to work with her.

"It's okay, girl. When you're ready." Backing out of the stall, he fumbled with the finicky catch and let himself out. Coop set the apple down on a bench to try later.

In the aisle, he sat on the chest containing cleaning equipment and pulled out his cell phone. After scrolling through messages, laughing at a stupid joke one of his teammates sent, he clicked onto a news station from Palm Beach County.

Needed to see what else he could find out about Meg.

And then he saw a headline screaming in bold type: Palm Beach Millionaire Found Shot to Death.

Coop's heart raced. He read through the article, and then set his phone down, burying his face in his hands.

Damn it. There went his hope of getting to Jacobs and finding out how to track down M. E. Franklin, owner of Combat Gear Inc. Digging into this company was like a game of Chutes and Ladders he'd played as a child, and he'd just slid down a very long chute.

He dug into his pocket and withdrew a jeweled figure no bigger than his thumbnail.

It had a gold halo, a white crystal for a head and body, and two blue crystals for wings. His guardian angel.

"I'm sorry, Brie. I let you down again," he whispered. "God, I wish you were here. I'm sorry I couldn't be there to keep you safe."

Brie had bought it for him the day he enlisted. She'd pressed it into his palm as he slung his duffel over one shoulder. "To protect you, Super Cooper. No being the hero, okay? You come home to us," she'd told him, and then hugged him tight.

He treasured it as much as he did his Budweiser SEAL pin. He'd tucked that angel into his uniform pocket and it had traveled with him ever since. The little angel had seen him through BUD/S, the Basic Underwater Demolition/ SEALS training all SEALS endured, and was in his uniform when he'd taken a bullet in Ramadi that should have killed him. Jarrett had teased him about it at first, but later, his LT started thinking maybe that angel pin pulled Coop out of a bad scrape or two dozen.

He'd been banged up bad, came through it intact. But no angel pin could keep Brie safe. Only a damn vest that should have never been sold.

Coop ran a hand through his hair, his guts churning. He looked at the little guardian angel charm and felt his throat close up.

A noise at the barn door jerked him out of his ruminations. Coop pocketed the angel and stood, muscles tensing, his hands itching for a weapon as the barn door opened.

Wind blew the snow inside as Meg and her dog ran into the barn. Meg struggled to close the doors.

He stood, alarm pelting him. "What's wrong?"

Had to be a hell of a reason to bring her out of the nice, warm cottage in this mess. Scanning her body, he felt relieved to see no obvious injuries, nothing but a hint of distress in her green eyes. At her side, the dog wagged her tail and then shook, spraying melting snow everywhere.

"I need to talk to you."

She braved this snowstorm for a chat? Exasperated, he shook his head. "I told you, I'd be by the cottage later."

"I know." She came forward, snowflakes dusting her soft brown hair. "I also wanted to see how Betsy is doing."

Nice of her to check, but he resented Meg's intruding on his personal space, his retreat away from the world. "She's good."

Cooper splayed his legs and tensed. "Go back to bed and

stay warm. You've just been through one bout with exposure. Unless you want me warming you all over again."

*Not a bad idea,* his body cheerfully agreed. Amid the earthy scent of horses and hay, he caught a tendril of her fragrance, all floral and feminine. Yet another reminder it had been a long time since he'd had a woman warm his bed. Or warm anything of his.

Meg flushed a little and she bit her lip. He caught sight of her pulse pounding at her temple, as if she thought it was a great idea as well.

*Right. Put that thought out of your gray matter, chum, 'cause it ain't happening in this lifetime.*

He heard a *whuffing* sound and hooves clicking against the cold cement floor, and his heart dropped into his stomach. Adela had nosed her way out of the stall and now stood in the aisle, right in front of Meg and her furball.

Son of a...should have fixed that damn latch. But it had been yet another thing on his long to-do list.

"Stay where you are and don't move toward her," he warned in a low voice, not wishing to alarm Adela.

Wariness faded from Meg's expression. Instead, she pulled off one glove and started toward the horse. *Terrific. Now I have to save you a second time tonight?*

He murmured to the horse, hugging the left side stalls, not wishing to get kicked by Adela's hind hooves.

"Hey there, pretty girl," Meg crooned. She picked up the abandoned apple.

"Careful. Back off, now," he warned. "She's a rescue and had a tough time of it."

"A rescue horse?" Her face lit up and she smiled with such warmth, it nearly took his breath away.

What would it be like to be greeted with a sweet, sunny smile like that every day? Marriage, family, a wife who would stick by his side, someone he could talk with, encourage her hopes and dreams like she did to him. Not the women he'd taken to bed and watched walk away, women who simply wanted sex because he was a Navy SEAL.

Shaking free of the thought, Cooper watched Meg with wariness. Adela had been a rescue from a group out West. Her owner failed to care for her, leaving her alone in a pasture without enough water or feed. Ribs stuck through her skin, and Adela had huge trust issues.

One didn't simply walk up to a horse, let alone an abused one, and start chatting. But Meg walked toward her, nice and easy, approaching from the side, talking slow and soothing.

Adela trembled at Meg's approach, her ears pinned back. Meg stopped and stepped to the side, her gaze averted.

"I know, pretty one. Someone was mean and hurt you. I'm not going to hurt you, baby. I just want to offer a little treat. A nice, fresh apple."

Meg took the fruit and held it out. "I'm going to stay right here and let you see me, see I'm not going to do anything until you give the okay."

She kept talking in low, soothing tones to the horse. Finally the mare's ears returned to the side and she lowered her head.

Meg kept palming the apple. "I've got a good friend who really likes horses, just like Cooper here does. She's small, so you have to be real careful around her. Sophie, go say hello to Adela, nice and slow, like I taught you."

The mare didn't retreat, and her muscles didn't tense.

Tail wagging, Sophie went to Adela, approaching very slowly from the side to avoid the horse's blind spot just as Meg had. The dog stopped about thirty feet away, watching the horse, as if gauging her reaction.

Ready to spring into action—it wouldn't be good if the horse trampled the princess's furball—Coop tensed.

When Adela relaxed, Sophie loped over to the horse. For a moment, the pair sniffed at each other. Jaw dropping, he watched as Sophie nuzzled the horse's neck and Adela responded by playfully butting the dog.

Well, look at that. The dog and the horse. Remembering what Meg had said about Sophie being abused, Coop shook his head. Animals never ceased to amaze him. All the times he'd worked with Max, the Belgian Malinois who had been an integral part of the teams, he'd learned a lot.

But he'd never seen anything like this. Instant friendship. His gaze whipped over to Meg, whose attention remained riveted to the dog and the horse.

Meg made a hand gesture to Sophie, who moved away from the horse. Then Meg continued sidling up to Adela, holding out the apple. Adela plucked it with her big white teeth and munched. Meg stroked her neck, continuing to murmur soothing words.

With a reassuring pat to Adela, Meg left, Sophie trotting on her heels.

He must look like a fool, standing there with his mouth open. Coop approached Adela after she finished her treat and led her back to the stall. She went docilely, and he made certain to latch the gate firmly.

Then he turned to Meg, who was crouching down and petting Sophie. "Where did you learn that trick?"

She stood up. "I work with a local animal rescue group in Florida for abused horses, everything from feeding them to caring for their needs. Sophie has been a natural at getting the horses to calm down. I spent a lot of time at the stables training her to get horses to trust again."

"You don't look like the type to muck out a stable. Weren't you worried about chipping a nail?" His gaze shot up and down the length of her body, from those well-manicured hands to her dainty feet.

Meg's pouty mouth flattened. "My grandparents owned a farm up north and I grew up there. I know just as much about shoveling manure as I do about hosting a charity benefit, Mr. Johnson."

Coop leaned against a bale of hay, slightly ashamed of jumping all over her. Maybe because he was attracted to her, too attracted, and felt a natural need to put distance between them.

Like between now and next week would be good.

"Adela's had it rough. Thanks for that." From beneath the brim of his Stetson, he gave her a meaningful look. "But next time, do as I say. I don't care if you rescued all the wild mustangs in the West and tamed them, you don't go walking into a man's barn and approach any of the horses until you know their background. Deal?"

He removed his right hand from his pocket and shoved it out at her.

But she did not take his hand. Rather, the princess looked at his palm the way Adela had regarded the apple earlier.

Fine. He was here to keep her safe until the next step of her journey. Nothing more.

Meg went to a bale of hay and sat, Sophie at her side. She scratched the dog's head. "What happened to her?"

He glanced at Adela. "I bought her from a kill pen last month. She was scheduled to be shipped to Canada to a slaughterhouse."

Yeah, kinda harsh. He winced as her mouth trembled and she blinked rapidly. "I hate kill pens. I've bought a few horses from a kill buyer and managed to save them. But it's never enough."

Now it was his turn to be surprised. "You know about the business?"

"The foundation I helped was very involved in rescuing abused and abandoned horses, and horses sold by their owners for the slaughterhouse. Mainly older horses who had outlived their use, as seen by their owners. I've rescued a few. Once, I actually staged a protest outside the polo grounds to raise awareness." Meg gave a rueful smile. "It didn't win me many friends with the polo set, and I was banned for a month."

His respect for her grew and he felt a little ashamed for judging her so quickly. "Good for you."

Her expression fell. "When my husband found out, he was infuriated, because he had business dealings with executives who played polo. He said I did it deliberately to mock him." Meg looked down, rubbing her hands against the jeans he'd lent her. "He wasn't one for saving any stray animals. With him it was all business and all money, all the time."

Cooper leaned against Betsy's stall door. "That guy sounds like a total loser. Then why did you marry him?"

Meg bit her lush lower lip, and the little movement fired his blood. "When I first met him, he was urbane, charming and caring. He swept me off my feet. He was the first person to really listen when I talked to him about my plans and my dreams. He put my needs first, or so I thought."

A faint flush tinted her cheeks. "He even fooled my grandmother, who approved of the marriage. She had hired him to take over the reins of the family business, and he saved our company when we were headed into the red. But a year after we married, my husband showed his true colors. And yet I stuck it out for two more years." Her voice lowered, as if she were ashamed to say the words. "I thought I loved him. I was a fool for not leaving him sooner."

Anger raced through him. Some men weren't fit to have a relationship, no matter what their background. "It takes a lot of courage to leave. Don't be so hard on yourself."

She looked him in the eye and said clearly, "I kept hoping he would change. He used to promise never to do it again."

He'd heard that story before, and it rankled him that this pretty, seemingly frail woman had endured such abuse. Coop had been raised to respect women, and never hurt them, no matter what. The hardest thing for him to do as a SEAL was turn off that ingrained belief, and do his job in enemy territory when facing a woman holding a grenade...

He gentled his voice. "Someone like your louse of an ex will never change. The behavior is too ingrained in them. Like drug addicts, they find it hard to kick the habit."

"You seem to know a lot about abuse."

He glanced over his shoulder at Adela. "I have more than a nodding acquaintance with it. My sister was with a guy who used his fists when he got drunk."

Meg's eyes went round. "And how did she end the relationship?"

"She didn't. I did, by showing the guy the business end of my nine-millimeter." Cooper offered a grim smile. "Brie wasn't happy I muscled into her life, but later, she thanked me."

"You were being a concerned brother," she said gently.

His smile dropped. Yeah, but he'd failed Brie in the one area he'd felt confident of protecting her. That little reminder truly rankled him. "Why are you here? You said you needed to tell me something. So talk."

Inwardly he winced at his curt tone. The softness fled from Meg's heart-shaped face and she looked wary. Even the dog growled at him.

"I came to tell you I'm only spending the night and leaving in the morning as soon as my car is fixed. That's all."

She turned on her heel, and the dog followed. Coop rubbed the nape of his neck.

Ah, damn. He was supposed to protect a woman for Project SOS and offer her safe refuge from an abusive spouse.

And she was going to bolt.

Cooper ran after her, blocked her from exiting the barn. He held out his hands, kept his body relaxed and loose.

"Don't go because I'm an ass. Stay. You came here to find a safe place and I promise, you will be safe here."

She watched him with narrowed eyes, and he could read the doubt in her expression.

Spreading out his hands, he wriggled his fingers. "Look at me. I'm not armed, and I will listen to you. If I say something stupid again, you can go ahead and do what my mom always does when I'm being dumb."

Meg's mouth twitched in a ghost of a smile. "And what's that? Send you to bed without supper? Is that what I should do?"

*Sending me to bed with you would be a most pleasant punishment.* Desire surged through him, and his grin tightened as he struggled to maintain a grip on his emotions. There was something about this woman that scrambled his senses and made all his tightly held control go southward.

Straight to his groin, in fact.

He wasn't the charming type like his teammate Stephen, or a ladies' magnet like LT before LT had married Lacey. He'd always been quieter, more drawn to animals than people, and relationships were brief because of his time downrange with the teams. When he did have leave, it was always spent with family, not partying and impressing women.

But something about Meg drew him like a lodestone. Oh yeah, she was a beauty, but it was more than that. He'd had his share of beautiful women, some of whom were vapid as an air bag. Maybe it was the wounded look in her eyes he wanted to erase, or her sheer pluck, or the fact that she refused to cower.

That "no retreat" attitude he both admired and recognized.

But she'd fled a bad marriage and a man who treated her like a punching bag. Last thing Meg needed was unwanted male attention. Coop cocked his head.

"What you should do with me is tell me what drove you in here, in this storm, 'cause you had something you wanted to tell me before I went all ape on you. What happened?"

Her gaze darted away, a sure sign she was nervous. "It was nothing."

Suspecting he wouldn't get much more out of her, Coop opted for a different approach. He crouched down to Sophie and spoke in a low, soothing voice, the kind that coaxed women into his bed and animals to his hand. "C'mon, pretty girl. Did something scare you? Because if it did, I need to know so I can make it right. I want you to feel comfortable here in my home, and I sure do want you to stick around because my mom makes the best breakfast this side of the Mississippi. You can't run off before you taste her cranberry-orange-nut muffins with honey butter."

Sophie's tail waved ever so slightly. She bent her head and sniffed in his direction. Then she cautiously approached him and smelled the hand he held out.

Meg watched as her man-hating dog licked Cooper's hand. He glanced at her and winked. "She wants me to tell you. See?"

"I don't understand. Sophie doesn't like men."

Scratching behind Sophie's ears, he nodded. "She's been burned, but animals are smart. They know which people will hurt them and which ones to trust."

At his meaningful look, Meg sighed. "You're not going to let this go."

"Nope. I can be real stubborn that way."

"There was a crash outside. I think it was the wind." She looked away. "Or not. I had this feeling of being watched."

Immediately he assessed the situation. She'd been alone in a strange place, all sorts of noises outside in the storm where anything could sound like a threat. "I'm sorry," he told her. "I shouldn't have left you alone like that. I'll come back with you now."

"What about Betsy?"

Much as he wanted to remain in the barn, he couldn't leave Meg alone. The horse seemed to be over the worst of the colic. "She'll do fine. Come on."

"It was nothing," Meg repeated. "Just the wind knocking something over."

Straightening, he turned toward the door. "Show me."

The wind had died down, and the clouds had scudded across the night sky, showing a pale full moon as they made their way back to the cottage. The path was only a few hundred feet away, but he thought of Meg making her way to the barn in the dark with only a thin pencil beam from the flashlight to illuminate the way, and his guts churned.

He should never have left her alone.

At the porch steps, she gestured to the broken clay pot. Brie had planted marigolds in the three pots on the steps, and when they'd died, he simply hadn't had the heart to do anything with them. Same reason he hadn't cleaned out Brie's closet or, against his mother's wishes, gone through any of her personal things.

Cooper saw Meg's trim boot prints in the newly fallen snow, and a set of paw prints leading from the front steps.

Nothing obvious. But he'd check the entire cottage to make sure.

"Go inside, get warm. I'll be in shortly."

His no-nonsense tone indicated business. Meg bit her

lower lip again and then held out the flashlight. He shook his head. "Don't need it."

"It's dark out here."

"Yeah, and it's how I roll. Go inside. Lock the door behind you."

He was relieved to see her unlock the door and head into the cottage, the dog on her heels. Soon as he heard the lock click, he began a perimeter check. The new snow made it easy to spot any disturbances. And using a flashlight would be like a neon sign if there was anyone, or anything, lurking outside.

Cooper made his way around the cottage, using the light of the moon as illumination. Nothing. Maybe it was the wind. But he didn't like it. Took a mighty strong wind to knock over a pot that heavy.

As he walked to the east, hooked around the house and examined the grounds, he got a prickly feeling on the back of his neck. Gut instinct saved his butt more than once in the field, so he paid attention to the night sounds, the quietness, the smells...

He inched toward the living room window that was parallel to the sunporch. And then his blood ran cold.

Another set of prints in the snow, these much larger.

As if a man had been standing outside the window, trying to peer past the curtains at Meg...

Using the spare key, Cooper let himself into the house. Meg sat at the kitchen table. "Did you find anything?"

"Maybe." Coop headed to the closet and opened the gun safe where he'd stashed Brie's .38 special. After loading it, he returned to the kitchen and showed her the gun. "Ever use one of these?"

Meg's eyes widened to dinner plates. "No. Is it necessary?"

"Not as long as I'm around. It's for when I can't be at

your side." He showed her the safety. "Click this off and point and shoot, but only if you're certain your target intends harm."

She looked at the gun as if it were a cockroach. "I can't use this."

Coop considered. "Fine. Need you to do something. Ever make plaster of paris?"

At her head shake, he told her where to find the flour and bowls, and to warm the water. Taking the flashlight, Coop next returned outside.

After making another thorough perimeter check, he fetched the bowl of plaster, Coop poured the liquid into the footprints to let it set. Then he returned inside, locking the door. Pulling out a chair, he joined Meg at the table.

"You asked if I found something. I found a set of man's footprints, size 14, in the snow. I wear size 11, and no one I know, even the hired help, wears shoes that big."

Blood drained from Meg's face. She hugged herself. "Prescott wears that size shoe. He's found me. Oh God, I knew I never should have come here. He killed Randall and I'm next."

Coop's suspicions flared. He knew that name, all too well… "Randall?"

Meg's gaze darted away. Bingo. Cooper leaned forward, all business now. She knew something and he was going to find out what.

"I think it's time you started leveling with me about your ex. I need to know exactly why you ran away from him, who he is and what his business is. Starting now."

## Chapter 5

The little cottage was warm, but Meg felt only a deep chill at the intense look in Cooper Johnson's blue eyes. His body was tense as he leaned toward her, and she suspected he would not let this go until she told him the truth.

At least a portion of it, what she could tell him.

"Who is Randall and why did your ex kill him?"

Meg said nothing.

"Who is your ex-husband?" That blue gaze pinned her like a laser. "Jarrett didn't tell me anything other than to send me a photo of you and that you were in trouble and needed a new ID. I know your last name isn't Caldwell."

Meg battled with her need for secrecy and the need to warn this man and his family what they were up against. She decided he needed to know, because by coming here, she had put him in grave danger.

"No. It's Meg August, or was Meg August. My ex is Prescott August." She licked her lips. "The CEO of Taylor Sporting Goods. And Randall is Randall Jacobs."

Cooper sat back, looking stunned and then his mouth flattened in apparent anger. It was like someone had flipped a switch. Meg shuddered.

"You're Prescott August's wife? The Prescott August?"

The look of dismay on his face indicated his low opinion of Prescott. "Soon to be ex. Obviously Jarrett didn't tell you."

"Jarrett was tight-lipped when he asked me to take you in. He said he leaves it up to the women he helps to give out information on an as-needed basis. It's safer that way." Cooper's expression remained guarded. "And you think he killed Randall Jacobs? Why?"

Her trembling hand reached down to stroke Sophie, who whined beneath her touch. Sophie had always sensed her moods, knew when Meg was distressed.

"Randall had very important information that would put Prescott behind bars." *And me, but you don't need to know that.*

"What kind of information?"

She shook her head. "That's all I can tell you for now. I don't want to involve you."

Cooper drummed his fingers against the scarred wood tabletop. "Meg, I'm already involved. Those footprints out there tell me someone was here tonight, watching you. It could have been someone lost on the way to the inn, or someone who was checking up on you."

Asking her to trust him was too risky. "The information is very sensitive."

"Randall worked with Taylor Sporting Goods. Did he know your husband well?"

Goodness, the man was as tenacious as Sophie with a bone. "Randall was a very wealthy man who did contract work for several companies." True enough.

"But he invented the fiber that your grandmother's company used for sports equipment." Cooper's gaze narrowed. "Randall Jacobs was in business with them. And he was vice president for Combat Gear Inc., the company that manufactured the faulty bulletproof vests that were just recalled by the government."

Her stomach began to pitch and roil. She didn't expect the government to act this quickly. "How do you know this?"

"I heard about the recall on the news. As for Jacobs, he applied for a government patent for the fibers. He listed his title as vice president." Cooper leaned forward, his posture tense.

Meg tried to calm her galloping pulse. "I didn't know that."

A grim smile touched his mouth. "I have a vested interest in that company, pardon the pun. I've done some thorough research."

Wide-eyed, she stared at him, wondering what his interest was. What would Cooper do if he knew she was the one responsible for creating the company? She was the only one on the corporate documents, even though the name was false.

Would he call the authorities? Have her arrested? And then Prescott would remain free and would find a way to continue his dirty dealings. Prescott had made sure no one else would be linked to the company. But Randall had obviously changed that and provided a clue.

She was in deep and couldn't trust Cooper. Not until she could gather the proof to put her ex in jail.

Giving him the cold look she did to flattering social climbers at parties, Meg lifted her chin. "Is this how you question the enemy, Mr. Johnson?"

A grim smile touched his mouth. "Oh, Princess, my methods of interrogation are much, much worse," he said softly.

Meg backed away at the intent look. She blinked hard. "It's late and I'm really tired."

Cooper rubbed a hand over the slight bristles on his taut jaw. "Okay. You need shut-eye. I'll bunk down here with you in one of the other bedrooms and we'll talk more in the morning."

He didn't seem the type to give up, but the reprieve made her grateful. "Thank you." She lifted Sophie into her arms and the dog wriggled in protest. "Thank you for everything. In the morning when your tow truck driver delivers my car, I'll be gone."

When she was inside the guest bedroom, Meg closed the door and set Sophie down. Tired as she was, she dug her laptop out. Randall's death changed everything. Until she got the car back, she had to get an idea of what those mysterious numbers he'd given her were.

She clicked on the Wi-Fi and began surfing the internet news sites to discover what Cooper knew. A small article caught her eye. The FBI had opened an investigation into Combat Gear Inc., and the federal government had issued a massive recall of body armor manufactured by the company, for some of the vests were purported to be faulty.

A law enforcement officer had been killed in the line of duty while wearing the vest when responding to a domestic disturbance call. The dead officer was a woman named Sabrina Fletcher.

Sorrow mixed with relief, relief because no one else would put their lives at risk with the vests, and sorrow for the fallen officer. She looked at the photo of Sabrina Fletcher, her pretty, wide face and laughing blue eyes. So young. Only twenty-six.

*She was my age. Her life was beginning, and now it's cut short.*

Her family refused to talk with the media and had sent a lawyer to give a statement.

Suddenly overcome with exhaustion, she powered off

the Mac and set it atop the antique dresser. But long after she had climbed into bed, Sophie at her side, Meg lay awake staring at the ceiling.

Tomorrow, as soon as her car was fixed, she'd leave. But where could she go, when it seemed no one was safe from her ex?

Waiting until Meg's light had gone out, Cooper sat in the kitchen trying to control his raging emotions. Knowing the abuse she'd suffered, he didn't want to show the fury he felt inside.

So he waited in the kitchen, trying to calm down, though everything inside him churned like a volcano about to explode. He was a SEAL, and he knew emotions were bad on the job.

When he finally calmed down enough, Coop called his former boss. The plaster of paris cast was safely inside, showing a detailed footprint of a flat-soled shoe.

When Jarrett had asked him to shelter Meg for a few days, he immediately said yes because it was Jarrett. He'd have walked to hell and shot Lucifer himself for LT.

But Cooper didn't realize what kind of assignment he'd taken on. Jarrett said Meg was a frightened woman. Meg didn't act like any frightened woman he'd ever known, and her personality, her kind heart for animals and her body kicked him behind the knees. Those curves, that mass of soft ash-brown hair he imagined spread out on his pillow and those sleepy green eyes dazed with passion after they'd made love...

*Do not go there.*

The woman was terrified, that was obvious. But he also sensed she hid something pretty damn big.

Jarrett answered on the first ring. "Coop. How's Meg doing? She seemed scared when she called Lace earlier."

"She's safe in my sister's cottage. I'm keeping a close eye on her."

"Don't let her out of your sight. She will run, and she needs someone to watch over her."

"You told me she was shy and timid," Coop accused his former boss. "She's as timid as a machine gun."

He could almost see Jarrett's eye roll over the phone. "I said Lacey told me she used to be shy in college. Not anymore. Dude, don't you listen? Where the hell is your head at? You've been spending way too much time communing with the animals."

"I like animals. They're less trouble than women."

Jarrett sighed. "Whatever you do, do not let Meg off your farm. I don't know exactly what she's tangling with, but her husband is powerful and loaded with money."

He thought of Prescott August and his immense wealth. CEO of one of the country's largest sporting goods suppliers. The man might have a tennis racket, but he had a nine-millimeter. "And I'm locked and loaded."

He could protect her from threats, but the greatest threat could be himself, because Meg had started to worm her way past his guard. Her obvious love for animals made him see her in a new light.

*Focus on the job,* he reminded himself. *Keep her safe, hidden, and then she moves on.*

"Keep it that way, Coop. I don't know what threats she faces, but I suspect they are big ones. She needs protection."

"Damnit, then tell me what you know! I'm working in the dark without anything to go on. Give me intel, LT. She said she was supposed to meet up with Randall Jacobs to get information." Coop paused, struggling with his temper. "I didn't know Prescott was her ex. He employed Jacobs as a research engineer, and Jacobs was VP for the same company that made the vest that killed my baby sis. I know there's a link. I just need to find that M. E. Franklin."

Silence on the other end, as if Jarrett assessed what he'd told him. Then his former lieutenant spoke in a slow, clear voice. "What did you find out so far?"

"Jacobs made a mistake on the initial patent application. He used the mailing address for Taylor Sporting Goods, but the company name was Combat Gear Inc. Might have been done on purpose."

Silence on the other end of the phone. Finally Jarrett spoke in a low voice. "I did a little checking about Meg's ex. There are rumors he likes to snort away his income and got tangled with some pretty bad elements. The kind of guys you don't mess with because they have tentacles everywhere. That's why you need to keep your sidearm loaded at all times, Coop."

"Drug-related?"

"They're tangled up with heroin, money laundering and loan-sharking. They keep their noses clean, and law enforcement has a hard time pinning anything on them."

This news startled him. "Which family?"

"Miles O'Neary. Head of a smaller but very dangerous Irish Mafia family. They have a house in Palm Beach they use in the winter, but their main base is Boston."

It made sense now. If Prescott was in bed with organized crime and worried his research engineer could turn him over to the Feds, Randall Jacobs was a dead man from the moment he signed the patent application.

*If I didn't get to him first*, he thought grimly.

"Any idea what Randall had on Prescott August? Meg refused to say."

"No. It had to be big. Work on her tomorrow, Coop. Be subtle."

"I'm the master of subtle," he said drily, which earned a big laugh from his former lieutenant.

"If you sense she's getting upset at your questions, back off. It's more important you keep her from bolting. If she leaves your farm, she's got a bull's-eye on her back."

Deeply troubled, his anger slowly abating, he thumbed off his cell. This was no longer a simple case of protecting a woman running away from an abusive husband who needed a new life.

Meg August was linked to a man connected to the Irish mob, and a dead man who filed a patent for the same vest that killed Brie. A vest produced by Combat Gear Inc.

A ghost company no one seemed to be able to trace, without any executive staff, but for Randall Jacobs.

Somehow he suspected Meg's ex, Prescott, was involved in all this. How, he couldn't tell.

But soon, he would find out.

Sunlight dappled the oak floorboards of the room when Meg awoke the next morning to a dog licking her face.

Laughing, she flung back the covers. "Okay, girl, I know, you have to go outside."

Sophie barked and jumped down from the bed.

She tiptoed into the hallway, not wishing to awaken Cooper upstairs, and was startled to see him sprawled on the plaid sofa. Meg's breath hitched. He was a very nice sight in the morning. Long lashes against his cheeks, those angular cheeks, his mouth relaxed in sleep, his big body clad in gray sweats and a baseball T-shirt.

He opened one startling blue eye. "Morning."

"I didn't mean to wake you."

Cooper sat up, rubbed a hand over his tousled hair. "Got enough sleep already. I never need more than five hours. You okay?"

"Just letting Sophie outside." Meg couldn't help gazing at him. So handsome, the dark stubble covering his lean cheeks and firm chin.

"Why are you on the couch instead of bed?"

He gave her a steady look. "I slept out here to keep watch after what happened last night."

Her heart gave a happy little jump. Cooper looked solid and strong, and the idea that he was on guard, protecting her against a possible threat, eased her fears a little. Nothing would get past this man.

*Not even you. If he keeps questioning you, you have to give evasive answers. Don't trust him. Plausible deniability until you find the evidence.*

*Trust only yourself.*

"I'll come with you." He reached beneath one of the plaid pillows and withdrew a gleaming metal gun. The sight of it made her stomach churn.

She hated guns.

"Do you think someone was spying on me?"

Cooper shook his head. "I followed the footsteps to the inn. It was probably a late-night guest who got lost on the way to the main inn. It can happen, if they come in the back road leading to the barn. Gate's always closed, but never locked."

Meg pointed at the weapon as he tucked it into his waistband. "Then is that necessary?"

"With me, it is." He stuffed his feet into his boots and stood, yawning.

When they were outside, she looked at the indentation in the snow near the living room window where he had poured a plaster cast. Cooper watched her with a guarded look. He was a tall man, and she barely came to his chin.

Meg didn't like big men, because they reminded her too much of Prescott. But Cooper Johnson had shown her only respect. With his tall, leanly muscled body, he reminded her of a long-distance athlete. Her gaze flickered down to those lean fingers and the wicked scar on the back of his right hand.

Except long-distance athletes didn't carry guns. Cooper showed a casual confidence in handling the weapon. He was a US Navy SEAL and knew how to inflict violence. From what Lacey had said about the SEALs, they were a deadly force, and part of their strength came from a determination to never give up.

"I have a question," she told him. "Do you mind answering?"

"Shoot."

Very bad metaphor. "Have you ever killed anyone?" she blurted out.

Cooper blinked rapidly. "Whoa. That's an eye-opening question. I thought something along the lines of 'What's for breakfast?'"

Heat crawled up her neck. "I was thinking about the gun."

Those blue eyes were steady as he gazed at her. "I'm a Navy SEAL, Meg. I have engaged the enemy and did what I had to do to keep my country and my teammates safe."

"Of course, you are a professional soldier. I would expect you to carry a gun and do your job. And I didn't mean to open my mouth and insert my foot, especially this early in the morning before my brain cells actually awoke." She spoke in a rush, embarrassed at her gaffe. "And I'm a professional idiot for asking something so personal before you've even had your first cup of coffee. I didn't mean to offend you."

Cooper rubbed his neck and looked amused. "No offense. You're not a professional idiot, Meg. I've been asked much worse by a pretty woman when I first got out of bed."

Curiosity chased away her humiliation. "Like what?"

He considered. "What was your name again?"

At her stare, he laughed and winked. "Let's grab showers and we'll move your gear up to the inn after breakfast. I have a feeling your car won't be ready until tomorrow. Mikey's good, but always backed up."

"Okay. Now I'll ask what's for breakfast."

He gave her a sheepish look. "If you stay here, lumpy oatmeal. I'm not a good cook. But my mom is terrific in the kitchen."

Meg smiled. She was beginning to warm up to this man, who had a quirky sense of humor she enjoyed.

Her smile dropped as she thought of staying in the inn by herself, surrounded by strangers. Cooper had a protective air that made her feel safe. "And where are you sleeping?"

Cooper jerked a thumb toward the inn.

"Do I have to move to the inn? I'd rather stay here. I'm not sure if I'm ready to be around so many…people."

He gave her a long, thoughtful look. "You can stay where you're more comfortable, but that means I have to stay here as well."

"Is that a problem?"

A subtle ripple of tension went through him. "Not really."

Clearly remaining here in the cottage disturbed him.

"Inn's quiet now, but we have three guests arriving later. And tomorrow, there's Aimee. Once she sees you, she'll never leave you alone because of that."

He pointed to Sophie, who barked.

"Aimee?"

"My kid sister. She adores dogs. She's been away for a couple of days on a class field trip to Boston, but they're coming home tomorrow."

The sound of snow crunching beneath footsteps made

her tense. Cooper, too, until he saw who approached. Then he grinned. "Hey, Mom. What are you doing up this early?"

The petite woman in a navy jacket had black hair liberally streaked with gray, and warm brown eyes. She held out a basket covered with a checked cloth. Delicious smells wafted from the basket. Sophie sat down and looked at the woman, her little nose twitching.

Cooper took the basket and lifted the cloth. "Oh wow, cranberry orange! Thanks, Mom!"

"I figured you and your guest would enjoy fresh muffins straight from the oven." She smiled at Meg. "That way you wouldn't have to walk all the way in the cold without something warm inside you. Make sure he doesn't devour all of them before you even get a bite."

Cooper drew her forward with his left hand. "Mom, this is Meg. Meg, this is my mother, the owner of Sunnyside Farm, Fiona Johnson."

"Hello," Meg said, liking the woman's friendly face and the warmth radiating from her brown eyes. "Thank you for the treats."

His mother glanced down at Sophie. "Hello there. What a cutie you are."

Sophie wagged her tail. "This is my dog, Sophie," Meg told her.

"You don't look vicious." Fiona patted her head.

"She bit me last night." Cooper made a mock scowl.

"You're lucky she only bit your finger. Normally Sophie prefers to snack on other body parts," Meg jested.

As Cooper grinned at her, Fiona gave Meg a long, thoughtful look. "If you're still hungry after the muffins, come over to the inn. We had a new guest show up late last night, a nature photographer. I'm making a big breakfast. Scrambled eggs with hard cheddar, fried potatoes with peppers and onions, and biscuits."

New guest? Maybe he was the one who was outside the cottage last night. Cooper must have thought the same, for he asked his mother if the man had trouble finding the inn.

"He did mention it was difficult," Fiona said.

Well, that was it. Simply a case of a lost guest. Meg breathed a sigh of relief. "Your breakfast sounds delicious."

Cooper grinned. "See what I have to contend with? All this home cooking, it's a marvel I don't gain fifty pounds."

Fiona's smile grew troubled. "Hard for you to do with all the work you take on, Cooper. I wish you'd let me hire someone else to help around the farm so you can relax and enjoy your vacation."

"It's not a vacation. It's leave, Mom, and I told you, I'm here to help. First we need to hire more help for you." He dropped a kiss on his mother's cheek. "I've got things handled. You're the one who needs the rest. You work too hard."

Rolling her eyes, his mother smiled. "I'm not ready for a nursing home yet, Cooper. Hard work is good for the soul. Stop trying to make me feel ancient."

Seeing the respect and affection mother and son shared reminded Meg of her childhood, before family relationships were torn asunder and she was left as a little girl no one paid much attention to. She missed this so much that it sent a fresh wave of grief coursing through her.

"Thank you so much for your hospitality, but I'm not a big breakfast eater. And I'll be leaving as soon as my car arrives from the tow shop. If I'm lucky, maybe this afternoon," Meg told Fiona.

Mother and son exchanged glances. "It may not be that early," Cooper said. "Meantime, I thought I'd give Meg a tour of the farm. Maybe even go riding later. She's worked with horses before."

Fiona gave Meg another long look. "You're more than

welcome to stay, and some of our mares need exercising, so you'd be doing us a favor. Cooper told me you need a safe haven from your husband."

"Soon to be ex," Meg said, her gaze darting away.

"Hopefully sooner than later. Do yourself a favor, my dear. Don't judge all men by one bad apple." She looked at her son. "There are good men in this world, like my Cooper. Of course I'm biased, but he's a great catch."

At her smile, Cooper actually flushed. "Mom…"

"Do you need anything here? Fresh sheets, linens…" Fiona's eyes glinted. "Or perhaps bubble bath? There's a lovely claw-foot tub on the second floor. Very romantic."

"Meg's fine on the first floor," Cooper interjected. "She's already settled. I'm going to train her dog."

"I hope Sophie won't be a problem at the farm," Meg told her. "When Cooper doesn't have her, I'll keep her with me at all times so she won't bother the other guests. I was planning to find other lodging as soon as my car is ready."

"No problem," Cooper and Fiona said at the same time.

"What are your plans for today?" Fiona asked.

"I'm taking her into town to buy some boots and warm clothing, as soon as I finish feeding the animals and fixing that fence post," Cooper said.

The other woman's gaze sharpened. "Hank can take care of that. Long as you're in town, why don't you two have lunch at Minute Man Diner?"

Cooper glanced at Meg. "Sounds good."

"I don't want to be a bother," Meg started.

"No bother," Fiona told her. "I can handle things around here with the staff. Later, you can move up to the inn, if you like. Breakfast at the inn is from seven to nine-thirty. Don't forget."

His mother wagged her fingers in a goodbye gesture and set off toward the inn.

Meg glanced at the still-flushed Cooper. "She's always trying to set me up," he muttered. "God love her."

They went inside and Cooper set the muffins on the kitchen counter and then set about making coffee. Then he grabbed a muffin out of the basket and bit into it, moaning, an expression of pure ecstasy on his face. Meg had a naughty image flash through her mind—Cooper with the same expression, only naked as he moved atop her, all strength and smoothness, those muscles rippling as he flexed deep inside her in a bout of long, slow lovemaking. The kind of tender, explosive love she'd always longed to experience.

Dismissing the thought, hoping he'd blame the flush on her cheeks from the cold, she looked at the treats.

"Wow, these are amazing. I sure miss her cooking when I'm gone," Cooper told her.

She took a bite of muffin and agreed. Fiona was a superb baker.

Cooper fetched two mugs of coffee and poured a fresh bowl of water for Sophie. Meg added sugar to her coffee and joined him at the table. She sipped the coffee and coughed.

"Too powerful?" he asked with a knowing grin.

"A little." She went to the fridge and found milk, adding it to her cup. "Your mom must have missed you a lot while you were gone."

He nodded. "But she knew how much it meant to me to join the teams, and she was real proud when I got my Budweiser, my pin."

"What kind of qualifications do you need to become a Navy SEAL? Do you dive all the time? Lacey told me Jarrett is an expert diver."

"Diving is a big part of SEAL training. I like diving in the Caribbean for fun, but I grew up around here and learned to dive in the lakes. They're pretty cold and murky, so I was prepared for BUD/S."

At her confused look, he added, "Basic Underwater Demolition/SEAL, the training you go through to become a Navy SEAL. We also have specialties. Mine was radio communications and working with dogs."

"You have a real affinity for animals," she told him. "Sophie usually doesn't like men."

"I'm better with animals than people." He jammed his hands in his pockets. "I've had women in my life, but nothing long-term. I specialize in short-term. I'm warning you that even though my mom knows you're my assignment with Project SOS, every time she sees me in the company of a woman, she starts planning my wedding."

Meg tilted her head. "So that's the sound I heard when she brought over the muffins."

"What sound?"

"Wedding bells." She grinned and he gave a self-conscious laugh.

A dull flush covered his cheeks. "She's been trying to fix me up for years and says she's getting older and wants grandchildren. I told her to nag Derek, my older brother, if she wants grandkids. Most of my relationships have been pretty short. Women don't like that I am constantly gone, or knowing I might not return."

Meg felt a tinge of sympathy for Cooper, leaving on a deployment with no one to wish him goodbye, no one but his family to think about him while he was gone.

"So that remark about 'What's your name again' is really the truth, huh?" she teased.

"It has happened." He gave her a steady look. "Not saying it feels good, because I know then that my date just wanted to spend the night because I'm a SEAL. Usually I avoid the groupies who hang at the bars near the base, but sometimes after a deployment, a guy just needs to blow off steam and find someone who wants him, even if it's only for a night of sex."

Such honesty. Against her better judgment, she found herself liking him more. And the tender regard he had for his mother, worrying about her welfare, was worlds apart from someone like Prescott, who cared only for his own needs.

"About what I said earlier…" She raised her face to his. "I am sorry for asking it. I'm not a fan of guns. My brother died in combat and my grandfather was shot to death when I was only eight. His hunting partner accidentally killed him after getting drunk while they were tracking a buck. After, Gran threw out all the liquor in the house and got rid of all the guns. I never saw another one again until I married Prescott. He had a collection."

Quiet blue eyes assessed her thoughtfully. "And you were afraid he might use one of his weapons on you some day."

Meg hugged herself. "He never got violent when Gran was present. I was too ashamed to tell her what Prescott did. She thought he was terrific because he helped to save the company. When she died, I hoped I'd be free of him. But she left him everything in her will. The company's future was more important to her. It was devastating because she left me vulnerable. And penniless."

Cooper's mouth flattened. "I'm beginning to dislike your ex more and more. Did you hire a lawyer to contest the will?"

"I was more concerned with finding a good divorce attorney." She licked her lips. "I'm not helpless. With all his late-night meetings, I figured Prescott had a little something-something on the side so I hired a PI to find out."

"Good," he said softly.

"He showed me grainy photos of some brunette kissing Prescott. They were pretty far away, but I had enough grounds to file for divorce."

He gently touched her arm. "Prescott's answer to being served with the papers was to do this to you."

Shame crept through her. "He told me he could have all the mistresses he wanted, but I would always be his wife. If I tried to leave, I would wake up one morning with my arms and legs broken and Sophie would have a bullet in her head. So I...did what I had to do."

Emotion clogged her throat, but she pushed on, wanting this man to understand why she did what she did. Even Lacey didn't know the extent of it. Meg had been too ashamed to say much, but Cooper had a way of disarming her and making her open up.

"I hated being with him. I had to pretend around him all the time, smile like an obedient doll, while inside I screamed."

She saw a tensile change in his body, how he went from being loose and relaxed to alert and rigid. Jaw grinding, he dropped his hand.

"No wonder you dislike guns." He looked around the kitchen. "I made a promise to LT, Jarrett, that I would protect you from all harm, and I intend to keep that promise as long as you are under my watch."

Such quiet assurance. After two years of constantly watching over her shoulder, fearing her husband would explode into a tirade, this kind of vigilance felt comforting.

"Thank you, Cooper. I mean it."

He nodded. "We'll work on your alias and your new identity. It'll take days to get the right documents. But when we go into town, I'll introduce you as your new name. Megan Conners."

Not much different from her real first name. "I thought

I'd be something more exotic like Bunny or Buffy. Or how about Billy Jo? I can fake a Southern accent."

He didn't smile at her little joke. "First rule in black ops is blending in. Easier to have a new first name like your old one, so if someone calls you by your old name and you turn around, your cover isn't blown."

He looked deadly serious. Gone was the smiling, friendly man who teased her about shoes. In his intense expression she saw a glimpse of the warrior he must be.

"Megan Conners." It rolled easily off her tongue.

Cooper polished off his muffin and stood. "I'm grabbing a shower first because I have to look after the horses, Hank or no Hank. Stay here, relax, and we'll head into town in a couple of hours. There's a whole bookcase filled with paperbacks if you like to read, and the fridge is filled with food. I advise you to wait a good half an hour to shower after I'm done unless you like ice water. The heater is a little finicky in this cottage."

"I like hot showers, thank you very much."

She watched him walk away. For such a big guy, he was quiet. Soon, sounds of the shower upstairs began. Meg shivered, not from the cold, but thinking about his large, naked body beneath the spray, those tantalizing abs rippling as the water beaded against his skin, slowly trickling down to his...

"Stop it," she said aloud. "He's off-limits."

Taking another muffin back to her room, she fed small bits to Sophie. Meg ruminated over what Randall told her.

The microchip with the documents was close to her heart. She glanced down at her heart-shaped necklace. Randall had been to the house many times; was it possible...? Excitement hummed through her as she removed the necklace and found a nail file. Meg pried the diamond away from the setting.

Nothing. She put both away into her suitcase, trying to keep her spirits up. Perhaps the numbers would prove more useful. They must be a combination to a lockbox somewhere on Randall's property.

She studied the paper with the numbers. What if they weren't a pass code to a lockbox in his house, but something else? Randall was fastidious with his work. He wouldn't hide something as valuable as documents in something as obvious and accessible as a safe.

Powering up her Mac laptop, she accessed the cottage's Wi-Fi. Meg typed up the numbers, and sighed as random websites sprang into view. It made no sense.

She solved problems best when her mind was otherwise occupied. Meg surfed the internet news sites, glad to see another article about how federal authorities were investigating Combat Gear Inc. for manufacturing faulty body armor.

Prescott would be infuriated if he knew who had made that call to the authorities…

Shivering, she powered down the laptop. She needed to find those documents before she ended up like Randall.

Cooper drove her in his black Ford pickup to downtown New Falls. They parked in front of a flower shop and went into a department store so she could purchase two sweaters, a good pair of jeans and a warm jacket. Cooper wanted to buy them, but she insisted on paying for them herself, though the purchases severely dented her supply of cash.

Next, they walked to a shoe store a few doors down.

When they entered the shop, the cozy smell of fresh leather and shoe polish hit her nostrils.

A balding man with a slight paunch and a gold band on his left hand scurried over to greet them. "Coop! I heard you were in town. How long you home for, Coop?"

"Long enough, Roy."

Roy looked at Meg with interest. "So you need new shoes?"

Meg frowned. "How did you know?"

"Small town." Roy chuckled. "Lucy at the general store called and told me you were shopping for shoes."

"She needs work boots," Cooper said.

She was grateful he didn't introduce her. The less attention paid to her, the better.

"Work boots?" Roy's brown gaze lit with interest. "You're new around here? Just start working at the farm?"

Okay, not getting around this fishing expedition. Meg stuck out her palm. "Megan Conners. A pleasure to meet you."

Roy's hand was slick with sweat, and she quickly withdrew her hand. So different from Cooper's warm, firm handshake.

"She's staying at the inn," Cooper said smoothly. "About those boots, Roy. I know you stock them. Leather, brown, steel toe's best around the farm animals."

"But something I can wear off the farm as well," Meg added. "With nice stitching that's decorative."

Cooper grinned at her. "Ever the fashion princess."

The clerk pointed to a row of boots on display against the wall. "Pick out something you like and I'll get them from the back."

He joined them at the display. This man made the hairs on her nape stand up. There was nothing overt in his behavior, and Cooper knew him, but her instincts fired up.

She chose two pairs of boots. "Size six, please."

Cooper turned his attention to the men's shoes. "Say, Roy, anyone come in here lately and purchase a pair of size 14 men's flat-soled shoes?"

The salesclerk raised his brows. "Not that I know of.

No one I know has feet that big, except Hank, and I special order for his clodhoppers when he needs them. I never stock size 14."

Hank. The hired man. Meg wondered if it was Hank who spied on her last night.

As Roy disappeared into the stockroom, she sat in one of the chairs.

As she started to pull the suede boot free, he shook his head and swept a low bow.

"Allow me, madam."

Kneeling at her feet, he tugged off her boots. Meg wriggled her toes in the cotton socks.

Then Cooper examined her feet, pressing each toe with his thumb and forefinger.

"What are you doing? Making sure none of them fell off from frostbite?" she asked in amusement.

"Giving you a massage to circulate the blood. I'm real good with my hands, Princess." He winked.

He massaged her toes, and the feel of his big, rough hands made her bite back a moan. It had been a long time since anyone paid this much attention to her.

The right kind of attention, anyway.

When Roy returned, Cooper was all business. He refused to let Roy aid her in trying on the boots and helped her tug them on. She chose a pair of sturdy leather boots with a pretty Western stitch pattern and square steel toes. They were comfortable and soft, and they fit perfectly.

Then she looked at the price tag. Meg turned her head to see the nosy Roy lingering at a display stand close by. "Three hundred dollars?" she whispered. "That's too much money."

Cooper shrugged. "I'll pay for them." When she protested, he shook his head. "You're my girl now, Megan," he said in a strong voice, loud enough for Roy to overhear. "I always take care of my own."

A pleasant shiver went through her.

"You'll need a good pair of sneakers as well. Something good for running."

Meg frowned. "Running?"

"When I chase you around the bedroom, darling."

A heated flush ignited her body. Cooper winked, the act all plainly for show for the overbearing and too-curious shoe salesman, but her sorely neglected libido perked up at the image of Cooper catching her in the bedroom and the delicious price she'd pay for being caught.

In the end, she chose a pair of less expensive sneakers. Roy took the boots and the sneakers into the back room to find the right boxes to wrap her purchases.

At the cash register, Cooper gave Roy his credit card. Cooper was playing the part, of course, but the possessive note in his voice clearly warned off the other man. She wondered what it would feel like to really belong to a man like Cooper Johnson, who seemed extremely protective of his family and his privacy.

Wearing her new boots, she walked with him to the Minute Man Diner. A little silver bell tinkled over the glass door as they walked inside. There were two men at the counter, but other than that, the café was empty.

Behind the counter, a woman in a teal uniform and a white apron waved at him.

"Hey, Coop!" she called out. "Good to see you."

He lifted a hand in casual greeting. "Hi, Jackie. You serving lunch yet?"

"Sure thing." She put a hand over her heart and fluttered her eyelashes. "For you, darling, it's lunch all day long."

He laughed. "Don't flatter me, Jackie. You know you're taken."

They slid into a booth at the back, Cooper sitting with his back to the wall, looking over the café. Posture erect, gaze alert, he was relaxed, yet she sensed this man never fully relaxed except at home.

Jackie brought over two glasses of water and they ordered the special: chicken potpie with salad.

The waitress smiled at her. She had iron-gray hair, leathery skin and a friendly air. "You're new in town," she told Meg. "Staying at the inn?"

Cooper slid a hand across the table and covered her palm. "This is Megan, my new love. Sorry to break your heart, Jackie."

His new love? Good cover story, but could they pull it off? Certainly Cooper's hand over hers felt reassuring and real, even if it was only playacting. She wasn't certain how she felt about this. She liked Cooper, and felt attracted to him, but she'd suffered through too much of Prescott's beatings to even think about another man in her life.

She barely had met the man, yet he seemed rock steady and had a charisma that naturally attracted her. Her female parts tingled at the subtle pressure of his hand.

Once she'd felt like this with Prescott. Instant attraction. Meg forced herself to dial it down. Attraction could be deadly. Hadn't she learned that?

Far from looking heartbroken, the waitress looked interested. "About time you stopped waiting for me, Cooper. Pleasure to meet you, Megan."

"Pleasure to meet you, as well. I'm so happy I can finally meet Cooper's family and friends," she said, playing the part.

"Well, you get tired of Cooper's meals, you just come out here for the best home cooking this side of the Mississippi. Cooper's cute, but he could burn water. Even his mother says so." Jackie grinned.

"Hey, I can cook," he protested.

"Cutie pie, a man like you doesn't need to cook. You just blink those pretty blue peepers of yours and you melt hearts." Jackie sighed. "Including mine."

He lifted her hand and kissed the back of it. "I'd date you in a heartbeat, darling, if I wasn't worried about Mark coming after me with a stick."

The waitress rolled her eyes. "That would mean Mark parting from his recliner and the widescreen. You're free to flirt with me until football season is over, Coop."

Winking at Meg, she strolled off, pad in hand.

Meg smiled. "She's nice."

Cooper sipped his water. "Most people in town here are. Nosy as hell, too, which goes with small towns. A few you have to watch. Like Roy."

"I didn't like him," she admitted.

"Roy's married, but he's a hound dog who roams. He thinks he's a gift to women." Cooper snorted and drank his iced tea. "The kind of gift you wish you could return."

"He seemed awfully interested in how long you're home."

Cooper shook his head with disgust. "Roy knows I'm Navy, but he, like everyone else in my family, thinks I'm an ordinary sailor. He likes bragging he was a Navy SEAL. Went around telling everyone he took a bullet that dented his Budweiser when he was on a mission in Iraq, and he had to retire. Bunch of bunk that gets the ladies oohing and aahing. I just let him talk, make a fool of himself."

"Didn't you tell him you know what the real deal is?"

He lowered his voice. "Real SEALs don't brag about themselves. I have no desire to broadcast what I do for a living. The fewer who know, the better."

Her respect went up a few notches. Prescott always bragged about himself. It was refreshing to meet a man who did not, and instead, demonstrated his abilities through his actions instead of words.

They talked about the town and their favorite meals during lunch. Meg enjoyed his company. Cooper had a sincerity about him, but the entire time they were at the café, he never lost his aura of watchfulness. His quiet, solid presence was reassuring. She liked this man and felt safe with him.

But she knew soon enough, she'd be gone.

Cooper paid the check and they left the diner. Jackie called him back inside for a moment, asking him for a word in private. He glanced at her. "I'll be only a moment."

"Go on. I'll stay here." She nodded at the shop next door. "They have a wonderful collection of quilts. Time for a little window-shopping. Something a guy can't understand."

"I'll be back in a moment," he told her, and vanished inside.

The store had a lovely display of handmade quilts. Meg studied the creations, wistfully thinking of her grandmother. For a woman who ran a multimillion-dollar sporting goods company, Gran had never lost her country roots. She'd passed that on to Meg, along with a dose of common sense.

She moved on to study a blue-and-white wedding ring quilt hanging from a rack when she saw movement reflected in the window.

A man was standing in the street behind her. A man wearing an expensive camel-hair overcoat, dark trousers and polished loafers. Big loafers.

Meg's breath caught in her throat. Her fingers curled tight as she fought for control.

Impossible.

She glanced to the right at the overhead traffic light, which turned red. Guy in the street, no traffic, nothing unusual. He was probably crossing the street.

Guilty of jaywalking, nothing more.

*Turn around and see who it is. Just a guy, out for a walk. Maybe he wants to go into the quilt shop and he thinks he'll look silly, a guy entering a sewing shop.*

*Do it. Turn around.*

One, two…

Three!

Meg turned. The light turned green and a stream of cars went past. She craned her neck, looking up and down the street for the man.

He was gone.

But for a split second, she could have sworn he looked exactly like her ex-husband.

Cooper thought he could teach her young dog new tricks. Meg hoped so, for if Sophie kept growling at men, she wasn't certain who would want the dog. And she needed to find Sophie a home if the worst happened and she went to prison.

Late that afternoon, Meg went into the barn to watch them work. In his jacket, Stetson and faded jeans, Cooper looked more like a rugged cowboy than a dog trainer. But Sophie watched him attentively.

"Sit," he told Sophie.

Sophie promptly sat.

"Good girl," Cooper crooned. He opened his hand and said, "Stay."

Sophie promptly got up and wagged her tail, ignoring him.

He tried it a few more times, his voice soothing and deep, never rising in tone. Sitting on a bale of hay, Meg marveled at the man's patience.

Finally Cooper ordered Sophie to sit, and then walked

backward, his gaze never leaving the dog. "Stay," he ordered.

Her dog never moved. Meg held her breath.

Cooper walked up to Sophie, gave her a treat and praised her, stroking behind her ears. Sophie seemed to enjoy the attention as much as the treat. Hope filled Meg. Perhaps after all this time of suffering shouts, insults and the occasional kick from Prescott, Sophie would heal under Cooper's gentle hand.

Cooper tugged at the brim of his Stetson, a wide grin touching his full mouth. He turned to her. "Hey there."

She smiled. "Hey there yourself, dog whisperer. You're good."

He gave a modest shrug. "Takes a little time and patience, but she's a smart furball. She's learning."

Jumping off the hay bale, Meg started for Sophie.

"Sit," he ordered in a mocking tone.

Meg scowled.

And then he laughed, went to her and clasped her hand. "C'mere."

He tugged a little too hard and Meg collided with his firm chest. She stared up into his dark blue eyes. "And what kind of treat do I receive for obeying?"

His pupils expanded, and his breath hitched. Unsmiling, he stared down at her. "When you're ready, Princess, I'll show you."

Deep and husky, his voice washed over her like a velvet stroke. Meg pulled her hand from his. This man was dangerous. Sexy. Charming. And he adored animals as much as she did.

All the more reason to keep him at arm's length.

"Thank you for working with her. Please continue. She responds well to your voice. I'm cold and need to go inside."

Wasn't true, for the heat of the man still burned through

her jacket. She turned, ignoring the whine of her dog. But as she walked away, she could swear Cooper tracked her with his gaze, as if he wanted to teach her a few commands of his own.

She spent two hours at the inn with her laptop because the Wi-Fi was better there. Meg surfed the internet, looking for news articles on her ex and any updates on Randall's murder investigation. The police seemed to think it was suicide.

Meg tried to put the odd incident in town out of her mind. Lots of men wore nice overcoats and looked like Prescott and had big feet. The reflection hadn't been clear, either, so it must have been her overactive imagination.

When she finally returned to the cottage, Sophie was inside the kitchen. No sign of Cooper. Meg went into her room to set down her laptop and noticed a red rose on her bed.

Meg went still, fear curling inside her. Prescott used to give her red roses.

But this was an inn, and she was being silly, her imagination going wild. It was a welcoming gift, nothing more. She picked up the bloom and inhaled the scent. Sophie looked up and wagged her tail.

"Look," she told her, holding out the rose so Sophie could sniff it.

But the dog growled and backed off, and then suddenly dashed for the open door.

Setting the rose on the dresser, she went into the bathroom. Sophie was hiding in the shower. "Silly girl, it's okay, just a little prickly rose," she crooned, gathering the dog into her arms. She placed Sophie on her dog bed and patted her head until she relaxed.

She'd mentioned how much she used to adore red roses as she and Cooper explored the pathway cutting through the farm, down the hill to the nearby river. Fiona had a greenhouse, Cooper told him, and she grew roses year-round.

So, to thank Cooper for going to all the trouble, she asked Fiona for ingredients to make dinner. His mother was happy to oblige. And when Meg asked her to join them for dinner, Fiona made excuses about eating earlier.

Meg whipped up a green salad and a casserole from chicken she'd found in the freezer, noodles and a can of mushroom soup. When she called Cooper from the upstairs bedroom to come to the kitchen to eat, he gave a sigh of relief.

"I was going to cook some canned ravioli. I bet your cooking has to be better than that."

"Even your cooking is probably better than canned ravioli," she teased.

Sophie joined them. Meg watched as Cooper opened a can of dog food.

He set the bowl down and made a hand signal. Sophie did not move.

Then he snapped his fingers and the dog began to eat. Delight shot through her. "You really made progress. Usually she's on me, jumping up and down, as soon as she hears that can opener."

"I've been told I'm very good with animals...and women," he told her. His voice went husky. "I can be very, very patient when it comes to getting something I want."

Wow, there certainly was a message there. Heat spiraled through her all the way to her toes, and it wasn't from the oven, either.

As they sat down to eat, he praised her salad and then spooned up the casserole mixture eagerly.

"This is very tasty, Princess."

"I grew up with a grandmother who believed in self-sufficiency," Meg told him. The nickname was beginning to grow on her.

He smiled. "Better than the chow I make myself. I swear my cooking makes Sophie's dog food look tasty."

She was beginning to like this man, who adored animals as much as she did. But Meg didn't dare trust him. He had made it clear his family came first. And he was too interested in Randall and what Randall had on Prescott.

She had survived too much to ever get involved again with a man who wouldn't consider her needs first, both emotionally and physically.

"Prescott hated my cooking. He called it simplistic." She chased around her food on the plate with a fork, her appetite diminished at the thought of her ex. "He insisted on hiring a French chef."

"Idiot," Cooper muttered. "Not that he wasn't a big enough of one for what he did to you."

Meg kept her gaze focused on her plate, uncomfortable with talking about her past. "I should have learned to defend myself, but never did."

"Not necessary. Men should protect women, no matter what." His gaze darkened as she glanced up. "Not hit them."

"But a woman should learn to handle her own problems." Meg wasn't about to make excuses for herself.

"A good husband cares for his wife and is a shoulder for her to lean on, and he should take the burden off the woman."

"So you think the little woman should stay in the house and the kitchen? How very 1950s of you," she shot back. "Most women these days can fend for themselves. I certainly can, and so could my grandmother. She headed up a major business and knew how to do more than sew a quilt or bake."

Cooper looked at her calmly. "I didn't say that. I meant

a woman shouldn't have to do all those things by herself. God knows my mother shouldn't have to run this place alone. It's one reason I've thought about quitting the teams."

Glowering, he sat back and scrubbed a hand over his chin. Meg sensed she'd struck a very deep nerve. "Your mother sounds like she is a hard worker who could use a vacation."

Those broad shoulders relaxed the slightest. "She sent my uncle, aunt and cousins to Oregon to visit relatives for a month. One reason I returned home on leave was to help out while they were gone. But I wish she'd take a vacation, too."

Cooper's cell phone rang. He glanced at caller ID and told her, "It's Mike from the shop."

Finally.

But Cooper made a face as he talked with the man. "You sure? Okay, do what you need and send me the bill."

Meg's hopes shattered as he hung up. "Bad news. You bought a real lemon. I'm amazed you got this far without a problem. The good Lord must have been watching over you."

Her heart sank. "What is it?"

"Not your battery, but your alternator. It's going to take at least five days to get the parts shipped up here from the distributor."

Worrying her bottom lip, she felt her stomach roil. "I need that car back."

"Not going to happen right now, Princess. And you can't drive it with a bad alternator, because the car will keep dying on you." He gave her a pointed look. "I'm not going to send you out of here with a vehicle that will leave you stranded on the road like you were before."

Terrific. "I'm stuck here."

"For now." He leaned back, stretching out his long legs.

"I'll try to make it as pleasant as possible and not torture you. We only do that to our long-term guests."

Maybe she could spend the time searching on her laptop for other clues. She didn't like it, but had no choice because the sedan was her only means of transportation.

They made small talk about riding horses, and then he insisted on cleaning up. But she could see how weary he was, and she made excuses about retiring early. And then she remembered the rose.

"Oh, do you have anything here I can use for a vase?" she asked. "I need one for the rose."

A puzzled look came over him. "What rose?"

"The one you left on my bed. It was very nice of you, after I mentioned I used to like roses."

He frowned but quickly smoothed out his expression. "I didn't leave you a rose, Meg. But Mom is known to do stuff like that for guests."

Cooper hunted through the cabinets and found a dusty glass vase. Meg thanked him and rinsed it out.

"If you want dessert, there's apple pie at the inn. It's great heated up with vanilla ice cream," he told her.

Meg washed Sophie's dog bowl and set it in the dish drainer. "The pie sounds delicious, but I'm far too exhausted to have dessert. Good night, Cooper, and thank you for everything."

He nodded. "Going to check on the horses, and I'll be back soon."

When he left, she picked up the rotary phone and dialed the inn to thank Fiona for the rose. The inn's main number was on a sheet by the phone.

The woman answered in a brisk voice, "Sunnyside Farm."

"Hi, Fiona, it's Meg."

"Meg! How was dinner?"

"It went well. I wanted to thank you for the rose."

A pause came over the line. "What rose?"

"The one you left for me on my bed at the cottage."

Another long pause. "I didn't leave a rose. It must have been my son."

Meg felt her dinner start to churn in her stomach. "Probably. Well, good night and thank you again."

She hung up the phone, her hand trembling. Cooper hadn't left a rose, either.

If Cooper's mother and Cooper hadn't left the rose, who did?

# Chapter 6

The next morning after an early breakfast at the inn, she took Sophie for a long walk by the cottage. The forest flanking the drive to the cottage looked pretty, and the grounds were private, far enough away from the inn's other guests who arrived last night.

Remembering how Prescott had hired people to watch her every move, Meg had asked Fiona about the guests. There was a couple from England taking a second honeymoon, the reserved and taciturn nature photographer who'd arrived the same night as Meg, and a lonely gray-haired widow from Georgia who wanted to escape the heat.

Cooper met her at the fence separating the cottage from the private dirt road. He handed her a prepaid cell phone that had been programmed with his phone number and that of the inn. "We keep an extra for emergencies. Fully charged and set to go."

With old-world courtesy, he opened the white gate and waited for her to walk through. "When you come here to walk the furball, make sure you keep this gate closed. Sometimes Pete, our neighbor down the road, forgets to lock up his dog. That dog has a mean streak when it comes to other dogs, but he's sweet as a pup with people."

She touched her pocket where the cell phone rested. He didn't know who put the rose on her bed, but said it could have been the maid. Still, the gesture made her uneasy. Meg hated the idea of someone going into her room.

Cooper promised to take away the housekeeping key to make her feel more secure.

They walked for a while, and she asked questions about his family. His older brother, Derek, was a police detective in Boston. And, Aimee, now eleven, had been a "change of life baby" for their parents. Their father had been killed when his convoy encountered an IED.

"Dad was retired Army, who re-upped after the September 11 attacks. He wanted to serve again. Mom was worried, but she knew how important it was to him. When he died, it broke her heart, but she knew he died doing what was important to him."

Two years later, Cooper had enlisted in the Navy.

It said something about Cooper and his own quiet dedication to serve his country. Meg felt newfound respect for him. Prescott hadn't wanted to serve anyone but himself. And his mistress. Good riddance to both of them.

"I'm sorry about the loss of your sister," she told him. "Was she younger than you or older?"

Cooper fell silent for a moment, and Meg sensed this was a difficult subject. He jammed his hands into the pockets of his jacket. "Younger. Brie was always tagging along after Derek and me. She was a real tomboy. Loved to ride horses, too." He looked distant. "Brie was a good woman. I've known too many good people who died."

Sympathy filled her. His loss wasn't only his sister, but soldiers he'd known and fought with overseas. From working with veterans at a volunteer group after Caldwell died, Meg knew many returned home harboring their own quiet grief.

"Losing someone you love hurts. Sometimes it takes everything you've got to get through the day."

Cooper's gaze grew distant. "Yeah."

He seemed uncomfortable with this conversation, so she changed the subject.

"When are you returning to base?" she asked.

He studied the sweep of horse pasture. "Four more weeks. I asked for a month of leave, but my new CO told me to take six weeks."

"That was nice of him."

He gave a short laugh. "Nice? No, he wanted to get rid of me for a while. He thinks I take too many risks."

"Cooper! Can I ride Adela later?"

At the shout, they turned to see a young girl in a navy blue jacket, jeans and boots running toward them from the direction of the farmhouse. The little girl wore a red cap with a bear's head in the front. Two red braids dangled from the hat. The effect was so comic, it made Meg smile.

"Hi!" She ran through the gate, closed it and rushed up to them, hugging Cooper tight. He embraced her, his expression fierce.

Then he set her back and tugged at one of the red braids. "When did you get back, Peanut? Thought you weren't arriving until later today."

"Last night around ten. Mrs. O'Malley dropped me off. Patty got sick and threw up all over the room so her mom came to pick her up early, and I asked to go, too. I missed you too much."

"Missed you, too," he told her.

"Every time I turned on the TV when you were gone, I was so worried something would happen to you, Super Cooper. Don't leave us again for a long time. Please?" The little girl's voice grew thick. "I don't want to lose you like we lost Brie."

Meg stepped back, not wanting to intrude and sensing this was a delicate matter between siblings. But Cooper straightened. "Peanut, meet Meg. Meg, this is my sister Aimee."

She stared at Meg with obvious curiosity. "Are you one of Cooper's late-night lady friends?"

"Aimee," he said in a low voice.

Amused at the sudden ruddiness on Cooper's cheeks, she saved him by answering, "No. I'm a guest here until my car is fixed."

The girl beamed. "You're prettier than the lady who was here last year. She was taller than you and had legs that wouldn't quit."

"Aimee!"

"Well, that's what Uncle Jack said!"

Cooper tugged again at one of the red braids tumbling from the girl's winter cap. "Never mind what Uncle Jack said. Isn't it a little early to be wearing this?"

Aimee rolled her eyes. "I like Buster Bear. And it snowed this week, so it's officially cold. Jenny, our new housekeeper, said she's freezing in this weather. She's never been this cold. Wait 'til February—she's gonna freeze her tuchus off!"

Meg laughed as Cooper scowled. "Don't say tuchus. It's a bad word."

"Uncle Jack says it all the time."

"He says a lot of things he shouldn't. It's okay for adults, but not for little girls who wear Buster Bear hats."

The girl looked at her with interest. "Jenny says it's a pretty hat. I heard her tell Mom she was down on her luck and needed a job to get her through winter. I think Hank likes her and hopes she'll stay longer."

"Don't eavesdrop, Aimee. It's bad manners."

Aimee looked at him with wide eyes as blue as his own. "Can I help it if everyone talks loudly?"

Meg laughed again.

Cooper's sister stared at her with the inquisitive look of a typical eleven-year-old. "I like your laugh. You should stay here for a while. They have the Christmas hayride at the fair next month and I'm going to help sell popcorn to raise money for the local animal shelter. Cooper's gonna give rides. He's real good at that."

Now it was her turn to blush as she imagined the kind of ride she'd enjoy with Cooper. Definitely not at a local fair.

"My brother is a real animal lover."

Cooper looked embarrassed.

"He's great with dogs. He once carried Max over the hot sand when he was deployed in Iraq so Max's paws wouldn't get hurt. Max was our Belgian. Well, not ours, he was a SEAL. His trainer died in the fighting, so Cooper took him in and worked with him. Poor Max died last year in the fighting. I miss him." Aimee bent down to let Sophie sniff her hand, and then petted her behind the ears. "You're sweet. I wish you were mine."

Cooper's sister looked up at her with the same bright, inquisitive look Fiona had given Meg. "Where are you from? Do you have a boyfriend or are you hitched?"

"Aimee, watch it," Cooper warned.

"Mom says Cooper should settle down. Interested? He's a real catch. He even knows how to load the dishwasher!"

Cooper sputtered as Meg shot him a teasing look. "Definitely qualifications for a life partner."

"Peanut, go up to the house and get ready for school."

"So, can I ride Adela later? You said I could," Aimee told her brother.

"Not for a while. Adela's still getting used to us. Give her time. You can ride Pepper after school and chores."

Making a face, Aimee rolled her eyes. "Pepper is boring."

"Well, boring can be good." He tickled her ribs and Aimee laughed, and then rushed off in direction of the inn.

Halfway there, she stopped turned and waved. "Hey, Meg, stop by later and I'll show you my collection of *Star Wars* bobbleheads!"

"Okay," she called, waving back.

"You made quite an impression," Cooper murmured. "Usually Aimee doesn't show those to anyone except friends and close family. If she takes out the Chewbacca mask, you're gold."

Meg laughed again. "I'll remember that. I like *Star Wars*, too."

He sobered. "Aimee has attachment issues right now. I was stunned she even wanted to go on that field trip. After Brie died, she cried for days and had nightmares. And they didn't stop until I got home on leave."

"It must have been very difficult for you to return to active duty after that."

Cooper's big shoulders tensed. "I thought about resigning because my family needed me, but I'm going to stick it out until it's time to re-up. Love being a SEAL and never thought I'd quit the teams before turning forty, but then again, never thought I'd have to bury my kid sister, either."

She touched his arm, her heart twisting at the shadows on his face, and the grief in his eyes. "I'm sure your family wants what's best for you."

He shook his head. "I know what's best for me. Staying here with them. Family comes first."

Such dedication, sacrificing career for his loved ones. Meg had never known such devotion and envied it. Oh, her grandmother loved her, and was good to her, but the business always came first. Always. Had it not, Gran never would have hired Prescott to run Taylor Sporting Goods and eventually take the company public, where they could become a billion-dollar corporation instead of a million-dollar one.

"Aimee's sweet," she said, wishing she had a kid sister.

"Never boring. Though boring with Aimee would be good, because she is always getting into one scrape or another."

Boring could be good, she agreed. *Boring would be excellent right now.* Meg felt a chill, thinking of wearing an orange jumpsuit. No Jimmy Choos with that outfit. Would she get bored in prison? What kind of sentence would they give her when she turned over the evidence?

Maybe they would send her to a white-collar prison where she could serve a useful purpose, other than learning to make shanks from toothbrushes and avoid dark corners...

He studied the barn. "I have work. Feel free to walk your dog on the cottage grounds. Or if you like, there are books in our private living room. Mom usually doesn't allow guests in there, but you're special."

She forced a smile. "Thanks. I think I'll use the Wi-Fi for a while."

"Signal's more powerful at the inn. I have a booster I'll install, but can't get around to it until tomorrow."

"I was planning on working at the inn, anyway. The coffee is better there."

Cooper sputtered. "My coffee isn't that bad."

"If you like coffee that could serve as road tar."

"Woman, you mock me." He heaved an exaggerated sigh and put his hand over his heart.

Meg gave him a sweet smile. "The truth hurts, doesn't it?"

Cooper leaned forward and touched her cheek, his gaze

growing dark and filled with sensual heat. "You're a dangerous woman, Meg August."

Then he turned on his heel and walked off, hands stuffed into his pockets.

Trembling, she touched her face where his fingers had burned into her skin. Never had a man's simple caress made her so alive, so aware.

*You don't need Cooper Johnson in your life. Stop this.*

She needed to figure out what those numbers meant. The sooner she found the evidence, the better.

And then what? Prison for her, most likely. But what would happen to Sophie? She'd have to find her a very good, loving home.

A lump clogged her throat as Cooper headed for the barn. He liked dogs. Maybe his family would be willing to adopt Sophie.

When she entered the inn, laptop in hand, a man sat in the living room, reading a travel magazine. Richard Kimball, the nature photographer. He was an odd man, on the opposite end of the attraction spectrum from Coop. With his squashed face, slicked-back salt-and-pepper hair and tall, thickset body, he didn't look like someone who made a living climbing mountains and photographing eagles. A 35-millimeter camera rested on the table beside him.

Looking up, he stared at her with cold, beady eyes.

"Hi," she said. "You're new. I'm Meg, another guest here."

Saying nothing, he returned to his magazine. She felt a chill rush down her spine. Not a friendly person.

Meg looked down at his shoes and felt another chill. Big feet. Perhaps size 14. Was this the man who had knocked over the clay flowerpot outside the cottage last night?

She tried again. "It's nice outside now, but that snowstorm was terrible! I hope you didn't get caught up in that mess."

"No," he grunted.

"Did you have any trouble finding the place? I've been told guests sometimes get lost by the cottage."

*Were you spying on me last night? You're wearing the same kind of shoes that made a print outside the window. Who are you?*

*Is it really safe to be here?*

"You ask a lot of questions," he muttered, never lifting his gaze from the magazine.

Meg headed for the second-floor common room where guests could use the Wi-Fi. On the landing, Aimee greeted her. "I'm off to school. Hey, someone left you a card on the hall table. It has your name on it."

Aimee handed her the cream envelope. "Maybe later I can walk Sophie for you. I love dogs. See ya!"

Meg waved goodbye as Aimee raced down the carpeted staircase.

In the common room, Meg removed her coat and placed her laptop on the desk. She sat there, studying the envelope.

Someone had written her name on it with an elegant black pen. Curious, she tore open the envelope and smiled. Hearts and flowers emblazoned the outer card, along with a message: "Someone loves you!"

The inside was blank, but the scrawled, ugly words in black iced her blood. "But it's not me, you stupid bitch."

Voices sounded in the hallway. Quickly she folded the card and stuffed it into her jeans pocket. Cooper and his family must not know about this incident. She was on her own and couldn't rely on anyone else.

Fiona came into the room. "I don't serve lunch to guests, but Cooper likes to eat at noon. Why don't you stop in the kitchen? He'll need some help. My son is wonderful, but he's not a very good cook. Not even for lunch."

Her brows drew together in a puzzled frown. "Not even sandwiches?"

"You should see, dear." Fiona sighed.

"All right. If you are going to…"

"Oh, I'll try, but I can't promise anything, dear. I have to start decorating the grounds for the fall. I'm very far behind. But I'm certain Cooper would love to have lunch with you."

If that wasn't a clear setup… Meg almost laughed. "All right."

Closing the door after Fiona, she returned to the desk. The hateful card felt like it burned a hole in her jeans pocket. Perhaps it was someone who was jealous of the attention Cooper paid to her. Doubtful that Prescott had found her this quickly.

But she knew the sooner she was on the road, the better.

Around noon, Meg went searching for Cooper. She went downstairs and saw Fiona in the dining room, setting out fresh flowers on the table.

"Try the basement. He mentioned working out. Cooper set up a home gym down there. First door on your left as you go into the hall."

The basement was large and had pine-paneled walls. In one corner was a set of weight equipment, along with a bench. Shirtless, Cooper sat on the bench, his calves lifting a bar saddled with weights. Sweat streamed down his temples and he stared straight ahead. Droplets glistened in the silky hairs on his chest. Meg's mouth watered as she watched his biceps move as he lifted a set of hand weights, timing the motion to the leg lifts.

So handsome. And strong. And yet there was a gentleness that contrasted with his male strength. She sensed he would never deliberately hurt her.

He seemed unaware of her presence, so she contented herself to watch as muscle and sinew flexed on his legs. Cooper had the wiry strength of tempered steel.

Finally he lowered the bar with a loud *bang* and set down the weights. Cooper reached for a white towel, wiped his face.

He glanced at her. "Enjoy the show?"

So he had been aware of her. Meg pointed her two thumbs into the air. "Very good. Two thumbs up. I'd ask for an encore, but your mother said you like to eat at noon and it's nearly noon now. Lunch?"

"My treat this time. I'll make it for both of us," he told her.

He wiped his chest and legs and flung the towel aside. Cooper picked up a bottle of water and chugged. Fascinated, she watched his throat muscles work. He wiped his mouth with the back of one hand and set the bottle down.

"I need a shower first."

Meg licked her lips, unable to drag her gaze away from his rippling abs. It had been a long time since she'd had sex. Good sex.

*How about you and I skip lunch and engage in another activity?*

And then she remembered the hateful card and all thoughts of pleasure flew away. Someone wanted to hurt her.

Just like Prescott had.

She managed to find her voice. "Sounds good."

His gaze turned watchful. "What's wrong?"

"How do you know something's wrong?"

"Your face," he said gently. "You had that same wary

look when you walked into the barn after you heard the crash."

Reluctant to tell him about the letter, she decided to focus on her main concern. "Is there a place where I can leave Sophie for the day where she won't get into trouble if I'm out? A place other than the cottage?"

"What happened?"

Astute. The man was quite perceptive. Meg rubbed her hands against her jeans. "I don't want her locked up all day. She's a people dog, around women, anyway."

"Mom loves dogs. She was great with Max when he came home with me. Why don't you get Sophie and leave her with my mom? Even if she has errands to run, Sophie can stay in her room."

Much better than leaving her alone, where someone might sneak into the cottage and hurt her. "Sounds good. Thanks."

As she turned to leave, he caught her wrist. The pressure of his hand was steady, but not punishing. "Meg, if there's something troubling you…tell me."

The raw command in his voice almost made her capitulate. Almost. Meg offered a bright smile. "I'm expecting a terrific lunch, Farm Boy. And I'm hungry, so hurry up."

Lunch turned out to be burned toast and half-cooked bacon on BLT sandwiches. Cooper had covered up his magnificent chest and abs with a gray-and-white baseball shirt. The sleeves hugged the smooth contours of his biceps, and she enjoyed watching him slice and dice tomatoes.

True to Cooper's word, Fiona was happy to watch Sophie. She took the dog and left them alone in the kitchen. Meg ate the sandwich, trying not to make a face as Cooper chuckled.

"Usually I'm used to eating MREs, meals ready to eat.

And with my mom around, I never learned to really cook much for myself. Except in the field when I had to eat bugs and leaves."

Meg set down the uneaten portion of her sandwich. "That sounds more appetizing than this sandwich."

"Are you making fun of me?"

She poked at the blackened toast. "If the shoe leather fits…"

Shaking his head, he finished his sandwich. "Princess, you're breaking my heart. Here I went all out to prepare a gourmet meal fit for a beauty queen, and you're looking at my fine creation as if I served you toasted grasshoppers on rye bread. Which, I might add, are very fine when you're starving on a training op."

As he placed a hand over his heart, she considered. "Burned rye bread and raw grasshoppers? Is that what the Navy teaches you? What an epicurean delight."

"Philistine," he told her in a mocking tone. "You have no appreciation for the finer art of field cuisine."

Meg laughed and sipped her hot tea. When he finished, she went to clean the table. Cooper caught her wrist. The warmth of his calloused fingers on her skin sent a delicious shiver down her spine. Such strong hands, and yet so gentle…

"I'll get the dishes, Meg. You're a guest."

"I'm not helpless. You said you have work in the barn, and I have two good hands."

Cooper's fingers slid up her hand, and then he raised it to his mouth, brushing her knuckles with a light kiss. Heat flared between them, so powerful it felt like the very air would combust.

"Thanks," he said in a husky voice.

Then, as if regretting the action, he gathered his coat and

hat and went out the kitchen door, heading to the barn. But there was a spring in his step she hadn't noticed previously.

Meg finished cleaning up and looked out the kitchen window as Cooper climbed on a ladder to attend to a broken light on the barn. Hearing a sound at the doorway, she turned to see an innocent-looking Fiona standing in the doorway.

"Did you have a nice lunch with Cooper?"

"The company was good. The food…"

Fiona went and began to put dishes away. "I'm afraid my son is spoiled when it comes to meals. We never let him cook on his own. He once almost burned down the kitchen. If I wasn't making him something, then it was his aunt—my sister-in-law Jean. Or Brie. Brie always liked to treat her big brother when he came home…"

Fiona's voice broke. She closed her eyes, her hands gripping the pot handle so tight, her knuckles whitened. Meg went to her and touched her shoulder. "I am so sorry about the loss of your daughter."

The older woman nodded roughly. "She's been gone only six months. I miss her so much, even though we seldom saw her after she began working in Boston's rougher areas. We weren't happy about it, but she felt compelled to do something more."

Meg picked up a dish towel and began to dry the dishes. She didn't want to bring up the subject of a diseased loved one, but if Fiona needed to talk, she'd listen. "She sounds dedicated."

"Brie was a lovely woman. Even after she married that… man…she never lost her sense of joy. We were very grateful when she finally got divorced."

"Cooper said something about a bad relationship."

"Her ex-husband used to hit her," Fiona said, clanking the pot as she put it away. "Cooper put an end to that. If he hadn't, well, I own a .38 and I know how to use it. No one hurts my children and gets away with it."

Driven by sympathy, remembering her own loss, Meg hugged Fiona. For a moment the woman hugged her back, her shoulders shaking. And then she finally stepped back, wiping her too-bright eyes with the back of her hand.

"You're a good person, Meg. I can tell about people."

Oh, how she wished Fiona were right. But good people didn't operate companies that killed police officers. And they faced up to those who hurt them instead of running away. Cooper wouldn't be afraid. He would not run away. He would have stood up to Prescott.

As she walked away, rolling down her sweater sleeves, feeling dejected, Fiona called out, "Wait."

Meg turned at the door.

Cooper's mother glanced at her left arm. The bruised left arm. Meg bit her lip, waiting for the questions she didn't want to answer.

"I want you to know you're safe here, from whoever and whatever is in your past," Fiona said gently. "My son is a good man, and he'll protect you."

Awkward. She liked Fiona and the woman's warmth, but this was too personal. Nothing could protect her once Prescott found her. And she didn't want to hurt these kind people.

"Thank you," she said quietly. "I'm not staying once I get my car back."

"It's not easy to pack up everything and leave your family, Meg. Sometimes the familiar proves too tempting. It takes a great deal of courage to put it all behind you. Especially when you have no one backing you up and your own family turns away from you."

There was such frank bitterness in her words it made Meg wonder if Fiona referenced something even more personal. Yet Cooper said his father was a good man, and the way Fiona had fondly recalled her husband as they talked about life on the farm indicated he wasn't anything more than an ideal husband. "I don't have any family left, so that made it easier."

"There are good men out there, Meg. Learn to lean on them when you need it."

Nodding, she raced out of the kitchen, not wanting to pursue this conversation anymore. There were good men in the world.

Cooper was one of them.

But he wasn't meant for her.

# *Chapter* 7

While waiting for her car to get a new alternator, Meg kept busy over the next two days in the barn, working with Adela. She enjoyed horses, and teaching a traumatized horse to trust again proved one of her great joys.

She'd created Combat Gear Inc. to show herself that she was more than a Palm Beach socialite and a pretty decoration for her wealthy husband. Knowing she produced a product that would protect law enforcement officers and soldiers gave her a sense of peace she hadn't felt since the terrible day Caldwell died. It gave her empty life purpose and a quiet sense of pride.

But working with animals that had been unwanted, abandoned or abused made her feel an equal sense of accomplishment.

After an hour, Cooper left her alone with the horse. His trust fed her confidence. No more incidents had happened to alarm her, and she was beginning to relax. Still, it would be best once her car was fixed and she was on her way.

She was beginning to like it here too much. The farm was peaceful. Fiona was friendly and motherly, and Aimee was a bright, intelligent girl.

And Cooper...the man was hot, honorable and quietly

protective. Each time she was near him, the air snapped and sizzled with the attraction.

They fell into the habit of riding each afternoon, exploring the trails along the river. She rode Snowflake, a frisky young mare, while he rode Farmalot, a big gelding.

Cooper was a mighty fine sight in a saddle. Black Stetson tugged low on his forehead, sheepskin jacket hugging his broad shoulders, he looked like a poster for a rugged cowboy in Montana.

The previous night, Meg and Cooper had taken Aimee to enjoy a bonfire at the fire pit Fiona lit for the guests. The gray-haired widow from Georgia was Paula, a homemaker who lost her husband earlier in the year. Paula talked with a thick Southern accent and kept making eyes at Cooper.

Not a widow in deep mourning, Meg had whispered to the uncomfortable Cooper.

The nature photographer, Richard Kimball, even joined them, saying nothing and stuffing his hands into his pockets. The couple from England, Joe and Cathy Murphy, talked about their retirement dream of traveling the world. They offered peanut butter s'mores they'd made, but Aimee declined.

The girl had a peanut allergy.

After a while, she and Cooper had been left alone to the dying bonfire. They'd shared a bottle of wine, not of the expensive vintages Prescott stocked, but it has been aged in oak and fruity.

And the company had been far better.

Today Cooper was fixing things around the farm, but promised to be finished for their late-afternoon ride. While waiting, Meg decided to take Sophie for a long walk. She snapped on Sophie's leash and took her outside. The weather was brisk, but delightfully so. She headed for the cottage, waving to Cooper as she passed.

Randall had indicated he'd meet her at his family's summer home in New Hampshire. The house was located on a small lake. The evidence must be there, someplace around the house. If the documents were there, she had to act quickly before Randall's estate was settled and his heirs decided they might keep the house. But Meg was no closer to deciphering the mysterious numbers than she had been upon her arrival. If only Randall had given her more information before she left. It had been too risky. Prescott watched her every move, except when he went on one of his business trips to Boston or to oversee production of the vests.

Even then, she had to be careful because he had his staff watch her. A few months ago Prescott had left for Boston, and Meg went to a shelter for abused women. Just to check it out. Just to see what it was like, to see if someone could help…

That night during Prescott's evening phone call, he'd asked her why she'd gone there. Meg had stammered an excuse about charity work.

She walked Sophie down the driveway paralleling the horse pasture, enjoying the wind sending the dead leaves skittering across the ground.

Sophie sniffed at a tree and tugged on the leash, whining.

"Okay, let's go back. Maybe I can find you some nice…"

Meg stopped, every hair rising on her nape as Sophie whined. The gate at the end of the driveway swung open in the wind.

Barely one hundred feet away stood a black-and-white dog. Weighing roughly eighty-five pounds, it looked like a pit bull mix. All muscle. And he bared his teeth, big, bad teeth, growling low, starting to pace toward her.

His gaze locked on Sophie, who whined and backed

away, ready to run. Pete's runaway dog. He was going to tear Sophie apart. And maybe her as well.

Meg froze, but Sophie turned.

"Sophie, stay," she said in a low voice.

*Dear heavens, please let her listen to me this time...*

Her pet whined, but did not move.

Slowly, as to not anger the strange dog further, Meg crouched down and picked up Sophie. That gate wasn't open when she started her walk. Who could have opened it?

Terror iced her veins. No pepper spray. She had that back in the room, thinking the farm was a safe place to walk her dog. If she ran, she and Sophie were toast.

Her gaze whipped over to the horse pasture. Hank, the foreman, was at the barn. Too far away to shout. With her right hand, she reached into her pocket for the cell phone Cooper had given her. Meg slowly pulled it free and pressed the number one and the speaker button.

"Cooper," he said in a brisk tone.

"Nine-one-one," she said in a panic. "I'm facing a really angry dog right now who wants to tear into Sophie."

"Don't move," he told her. "I'll be right there."

Meg slowly pocketed the phone. The pit bull mix growled at Sophie, who struggled to free herself from Meg's grip. She knew the moment she put Sophie down, the bigger dog would attack.

Behind her, she heard Cooper pull up in a four-wheeler, heard him climb off, leaving the engine running. He reached her side.

"Meg, you okay?" he asked in a low voice.

"Yes, but in about one minute, I won't be. He has Sophie's scent and he looks ready to charge."

Cooper nodded. "Don't move. I know you want to run, but it'll trigger his chase instinct. Stay here. I know this dog."

He began sidling up to the growling animal very slowly.

"Easy, boy," Cooper murmured, avoiding direct eye contact. "You're not gonna get an inch near Sophie there, are you, Buddy? Not even to make friends. I'm your friend. You know me, Buddy. Remember me, Buddy?"

Keeping his body sideways, he kept talking in a low, soothing voice to the growling dog, approaching him cautiously. Cooper spoke over his shoulder.

"Meg, on my word, turn around very slowly. Once he can't see Sophie, he'll lose interest. I'm going to grab his collar and then you walk away. Don't run. Go back to the cottage. I'm going to take him back to Pete on the four-wheeler."

Cooper reached into his pocket and withdrew a biscuit. It was small, but she prayed it could distract the dog.

"Look what I got, Buddy. A treat, just for you. Bet you don't have many of those lately with ole Pete being so sick. You hungry, boy? You want a nice dog biscuit? It's good."

He tossed the biscuit to the dog, who loped forward and snatched it up.

"Now Meg, turn around real slow and walk off," he ordered.

Every cell of her body cried out to bolt for the house. Still holding Sophie, she turned around, her heart racing. That was a big, mean dog. She didn't see how Cooper could tame it to his hand.

Very slowly, she began to walk away.

"Gotcha!"

Daring to peek over her shoulder, she saw the most incredible sight. As he scratched behind the dog's ears, the monster wagged his tail, licking Cooper's face. The Navy SEAL had a leash attached to the dog's collar.

Relief spilled through her. Gripping Sophie, she walked slowly back, fighting the urge to race for the safety of the cottage. Once inside, she closed the door. Meg watched Pete's dog run alongside the four-wheeler as Cooper steered it through the gate. He got off, closed the gate and continued down the road, the dog barking joyously as he raced alongside him.

Trembling, Meg sank into the sofa in the sunroom and set down Sophie, who jumped onto her lap and crouched there, whining.

She stroked her dog's head, trying to calm her. Poor Sophie. First Prescott's nasty streak and now this. Was there any place safe for them?

"I know, baby. That was one huge set of teeth. I wasn't going to abandon you, sweetie. No way. Where you go, I go. It's you and me now. We're all alone."

Wagging her tail, Sophie licked her face.

Emotion clogged her throat. She could have lost Sophie today, and Pete's dog would have hurt her as well. Anyone who knew her knew she'd never sacrifice her dog to an animal attack. Knew she'd defend her best friend with her life.

Cooper drove up, parked the four-wheeler. He let himself in and looked at them.

"You okay?"

At her nod, he went into the kitchen and she heard water running. Cooper returned and joined her on the sofa. Sophie still curled up against Meg. She allowed him to pat her on the head.

"You washed your hands to get rid of that dog's scent," she guessed.

Cooper nodded. "Don't want to upset Sophie any more than she already is."

Meg shuddered. He stopped, sat beside her and slid his palm over hers. "You're still trembling. Can you tell me what happened?"

Meg told him about the walk, staring down at her hand

as he held it. Not too tight, with just the right comforting pressure.

"Who could have opened the gate? I never would have done that and endangered Sophie."

"I don't know." Cooper gave her hand a reassuring squeeze. "Everyone around here knows to close it. And the guests know this area is off-limits. I'll check into it with Hank, see if he saw anything. Pete's old and forgetful. I heard he had a relative come and stay with him this week and I thought things were better. I'll call Pete's daughter, who lives in the next town over, see if her family can take in Buddy. They have a nice spread, lots of room for Buddy to run without him getting into trouble."

It felt so good to have him here next to her, his solid body muscled and capable. For two years, she'd struggled on her own against Prescott's ill will.

Tempted to lean against Cooper, absorb some of his strength, she pulled her hand away. He had enough to contend with, and soon she'd be away from here. She liked his family. What would they think if they knew they'd sheltered a criminal in their midst? Fiona thought she was a well-bred socialite, accustomed to pampering. Not a woman whose trust fund founded a company that killed a police officer.

Meg gently disentangled herself from his arms. "I'd like to return to my room now."

His quiet gaze searched her face. "Are you sure you're okay?"

"I'll be fine. Thank you."

Meg headed for her bedroom, Sophie in her arms, glad the dog disguised her trembling palms.

Good Wi-Fi or not, she switched on her laptop.

Meg began surfing through websites about Randall's life and Randall's summer home.

For an hour, she found nothing that would indicate a favorite spot where Randall might hide the documents.

Her thoughts drifted to Cooper. Family man, devoted to his little sister and his mother. Holding it all together. The pull of attraction between them was strong, but she couldn't get involved with a man like that.

A man who would always put others first before her. Cooper wasn't self-centered like Prescott. Cooper's rugged, quiet determination and his heart-stopping grin could coax a legion of women into bed. Prescott had almost the same charisma, until you got to know him.

All Prescott cared about was money.

Cooper cared about his family.

She needed a man who would put her needs first. And she needed a man now, as the old saying went, "like a fish needs a bicycle."

Except Cooper remained in her thoughts as she dragged her index finger over the touch pad and kept surfing the web. Cooper with his solid body, those athletic legs and his hands that were so gentle in currying a horse…

So gentle and strong as he'd massaged her tired feet. His hands would feel wonderful against her naked skin, touching her every place she liked…

Meg forced her attention back to the computer screen. Randall was dead. Randall, who liked to fish and loved photographing nature. Sometimes when they were at his summer house for a corporate retreat, Randall had taken out the boat onto the lake just to get away by himself.

He'd bragged about the largemouth bass and how his little handheld GPS recorded the best fishing spot on the entire lake…

Meg stared at the screen. Could it be?

She plugged the numbers into Google Earth and her jaw dropped.

"GPS coordinates," she muttered. "Of course."

The longitude and latitude were from the lake fronting the corporate house. She stared in dismay at the water. Beebersim Lake was a popular destination in the summer, with lavish mansions peppering the property ringing the water. Only twenty feet deep at the center, the lake was stocked with smallmouth and largemouth bass and trout. In November, almost all the homes were closed up, and the wealthy left for the warmer climate in Florida.

He'd sunk the papers into the lake in a watertight container. It didn't matter if the papers were at twenty feet or two hundred feet. She had to see if Randall attached a buoy to the underwater container. If not, she was in trouble.

The water was ice cold and she couldn't scuba dive. But she knew someone who surely did.

A Navy SEAL named Cooper Johnson.

# Chapter 8

The next day, Meg asked Cooper to drive her to Randall's summer home in the next town. He'd refused to let her go alone. And of course, he wanted to know why she needed to see the house.

"It's for sale and I want to look around before it's sold," she told him as he drove. "I remember that house from when Randall invited me there."

Cooper gave her a skeptical look. "Do you always have a hankering for seeing houses you once visited?"

Meg tried to steady her shaky nerves. The man was far from stupid. He knew she was up to something.

"My grandmother used to visit here as well. Maybe I'm on a tour of memory lane," she shot back.

She gave him the code for the gate at the entrance of the exclusive community and they drove through. At the cul-de-sac on the next road over, they parked and walked along the deserted street. There were security guards here in the fall and winter, she remembered, but they patrolled only at night.

When she reached the woods adjacent to the property, Meg pulled out the binoculars Cooper had lent her. She scanned the lake. No buoy.

Though she'd expected as much, disappointment filled her. Meg tucked away the glasses.

Cooper studied her. "See anything interesting?"

"It's a lake." Meg gazed at the house, glad there wasn't a fence around the property. And then she remembered the security cameras.

"I have the code, but I don't want anyone to see us on the security cameras."

Cooper leaned against the trunk of a thick oak tree. "Meg, why are you really here? What's going on? You can trust me. My job is to protect you."

She gave a shrug. "I just wanted to have a look."

"If you wanted to look closer, you could contact the real estate agent and tour the house. What do you need from this place?"

*Nothing you can help me with because I don't dare risk your involvement. It's risky enough staying at your farm.*

"Closure," she finally said.

True enough. She needed to finally move on with her life, and the secret the lake held would aid her in doing so.

"When are you going to level with me, Meg? I'm not your tour guide. I want to help," he said gently.

She trembled as he stroked a hand down her chilled cheek, the longing to confide in him and have someone who could really help her warring with the instinctive need to protect herself.

"I will. Give me time, Cooper. I just wanted to see the house and the lake. Let's go now."

Cooper dropped his hand, his expression shuttered. He said nothing as they returned to the truck.

As they drove back to the inn, she kept thinking about the lake and the secret it held. So close and yet so far. And the man who could help her, the man who could get the documents she needed, sat beside her.

If only she could trust him. Meg wondered.

"Do you know how to scuba dive in icy lake water? You're a SEAL. Is that something you learned?"

The question, asked after their horseback ride later that afternoon, made him pause. Cooper finished currying his gelding and then checked on Betsy, worried about how she was slowing down. She'd made it over the colic, but he didn't like how much she was limping lately, and her appetite was poor.

"I grew up around here, learning to dive. Why?"

She tugged at one leather glove, avoiding his gaze.

"Hey," he said gently, and put a hand under her chin, lifting her face to meet his gaze. "Tell me."

A pretty flush tinted her cheeks. Meg sighed beneath his touch as he, unable to resist, stroked a thumb over her smooth skin. So soft. Fragile-looking, but strong. He wished she'd open up. That trip earlier to the Jacobs house wasn't about seeing a house.

Something was in the lake that she wanted. He knew she didn't want to see the house one last time.

Why else would she ask about diving in cold water? If only she'd open up to him, confide in him. Frustration filled him. Until Meg did so, he didn't know how to help her.

"Talk to me," he insisted.

"I'm going to need your help with something. But first, I need to get my car. Can we go there this afternoon? It should be ready by now."

"Let me call." He fished out his cell phone.

Meg walked over to give Adela a treat as he talked with Mike, his childhood friend who owned the shop.

"Give me two more days, Coop. New alternator is in, but the engine is still finicky. Need a loaner?"

"No," he said quickly, glancing at Meg. He didn't want her taking a loaner car and bolting. Jarrett told him to keep her on the farm, and he would. "Call me when it's ready."

He told Meg the disappointing news, glad of an excuse to keep her close.

Close enough to find out what she hid. And Coop knew she hid something important.

"What did you need help with?" he asked.

She nibbled on her lower lip, and the sight sent fresh desire shooting through him. Damn, the woman had the most kissable mouth. But he wasn't going to push her. Meg was still scared and wounded. Had to take it slow with her. Still, he had the fierce longing to wrap her up in his arms to keep her safe from the world—and beat the hell out of anyone who wanted to hurt her.

He didn't know who had left the gate open for Buddy to wander through. Perhaps it was a mistake. The latch was old. But he didn't want to take chances. Cooper had wired it shut until he could replace it.

This frail-looking woman with a spine of solid steel deserved someone who cared about her welfare. Not him. His first duty came to his family and his team.

But while she remained here, under his roof, he'd do his damnedest to keep her safe. Yesterday's incident haunted him. She could have been torn to pieces if she didn't have the common sense to remain calm and not run.

She still didn't answer him.

"Meg, you can trust me," he said gently. "I want to help however I can. Whatever is bothering you, tell me."

She hugged herself. "Later. Are you going to fix that gate latch now? I can help."

They walked out of the barn and over to the cottage gate

leading to the road, Meg following as he carried his tool bag. Time to go on a little fishing trip, see if he could get Miss Meg to loosen up and confide in him.

At the gate, he took out his screwdriver. The new latch would be much harder to unfasten, and no chances of it accidentally being left open.

She wanted to dive in cold water. Why? Was something in the lake that interested her? She'd shown enough interest in it, scanning it with the binoculars.

Coop removed the faulty latch as she opened the packaging for the new one he'd bought in town.

"If you want to learn how to dive around here, best time is summer. Days are nice and hot, and the lake water isn't too terrible. Not as bad as some. Why do you want to know about diving? You need to dive somewhere cold? Like that lake?"

Meg sidestepped the question with another question. "You must have been on some interesting dives as a Navy SEAL. What was your most dangerous one? Was it on a mission?"

Now it was his turn to clam up. "They all have risks," he said, studying her. "But you work as a team and no man gets left behind."

"Don't you miss it? The action and the adrenaline thrill, compared to working here on the farm?"

Startled, he looked down at this little spitfire, who had faced a dog attack without as much as a scream. No one ever asked that question since he'd left. Certainly not his family, who was happy to have him home.

"I miss the action. But it's worth it to help out my mom with the inn while I'm on leave."

"But you're going back. What are you going to do with your life when you finally do leave the Navy?"

Cooper stared at her, not liking this conversational thread. "What are you implying?"

Meg gestured to the pasture, the barn and the inn. "After my brother died, I volunteered with a veterans group. I know about soldiers, Cooper. In combat, you see horrific things most Americans will never witness. It's hard to adjust to being back, and even harder to find purpose once you leave the military."

He didn't like how this was going. "I'm good at adjusting. And my family needs me."

"You need them as well, Cooper. But you need more."

Her green gaze was calm, assessing. It felt unnerving, as if she could see straight through to his soul.

"I haven't known you long, but you don't seem like a farmer or an innkeeper. If you were, you never would have become a SEAL."

Anger simmered. He set down the screwdriver, mindful of how his hand shook. "You're such an expert, you tell me, Meg. Tell me what I should do with my life once I'm a civilian."

To her credit, she didn't back down. Instead, she folded her arms and shook her head. "You're a man of action. You have much to offer the world. Baling hay isn't going to keep you happy. Giving your life real purpose will."

That stung, because deep down, he knew she was right. Hell, the very thought had kept him awake, staring at the ceiling, since he got home. He stood and brushed off his hands, approaching her. "My family is my purpose. So butt out, Princess."

She didn't. Instead, she took a deep breath, as if going for the knockout punch. He waited, his body tensing.

"Sometimes you need a stranger to tell it like it is. Fiona won't. I suspect others won't, either. But I will. You don't like the idea of quitting the Navy because of family obligations. And perhaps it's made you a little resentful."

Whoa. That was way, way close. Fiona had mentioned that when he came home, hinting at the same thing. Cooper fisted his hands. Seeing her back off, the flash of fear in her eyes and remembering her past, he relaxed his hands.

Meg's shoulders lost some of their tenseness.

"I love my family and I'd do anything for them. Anything. Stop psychoanalyzing me and look at your own life, damn it."

"I have," she said quietly. "I've analyzed my own life for a long while now. And I know what I'm going to do. Leaving my house, everything I know, was the first step."

At a loss for words, he couldn't meet her gaze as she touched his arm.

"Cooper, I am sorry if I hurt your feelings. But I'm not sorry I said those things. On our rides, you talk of your teammates like they are your family…and how much you'll miss the action."

Stomach churning with grief and anger, he pulled away. Didn't want her soft, leather-clad hand on his arm. Didn't want this woman to get underneath his prickly armor and burrow in there like her dog burrowed into the sofa. She was too tempting, and he had a mission to complete.

Find the person responsible for Brie's death and go after him with everything he had.

"They are my family."

"There are vet groups that can use your skills. You have a calming presence and you're great in a crisis. Those skill sets can transition into civilian life."

"Right. I'll have headhunters knocking down my door to hire me just because I'm an ex-SEAL."

"They can't knock on your door if they can't even find

you. You have to try finding them, and trust me, you will have another career again."

"You're such an expert," he shot back. "And you know this because…?"

Meg's cheeks pinked at his sarcastic tone. "I know how to analyze skill sets and place people according to their temperament and their abilities. I was very good at it at the family business until I quit."

"SEALs never quit. It's part of our code. If you're so great at giving advice, why did you leave?" he snapped, the raw hurt spiraling through him all over again.

Wounded eyes stared up at him, big green eyes that were woebegone. Then she stiffened and drew off her coat and rolled up her sleeve.

The yellowing bruise made him flinch.

"Prescott didn't want a working wife. He wanted a trophy wife to arrange society parties and play hostess. And when I protested, he made sure to place the marks where no one would see them if I wore a strapless gown." She touched her arm. "Except this last time, he simply didn't care who saw the bruises."

Shame curled through him. He'd been so busy arguing, he'd forgotten her past. "Real men don't hit women."

"No, they just argue with them. And cook them burned BLT sandwiches." She shrugged into her coat again and looked up. "Truce?"

Exasperated, he nodded. Dang big green eyes, like a puppy's. All soft and woeful. She'd gotten under his skin. "Truce."

Meg gave him a real smile. "Your mom hinted about the new restaurant in town for dinner. I thought it would be nice to take Aimee out for a treat. So let me treat you and your sister, Cooper. I have a little money."

"Princess, save your money…"

"No." Her smile wobbled. "I want to do this, Cooper. Let me pay for a dinner in town. Your mom could use a night off from cooking, too."

There she went again, being all thoughtful. Hard to stay mad at her.

Cooper picked up his screwdriver again. "I've got this. Go back, get changed for dinner, and we'll leave at seventeen hundred hours."

She had poked the big bad SEAL in a sore spot. Cooper didn't make a move to hurt her. He didn't insult her, belittle her or worse, hit her.

They fought. But nothing more.

It was so refreshing to argue with a man, a big man, and not worry about him hitting her that Meg felt almost as giddy about that argument as their upcoming dinner.

She headed for the inn, where Aimee had been taking care of Sophie. Taking the porch steps at the inn nearly two at a time, Meg found herself humming. It wasn't a date, she warned her rapidly beating heart. Just dinner.

But the prospect had her blood surging through her veins. Alive. She was alive, and not lying six feet under. She could forge a new beginning and start all over. Date again.

Then she remembered the FBI and the elation fled. One didn't date in jail. She wasn't here to start a new life, but to ensure no other lives would be lost because of her company's criminal misdeeds.

Still, she could live for the moment. A moment of fun and laughter. Cooper made her laugh, made her feel like a woman again instead of useless trash. Only through her own determination and self-confidence had she managed to survive.

Her dog greeted her on the landing, wagging her tail, but Sophie did not bound down the stairs as she once did. Her dog had taken to Aimee, and was growing closer to the girl. Meg knew it was for the best if she left Sophie here permanently, but still, it hurt a little. Sophie was all she had left.

She petted her dog as Aimee burst out of her bedroom.

"Meg! Come see my collection!" Aimee was practically dancing up and down. "I got a new one today."

Not waiting for an answer, the girl led her into her bedroom.

The bed was neatly made with a *Star Wars* bedspread, and on a shelf above a desk and a laptop computer stood a neat array of bobblehead figurines. Aimee picked up a box from the desk. "Coop bought me this online and it arrived today! I wanted Rey for a long time, but Mom said only for my birthday and Coop said he'd make my birthday come early. He's the best!"

Meg smiled, agreeing with Aimee. "Tell me about your collection."

Aimee prattled on about the collection that her sister, Brie, had started and passed on to her when Brie graduated from the police academy and went to work as a patrol officer.

"I miss my sister," the girl said, looking solemn. "But she's in heaven now with my dad. That makes me feel a little better, knowing he's not alone anymore. And Max, Coop's dog."

Aimee's big brown gaze met hers beseechingly. "Do you think dogs go to heaven?"

Her throat tightened. "Of course they do. Dogs and horses and cats. They don't live as long as we do because they don't have as many things to learn as we do. They already know the important things."

"Like what?"

"Like how to love, and how to take care of themselves and each other. And how to not hurt each other unless it's very necessary. Animals never do, you know. They only do it to hunt and eat or to defend themselves."

"That's what Coop says. He said Max is in heaven, helping to take care of Brie and Dad, just like he took care of Coop. Max saved his life." Aimee bent down to stroke Sophie's soft, silky fur.

She blinked. "He did?"

"Max was on patrol with Coop when he sniffed out a bad guy hiding alongside the road. Max barked a warning and the bad guy went to shoot at my brother and Max leaped in front of the bullet. My brother and his team shot the bad guy, but they couldn't save Max."

Aimee's lower lip wobbled. "I wish I could thank Max for saving my brother. I don't want Cooper to die, too."

Meg hugged her. "He's too tough to die, sweetie. Cooper's going to be around for a long time."

"I know." Aimee hugged her back and then spun the box around on the table. "I wish he'd take care of himself, too. But he's too busy worrying about us. He's always worried about where I'm going and what I'm doing, and nagging me more than Mom."

Startled at the insight, Meg set the bobblehead box upright. "He's being a big brother. Maybe you and your mother should let Cooper know that you'll be okay."

"Thanks, Meg. I like you. You're not like Cooper's other lady friends, who wouldn't even talk to me."

She hugged the little girl back, liking her immensely, and then snapped on Sophie's leash to return to the cottage.

Inventorying her clothing in her mind, she knew exactly what to wear for dinner. Not the fancy designer clothing she'd purchased, but the soft powder blue sweater her grandmother had made her. It was the last item Gran had knitted, and Meg treasured it.

Using her key, she unlocked the side door leading to the

hallway where her room was. As she entered the cottage, Sophie hung back, growling.

"What's wrong, girl?" Meg looked around, her nerves frayed.

Cooper wasn't here. The cottage had been locked. But still, her dog growled.

Meg picked up Sophie and went into the kitchen, first locking the door behind her. In the kitchen, Sophie circled around the rag rug and then lay down.

Odd. Why did she growl at the entryway?

Shrugging it off, Meg headed to her room. It was exactly as she'd left it, the bed made in haste, pillows lopsided. Relief filled her. She'd done this on purpose to see if the housekeeping staff actually did as Cooper said, and didn't clean the room.

Humming again, Meg opened the closet door and froze. Her heart dropped to her stomach.

The powder blue sweater hung in tatters, shredded in useless strips. She removed it from the hanger and clutched it in horrified disbelief.

The tears were long and jagged, as if made with a serrated knife.

This was malicious and deliberate.

Someone wanted her to know she was being watched. And only one person knew how much that sweater meant to her.

Prescott.

# Chapter 9

The sweater fell from her shaking fingers. This kind of maliciousness was on Prescott's level. Or someone he'd sent to find her and give a clear warning.

The rose on her bed, like Prescott once gave her.

The card that looked sweet and romantic, until you read the inside message.

And now the shredded sweater.

All the same things that documented her wreck of a marriage over three years. Romance at first, then followed by a growing mean streak. Meg sat on the bed, holding the sweater and rocking back and forth, moaning. In the distance, she heard something, but the terror buzzing in her ears blocked out all else.

*He found me.*

*He found me. Not safe, never will be safe, no one can protect me...*

A shadow fell over her and she screamed. And then a furry body wriggled next to her and began licking her face.

Meg began to shake.

"Meg!" Two strong arms gripped her shoulders, but the grip was gentle, not punishing. Cooper's worried eyes scanned her face. "What happened?"

Still trembling, she held out the sweater.

"Someone did this." Her voice came out shaky and unsure. "And I locked the cottage, I always lock it. It's my ex. He's here."

"It's okay," he soothed. "Tell me what happened."

"He once ordered the maid to rip up a new dress I'd purchased for a business dinner because I had insisted on wearing it against his wishes." Her voice rose in hysterics. "This is exactly what Prescott would do. But he'd never lower himself to do it. He'd order someone else to destroy my things."

Cooper gently removed the ruined sweater from her shaking hands. "It's okay, Meg. Deep breaths."

Following his instructions, she forced herself to calm. He nodded in approval. "Good. Stay here. I'm going to look around."

"Don't," she begged. "If he's here, he'll kill you. He's ruthless."

"And so am I."

He left the room, and she heard him run up the stairs. When he returned, the pistol in his hand didn't alarm her, but proved reassuring. That, and his determined look, eased the tight knot in her stomach.

Hugging Sophie, she remained on the bed until he returned. Meg set the dog down on the ground and Sophie went into her little pink dog bed.

"No discernible footprints. But the lock is loose on the hallway door. Whoever did this must have tampered with it. It wasn't the housekeeping staff. They don't have a key to the cottage." Cooper holstered his pistol. "From now on, use only the front entrance. I'm going to nail this door shut."

As he set about securing the hallway door, Meg rubbed her clammy palms against the designer blue jeans. She should have purchased a suit of armor, because she'd need it to combat Prescott.

The man had tentacles all over the country, and he would find her if he hadn't already. Would send a legion of hired hands to find her. He could pay to make her vanish…

When he finished, Cooper returned to her room.

"All set. I doubt it's your ex. There's little chance of him finding you here."

"Then who was it?"

"Someone could be messing with you." He picked up the shredded sweater. "Or trying to scare you into leaving."

"Well, it's worked." Meg plucked the sweater from his hands and tossed it into the trash. "I'll pack my things and call a taxi. I can grab a motel room in town."

"Whoa, Princess." Cooper held out his hands. "Running now won't solve anything. You're safer here with me. I'll get a security system, cameras. Been meaning to do that for a while."

He sounded so determined and assured. "You'd do that for me?"

Cooper nodded, his expression grim. "When I take on an assignment, I finish it to the end."

An assignment. That's what she was. Exhausted and spent, Meg buried her face in her hands.

The bed dipped beneath his weight as he joined her. He pulled her against him and stroked her hair.

"It's okay, Princess. It's someone playing tricks on you, to rattle your cage. I'll find this bastard and deal with him. I promise I won't leave your side."

She wanted to burrow against him like Sophie curled up against her when she was scared. He smelled so good, spices and sage aftershave, and his arms were solid and reassuring.

Meg could remain here forever, secure in his embrace. It

had been far too long since anyone held her like this. Gran had been far too ill in the last year, and Prescott knew only how to hurt.

So she indulged in the comfort of Cooper's embrace. Tears threatened, rising in the back of her throat. Meg tried to blink them away, but the trauma of the unsettling incidents, coupled with the raw emotions over Randall's death, undid her.

She felt warm salt water trickling down her cheeks and sniffled as if she were Cooper's kid sister, not an adult who knew how to take care of herself.

"Aw, hell," he muttered. "Don't cry now, Princess. You and the furball are safe here, I'll make sure of it. If you want to cry over something, cry over my lousy cooking. It's enough to give a seasoned sailor a bad stomach."

Meg smiled against his chest.

He stroked her back in caresses that soothed, and began to stir different feelings as well. Desire. It tickled her insides like a feather and began to grow, pushing aside the mingling fear and dread. She raised her face to find him studying her with an intense and purely male look. But along with the sheer lust on his face was concern.

Tenderness.

Parting her mouth, she started to close her eyes as he dipped his head close. And then the image of Prescott flashed in her mind. His sneer of triumph as he threw her against the bed…

She jerked away as Cooper's mouth touched hers.

Flustered, Meg rubbed her hands against her legs. "I'm sorry. I—"

"No prob." He squeezed her hand. "Let's get you some dinner. Then we'll figure out plan B."

There was no plan B for her. She'd always lived from plan A to the hopeless feeling that there would never be a second alternative. Cooper was solid and strong, but he didn't know Prescott.

Meg glanced down at Sophie, her stomach churning. Was the dog next? How easy would it be to take the scissors and hurt her beloved pet? She might have lost more than a mere sweater.

It killed her to do it, but perhaps it was best for Sophie to adjust now to living with new owners. Meg pushed past the lump in her throat.

"I want to give Sophie to Aimee."

Cooper's keen blue gaze sharpened. "Why?"

"She'll be safer with Aimee. And with your mom at the inn." She caught his arm. "Please, Cooper. If this person had taken the scissors to Sophie…"

He rubbed a hand over her nape, and the gesture felt soothing. "All right. We'll tell her it's part of Sophie's training to get used to new people."

They took the dog and her belongings to the delighted Aimee, who began playing fetch with Sophie's squeaky toys.

But she canceled dinner and instead, she and Cooper grabbed sandwiches from the inn. Meg retired early with the excuse of a headache. As she lay in bed, staring at the ceiling, she couldn't fathom who would want to do this to her.

And if it was Prescott, why was he going to all this trouble?

Two days after the sweater incident, Meg started to feel the ever-present tension ease. Nothing more had happened. Cooper had installed security cameras and motion detectors around the grounds and the cottage.

He'd questioned all the staff. Jenny, the new housekeeper, admitted to being in the cottage. She said she'd gone there to borrow the vacuum.

But she denied touching any of Meg's things.

With the new locks on the cottage, Meg felt more secure. Sophie had adjusted to sleeping in Aimee's room and being with the girl. After receiving strict instructions to never let Sophie wander outside alone, Aimee promised to watch over her.

During the day while Cooper's sister was in school, Fiona kept the dog with her. Knowing her pet was in good hands made the separation easier. And Cooper's calm, steady demeanor soothed her frayed nerves. With Cooper, she felt safe. Cooper was so normal and easygoing, she could almost forget why she was at the Sunnyside Farm.

She was almost ready to trust him with her secret about the lake.

Almost.

The nightmares had finally receded, replaced by images of Cooper's lazy grin, the way he sat on a horse, his long legs easily guiding the gelding on their afternoon rides. His intense blue eyes would light up as he told her about growing up here and the winter sports he and his older brother played. And his voice would grow soft as he mentioned his mother and Aimee.

The only family member he never mentioned was the mysterious Brie. Meg didn't ask, not wanting to stir his grief.

His big, muscled body had power, but he'd shown her only gentleness in the small ways he'd touched her. Taking her hand to help her off the horse, or placing a hand at the small of her back as he escorted her into the inn for dinner last night.

*There are good men in the world,* Fiona had told her. She wanted to believe this.

He took to carrying his pistol on one lean hip in a leather holster when they went for their rides. Guns used to upset her, but seeing him with the weapon gave her peace of mind. Cooper was a trained warrior who knew how to handle a weapon.

And he'd given her a bright silver whistle to blow if she was in trouble and not within reach.

Meg hummed as she popped an apple pie into the oven that afternoon at the cottage. Fiona was hosting dessert night at the inn and she'd offered to help. She had spent hours in the kitchen, rolling the dough, recalling Gran's recipe as she peeled the apples. The pie would sit fine with a sprinkling of cinnamon and ice cream.

For once, she wanted to forget everything and enjoy herself.

"I'm headed outside to say good-night to the horses," she called up the stairs to Cooper, who was headed into the shower.

Betsy hadn't been faring well. Meg wished there was something she could do. She headed outside and shivered. The temperature had fallen and she could use a hat. Remembering Cooper told her to feel free to borrow Brie's clothing, Meg ran back inside and up the stairs. She found a ski hat that fit perfectly.

Coming out of the bedroom, Meg nearly collided with Cooper, who stood on the landing, toweling his hair.

Dripping.

Nude.

"You're naked." She felt her face heat. Smart observation coming from a college graduate who was summa cum laude.

He gave her a crooked grin.

"I like to shower naked. And I sleep naked, too, Princess. You said you were headed outside."

Meg tried to avoid looking at his lower extremities, which were on display like a shop's wares. Her breath came in jagged pants as she stared at him.

The very magnificent maleness of him. All tanned skin over smooth muscle.

Cooper leaned against the doorjamb, water dripping onto the antique wood floorboards. Drip, splash, rolling down his flat belly, following the thin line of dark hair that dipped into the much darker hair at his...

Her gaze riveted to the floor and his feet, she refused to look up. Nice feet, square toes. The man was a well-put-together package.

*Package. Don't think package; don't say it, either!*

"See anything that interests you?" he inquired.

"Very nice floor. Reminds me of Dade County pine and the Mizner cottages in Boca Raton. Those pine trees were very sturdy and..."

Like a bystander trying to avoid looking at a train wreck, her fascinated gaze whipped up to the very male part of him. Oh dear heavens, that part of him was getting aroused.

Meg hastily looked down again, staring at the curve of one strong calf.

"Thick," she finished.

A low chuckle from Cooper.

"I should leave for the bed. I mean the barn. I was going to the barn."

And yet she could not bring her feet to shuffle toward the staircase. Deep inside, the woman who had been neglected and longed for love cried out for attention, for a man to give her great sex and then hold her long after, making her feel cherished.

Or just loved, with lots of great sex.

Cooper studied her, the intensity in his gaze making her knees wobbly.

"What do you want, Meg?"

Dangerous. Forbidden. He had strength enough to snap a man's neck.

Or stroke a woman's thigh with equal focus, and bring her to such a pleasure that she'd scream and never stop...

She'd picked the wrong man to guard her and provide her with twenty-four-hour protection. Because she wasn't certain if she could protect herself against his raw sexuality. The man smoldered with it.

Authoritative without being overbearing or arrogant. Quiet and confident, unabashed at being caught with his pants down.

And much more.

"I wanted to go to the bedroom. I mean the barn."

His gaze darkened. Drip, drip, the rhythm echoing her heart beating faster.

"Alone? Or do you need warming up?" he suggested.

Her lady parts tightened in anticipation. *Oh yeah, lots of warmth. I'll get undressed and you can snuggle against me with all those delicious muscles and hot skin sliding over me, and then you can warm me up from the inside when I spread my legs open and you...*

"You look flushed. Hot," Cooper told her, his voice deepening.

Meg put her hands to her burning face. "I'm fine. Tired. I need to lie down for a while before dessert. I didn't sleep well last night."

She sounded like a fool. But Cooper didn't laugh, nor did he sneer as her ex would have when she babbled. He left his perch and came closer, the water splashing onto the floor. Water slicking back his dark hair, droplets clinging to his ebony eyelashes.

"Do you want me to check downstairs, make sure no one

else is there? Check the locks and double-check? I had the locks changed, and only you and I have the keys."

Cooper's body tensed ever so slightly. In a minute he'd gone from relaxed, playful in his sexual banter, to watchful protector. The offer startled her, made her scramble for her lost composure because she didn't know how to react around a man intent on protecting her instead of punching her.

Strong, she had to be strong, because men like Cooper Johnson were a blip on her radar. Here and gone. She had to rely on only one person—herself.

"No. Thank you. I'm fine. I came upstairs only to grab a hat before heading to the barn." She gathered her dignity around her like a tattered cloak, clutching Brie's hat.

And then she couldn't help it. "You're naked and wet, and it's got to be no more than sixty-five degrees up here. Don't you ever get cold?"

Cooper glanced down at his groin with a wry look. "Yeah, some parts of me do."

She sputtered as he flashed a wide, impish grin. Soft laughter followed her as she fled down the stairs.

Cooper watched Meg take the steps two at a time. Still dripping, he went to the bedroom to grab the spare hair dryer. His had shorted out.

Damn if that wasn't one fine, brave woman. Oh yeah, she was lovely and the air seemed to crackle between them when they were together. But there was depth to her, a depth that intrigued him.

Meg was a paradox, a puzzle. And Cooper adored solving puzzles. His brain wove through them, analyzing facts and figures, until arriving at the answer.

Nearly a week after he'd first found her, shivering in the car at the roadside, he still had not come any closer to obtaining answers about her past. Or the two men he was interested in knowing more about—Randall Jacobs and Prescott August.

Cooper sensed he would not be solving the puzzle of his pretty, brown-haired refugee any time soon.

She appealed to him, with her grit and confidence and refusal to be pampered. Meg fit into the farm more smoothly than any other woman he'd known.

*She's an assignment*, he reminded himself. Nothing else. No permanent attachments here, nothing that would interfere with his attention to family.

No snobbish airs about her like he'd seen in the wives of some Navy brass whose noses were so high in the air it was a wonder they didn't trip over their fancy heels. Meg was friendly, her warm smile lighting up the room, the cold pinking her pretty porcelain cheeks. Light from the overhead hallway light had picked up honey strands among her dark brown hair. She was as pretty as the first flush of spring growth poking through the sullen snow.

No airs and graces with this princess.

Yeah, he wanted her, not just for a quick one-nighter, because Lord knows he'd had those before, but something deeper and richer. More lasting, like the relationship his parents had shared, the deep love and affection that got a couple through the bad times and made the good times even more treasured.

Coop almost laughed as he dressed. Look at him. Only days with the princess and he started getting starry-eyed dreams of settling down. He'd been a SEAL for years, and relationships were out of the question. The only relationship he must focus on was his family and helping them out. He would not quit the teams for a pair of big, woebegone green eyes and a tempting mouth.

No matter how kissable it was.

Because Meg August hid something, a secret she hadn't yet shared, despite his coaxing.

He would get it out of her, one way or another.

And not just to protect her, but his family as well.

He only hoped he could protect the one organ he feared losing the most.

His heart.

# Chapter 10

The next afternoon, she joined Cooper in their usual afternoon ride. He'd said nothing more about catching him in the nude, and she was grateful for that.

Now, as they rode down through the empty fields on the dirt road leading to the river, she tried to figure out how to ask him about diving in Lake Beebersim to retrieve the secret Randall had stashed there.

Cooper tipped his Stetson back and talked about the crops the farm had grown.

"Land's been in my family for five generations. At one point, Gramps wanted to sell because the farm was nearly in foreclosure, but Dad refused. That's when they came up with the idea of a B and B. We all had to work hard to make it happen, but it was worth it to save the family land."

In his faded jeans, blue chambray work shirt and sheepskin jacket, he looked the image of a rugged cowboy sitting on his mount. She appreciated families who worked together and sacrificed to save their business or their land.

"My grandmother had a dream of taking the company public. It never happened. I wish she'd have seen it come to fruition before she died."

"What happened?"

Meg lifted her shoulders. "Prescott argued that the time wasn't right. You can spend up to two million to make a company's stock available for purchase. And the regulations…the federal regulations are extensive. More red tape.

"But I knew how hard Gran worked to keep Taylor Sporting Goods afloat when we went into the red. She and senior management cut their salaries rather than cut staff. She hired Randall Jacobs, a family friend, to research ways we could improve our products. I would work in the office after school, sending out shipping orders to our distributors. Eventually Gran hired Prescott to bring his business expertise to our company."

His blue gaze was steady. "Is that how you met your ex?"

The delightful sunshine suddenly seemed cold. She remembered that day well when Prescott first arrived in the office. "Yes. I was eighteen and he was charming, swept me off my feet. We dated, but I had to leave for college. All the time while I was away, he sent letters, called, showered me with attention."

Prescott's devotion had showered her with the loving affection she seldom knew growing up.

"When I graduated, we got married. He was wonderful that first year we were married, and then his true colors came out."

Silence fell between them for a few moments, broken only by the wind rustling the leaves on the ground and the horses' clopping hooves. How naive she'd been when they first met, and starved for attention. Prescott sensed that and preyed on her vulnerability like a snake attacking a fat mouse.

Later, she realized he cared only about himself. By then they were married, and fervent devotion had turned into excruciating domination. He would never let her go, and she partly suspected he held on so tightly to their marriage because he didn't like admitting to failure.

Divorce was failure in Prescott's eyes.

"Why didn't you leave him earlier?"

Leather creaked beneath her as she turned in the saddle to face him. Meg didn't know why it was important he understand why she'd stuck it out in a bad marriage.

"I kept hoping he'd revert back to the charming man I'd married. He was a hard worker and dedicated to the company. But one week while we vacationed at the Palm Beach house, we were invited to a private party. I didn't want to go, but Prescott went. He changed after that night. They had cocaine at the party and he started using."

She flushed remembering the other personality changes, how Prescott insisted on rough sex. Their sex life had been mundane until then.

"He insisted it was purely recreational. But then he got nervous and paranoid, and controlling. He insisted I quit working for the company and when I balked, he beat me. My only escape was my charity work, which made him look good to his business associates. I tucked away money so I could escape, but it was hard to escape his attention. And then Gran fell ill and I couldn't leave her."

Her voice cracked. "After she died, there was nothing to hold me there. So I ran."

Cooper halted his mount as she did. Admiration shone in his intense blue eyes. "You did the right thing, Meg. I'm glad you left that bastard."

Mouth wobbling, she forced a tremulous smile. "Me, too."

As they rode through the fields, they passed a distant pickup truck parked by tall stacks of hay. Hank, the hired hand, picked up the bales and put them into the bed of the truck.

She gave an appreciative look at the stretch of freshly mowed grass rolling in a gentle slope down to the trees banking the river. "It's so peaceful here."

Cooper flicked the reins. "I know. It's a good place to get your head on straight after deployment."

"I've always wanted to open a sports retreat center for veterans returning from the war," she mused aloud. "Many vets told me how difficult it is to return to civilian life. Even a simple trip to the average grocery store can be harrowing. Turning a corner and running into someone. We think nothing of it, but to a Marine who was clearing buildings, running into someone could mean that person was armed and prepared to kill you."

He gave her a warm smile. "It's not easy to come home and assimilate when you've been running on adrenaline for weeks, even months. Thanks for understanding."

Her chest felt hollow at the appreciation. Meg said nothing, feeling a pinch of regret. She'd founded Combat Gear to help military personnel and give them an advantage in the field. Instead, her product had hurt, not helped.

They cleared the field and came to the trail snaking through the woods. Snowflake tossed her head and danced with anticipation, knowing what was coming. The young mare liked to have her head, running through the woods to the pretty picnic spot near the river. "Whoa, girl," Meg said, laughing. "You want to race, huh?"

Cooper's cell phone dinged. He removed it from his pocket and glanced at the screen. "Mom asked me to tell Hank to get an extra bale of hay for the inn's porch because she wants to decorate for Thanksgiving."

"Why didn't she text him herself?"

"Cell phone service is iffy out here, so Hank never brings his phone."

She looked around. Silly to be afraid and paranoid here

when he was only a minute away. Snowflake, impatient to be off, pranced and pulled at the reins.

"Go on. I'll meet you at the picnic tables."

Cooper frowned. "I don't know, Meg."

"I'll be fine." With that, she entered the woods. Meg leaned forward in the saddle. "Come on, Snowflake, let's roll!"

She kicked the mare's sides, urging Snowflake on. Laughing, Meg enjoyed the rush of wind against her cheeks, the thrill of the thundering hooves kicking up the dirt.

Slowing her mount, she allowed Snowflake to stop. Meg dismounted, letting the reins drop. The picnic tables, set in a clearing in the woods, overlooked the swift-moving river. It was a lovely spot to eat lunch. Maybe she and Cooper could picnic here tomorrow.

She walked toward the tables, admiring the last lingering color on the trees. While she was here, she wanted to enjoy every single moment of freedom. Too soon, it would all vanish. But it would be worth it to bring justice to the young police officer who had died wearing a vest she thought would protect her.

A flash of movement among the trees caught her eye. She turned her head. About fifty yards away, a man stepped out from the thick bushes rimming the riverbank. He wore a camel-hair coat and had a large streak of gray lining his hair. Tall as her ex, and with the same paunch...

No. It couldn't be.

She couldn't breathe, couldn't think. Couldn't move. Black spots danced in her vision as her throat closed tight. Meg began to shake uncontrollably, but she could not move. Fear paralyzed her.

The man started forward.

It was Prescott. She knew it, surely as she knew he would kill her once he reached her.

*Do something!* The slow, stalking menace in the man's gait reminded her of the times Prescott would stalk toward her, leather belt in hand. The sounds, *thwack, thwack*, against his open palm…indicating what he planned.

Memories pushed through her terror. Never again would she be his victim.

Frantic, she whipped her head around, searching for any kind of weapon, wishing Cooper with his gun was with her. But he was at least half a mile back, and had no idea.

The whistle! Fingers shaking, she dug into her jeans pocket, but her hand shook too badly. Prescott kept walking, getting closer; he would lace his meaty fingers around her neck and squeeze until no air existed, and then he'd dump her body into the river…

The whistle wasn't in her pocket. She forgot it, and now would pay the price for her carelessness…

Closer still he came, shuffling through the dead leaves on the ground as if he had all the time in the world…as if he knew how much fear had paralyzed her…

The other pocket, the whistle has to be in the other pocket, c'mon, try it, get a grip…

There!

Her trembling fingers dropped the whistle. Oh God, where was it? There, a spot of silver in the leaves, had to be it…c'mon, c'mon, move!

Meg put the whistle into her mouth and blew with all her might. The piercing sound shrieked a warning, lending her courage. The man hesitated and stepped backward. Still blowing, Meg mounted Snowflake and galloped back toward the field.

On his gelding, Cooper raced through the woods, halting when he saw her. "Meg!" he shouted.

With considerable effort, she halted Snowflake. Cooper pulled up Farmalot beside her. "What happened?"

The calmness in his deep voice shattered her numbness. Opening her mouth, she watched the silver whistle fall to the ground. Her breath came in little gasps.

"Just breathe, Princess. Breathe and tell me what scared you."

Deep breaths. Finally she pointed in the direction of the picnic tables. "I—I s-saw him. Prescott. Over there."

Cooper wheeled his horse around and removed the pistol from his holster. "Stay here."

He galloped off. She tried to quell the panic clogging her throat, the rise of terror that always immobilized her when Prescott raised his hand to strike.

A few minutes later, Cooper returned. "I did a quick search. No one was there, Meg."

"But he was standing there in the trees not even ten minutes ago. I'm not going crazy. I saw him!"

She pressed a trembling hand to her forehead. Or was she losing her mind?

Could he have run off that quickly?

Cooper's gaze hardened as he scanned the forest. "I believe you. You say you saw him, then you did. But there's no trace of him now. He couldn't have run that fast. Unless he took to the river, and that current is ripping today. You'd have to be an experienced boater to tackle it."

"Prescott is an experienced boater. He owns a powerboat he docks at the marina in Palm Beach. He used to kayak in the Intracoastal as well."

Cooper gazed around. "Hank told me he already knew about the extra bale of hay. Someone used my mother's phone to send that message to try to separate us."

It worked. Someone had been watching her, knew that she liked to race Snowflake through the woods to the picnic table. Knew that Snowflake always got anxious when entering the woods, anticipated the gallop.

Meg knew if she let fear rule her, she'd always be a prisoner to it. "I need to see."

He shook his head. "I'm not leaving you."

"Then don't. If I run back to the inn, I'll always wonder if I was crazy and imagined it."

Cooper nodded. "Stay right by my side and obey my every word. If I tell you to run, you run. Understand?"

"Yes."

The woods were quiet as they rode along the trail, Meg trying to peer through the thick copse of hickory, oak and maple trees. Prescott could be hiding anywhere.

They dismounted at the picnic tables, tying their horses to a nearby fallen log. Taking her hand, Cooper instructed her to take him to where she'd seen her ex.

When they reached the area, Cooper scanned the ground.

Frowning, he bent over and touched the leaves. "Someone has been here, all right."

Relief filled her. She wasn't crazy.

They walked to the river. The bank sloped gently down to a man-made sandy beach. The area looked undisturbed to her inexperienced eye.

Cooper gazed at the sand. "Easier to make a landing here, but the woods aren't as thick. And current's ripping beyond the swimming area."

Meg followed him as he walked along the narrow bank. He held out his hand to assist over a large boulder.

She relished the warmth of his touch as his fingers encased hers. Cooper was strong and reliable, and Meg was glad he was with her. These woods spooked her with their denseness. Anyone or anything could hide here.

They reached another landing area where the river flowed at a more sedate pace instead of tumbling over rocks. Cooper squatted down and touched the muddy earth.

"Look," he said quietly. "Something's flattened the ground here. See that mark ending in a narrow point?"

Meg could barely make out the indentation in the ground.

Cooper stood, brushing off his hands. "Looks like a kayak. He could have brought it here, tied it up and floated downstream and then disembarked on the other side. Wouldn't take long for a skilled boater."

"But he was wearing an overcoat and dressed for business, not for anything athletic," she told him.

Not responding, Cooper kept his gaze focused on the ground. "He could have used the rocks to access the water, but he'd have to leave some kind of... There!"

Meg looked down to where he pointed.

At the riverbank next to a stone partly set into the water was a large footprint barely sunk into the mud. A flat sole, just like the ones outside the cottage the first night she'd arrived.

Cooper frowned. "Looks like the same size outside the cottage, the night you heard the crash. I don't know anyone who wears size 14 men's shoes with a flat sole. Everyone around here wears boots or shoes with traction."

Meg looked up at Cooper, her heart racing. "I told you before that Prescott wears that size shoe. He was here. He's been here all along for one reason. To kill me."

# Chapter 11

When they returned from their ride, Cooper thoroughly questioned all the staff at the Sunnyside Farm, and even questioned the guests.

As far as Meg's safety was concerned, he took no chances.

All the staff were accounted for and most of the guests. Except Richard Kimball, the nature photographer. Fiona had not seen him since breakfast. He'd mentioned something about shooting the scenery in the White Mountains.

Awfully odd for a nature photographer to take photos when the season was mostly over. Cooper made a note to question the man upon his return.

Cooper didn't want to let Meg out of his sight. It seemed too convenient that her ex had found her so easily, but one thing was certain. The series of disturbing incidents was aimed to deeply rattle or hurt Meg.

He checked all the security cameras, but saw only the staff and guests on the grounds. The river, though, was an unprotected area. Cooper vowed to never let Meg ride alone again. It was too risky.

Most troubling was the idea that his family was involved. His mother told him her cell phone had gone missing that afternoon. They searched the entire inn, and the staff searched the barn and grounds.

Nothing.

But later that night while Meg watched a movie with his mother and sister, he headed out of the inn to patrol the perimeter. Fiona's cell phone was sitting on the hallway table.

Cooper picked it up, checked it. Maybe someone had found it and placed it there for Fiona.

Or someone had stolen it to lure him away from Meg.

A noise sounded in the living room behind him. He whirled and saw a woman quickly head for the stairs.

Cooper caught up to her. "Hey!"

The woman turned. Jenny, the new live-in housekeeper, the same one who'd admitted to being in the cottage. She kept her gaze focused downward. "Sir? Do you need something? I was returning to my room."

He held out the phone. "Did you put this on the table?"

A head shake.

"Did you see anyone who put it there?"

Another head shake. "I—I have to go now."

"No. You're staying here until I get answers." Cooper softened his voice, but he wasn't letting her get away so easily. Not with Meg's life at stake.

He questioned her for a good ten minutes, but Jenny kept shaking her head and stammering she didn't know anything.

Finally, he told her to return to work. Jenny fled up the stairs as if the ghost of Cooper's grandfather, rumored to haunt the inn, chased her.

Was Jenny playing these tricks on Meg and her fear was all an act? Was she conspiring to frighten Meg, get her to run? If so, why?

He wasn't certain. But Cooper knew one thing. If Jenny was guilty, sooner or later he would catch her in the act.

* * *

"Do you think I saw my ex?"

The question, asked over dinner in the cottage the next day, made Cooper pause. He lowered his fork onto the table.

"I believe you think you saw him. That's good enough for me to take extra precautions."

Still shaken over seeing a shadowy figure who could have been her ex, Meg could barely enjoy the delicious meal Fiona prepared for them at the cottage. She'd spent the entire day glued to Cooper's side as he went about his work.

The fried fish smelled delightful and the buttered potatoes were thick and sprinkled with freshly grated cheese, but her stomach roiled.

"What kind of precautions? A tank would suffice."

The corner of his mouth quirked up slightly. "I can pull some strings, but that's a little excessive."

"True. And a tank wouldn't blend in with the pretty scenery." She forced a smile she didn't feel. "I could paint it orange and red, though. Fall colors. Your mom could put baskets of hanging flowers on the turret."

Cooper laughed. She enjoyed his hearty, deep laugh. It made the little knot of anxiety in her stomach loosen. "I was thinking more of motion detectors outside by the barn, and extra security lights."

Meg sipped her cup of tea. She hated that he had to go through this extra trouble just for her. Cooper and his family had shown her hospitality, and she felt safe here, until yesterday.

Prescott was a ruthless monster. She suspected he had killed Randall and would stop at nothing until he had her at his mercy again. Sweat dampened the palms of her hands, and her pulse became erratic. Prescott had power and money, and used both to get what he wanted. And if Randall had confessed the plan to give her the documents and cash to start a new life, Prescott would redouble his efforts to find her.

Stop her.

With a bullet to her head this time, instead of his fists.

"Meg, you okay? You're not eating."

Toying with her spoon, she waited a minute before answering. "Just woolgathering. I wish I had the money to give you for the extra security."

"Don't worry about it," he said quietly. "Been meaning to do this for a while. Never got around to it."

"Maybe there's something else you can help me out with. Something you can do that involves your talents as a SEAL."

His gaze turned thoughtful. Assessing. The man wasn't easy to fool. Sweat trickled down her back.

"Maybe. Tell me something though, Meg. Why did you want to come here? You could have requested a safe house farther west. Jarrett has a few in place."

She chose to tell a partial truth. "I grew up not far from here. My grandmother's farm is in northern Massachusetts." She helped herself to another turnover. "This smells delicious."

"Do you have access to any cash, Meg? The agency can wire some for you to start a new life."

*I won't need much cash in prison.*

"I can manage."

"Meg, where was your ex when you left Palm Beach?"

More questions. She grew even more nervous. "On a business trip to Boston."

Cooper blinked. "Boston? For what?"

"I don't know. He never told me why he traveled. Lately he's been gone more than home, which was why I planned to run when I did. I had to make sure I had enough time to escape with Sophie before he returned."

"Right. So let's get back to my talents as a SEAL. What aspect of my training are you interested in? Diving in cold water?"

She wasn't quite ready to share everything she needed. "Maybe."

The evasive answer didn't satisfy him. He held her gaze as he drank more of his hot tea. "Where do you want me to dive? What do you need me to find?"

She didn't want to talk anymore about it. Maybe tomorrow. "Let's talk tomorrow. I'm tired of all these questions."

They finished and cleaned up. Meg headed to the living room, staring at the fire. She didn't want to think about her ex, or her life in Palm Beach, which had been filled with hollow misery.

Cooper joined her. He touched her hand, his calloused fingers reassuring and firm.

"You're trembling," he said gently.

"It's been—" she gave a little laugh "—a little rough. I had hoped I'd never face Prescott again, except perhaps in court."

"He's not going to get near you. I promise."

She turned to him, letting all her feelings show. "Thank you. I feel safe with you."

Meg parted her mouth as his gaze grew intent. Cooper stared at her lips. He was going to kiss her. And this time, she'd let him do it.

Heat and desire spiraled in those intense blue irises, and determination etched his rugged features. Meg felt exhilarated and breathless as he drew closer. Her heart skipped a beat and all her female parts sat up and paid close attention.

Real close attention.

As he dipped his head down, she closed her eyes. Soft, firm lips brushed over hers, the sensations rushing through her. Arousal and need twined together like snakes as he feathered his mouth across her trembling lips. Light and airy, not punishing, not rough.

Almost as if he asked for permission.

Meg parted her lips on a sigh and lightly flicked her tongue across his mouth, giving him what he requested.

Cooper curled his right hand around her head, drawing her closer. His left hand slid around her waist and began stroking her back in calming caresses, like she'd seen him do to Adela when the mare got nervous.

She kissed him back as he deepened his hold on her, and she slid her arms around him to anchor herself. Giddy with the taste of him slipping deep into her mouth, Meg teased him back as he moved his mouth expertly over hers. Slow, yet demanding. Giving and letting her take, letting her set the pace.

Leather and sage, the scent of his aftershave wove through her senses. Cooper delivered the right amount of pressure on her mouth, subtle and yet authoritative enough to let her know he was in charge. But he didn't mash his mouth against hers, and he made no move to grope her. His hands on her were assured and firm, yet she sensed the moment she wanted out, he'd release her.

She didn't want to be released. Meg wanted to stay here a long time, basking in the way he lightly nipped her lower lip, then ran his tongue over it in a gentle stroke. Emboldened, she thrust her tongue deep into his mouth.

Held tight against the hard heat of his body, she felt another hardness at his groin. Old instinct urged her to struggle and try to escape, but her female hormones sang a different tune. This was a man who wouldn't hurt her. Every bone in her body sensed this. He would die before raising a hand to strike her.

Perhaps even die fighting to keep her safe from others who did. Cooper Johnson was a Navy SEAL who had sacrificed much for his country, and his code of honor extended far beyond his military service.

In the end, he broke the kiss, drawing in a deep sigh, the blue of his gaze darkened. Trembling, Meg stared up at him, licking her lips.

He pressed a finger against her wet mouth.

"Don't do that. Makes me want to kiss you all over again."

"What's stopping you?"

A rueful grin touched his own mouth. Cooper tugged at the jeans that obviously felt too tight. "A certain something that's urging me to do more than kiss you."

Disappointment speared her. "Maybe I'm wanting to do more than kiss, too."

"You're not ready yet, Princess."

Not ready, when every hormone in her body was singing a chorus of *let's get naked now*? Scowling, she narrowed her eyes. "And what makes you such an expert at telling me whether or not I'm ready to make love?"

"You're afraid. I still see it in your eyes now and then. You can't let go yet of that fear."

Cooper leaned forward suddenly and she flinched out of instinct. He sighed and then gently touched her wobbling mouth. "I would never hurt you, Meg."

Throat tight with emotion, she nodded. "I know. It's just…"

Cooper was a big man, and she'd seen him heft a bale of hay as if it were a sack of potatoes. But he'd been gentle with her, not rough. Ashamed of her response, she went to turn away, but he put his hands on her shoulders, staying her. When she looked up at him, his expression was intent.

"You've been through hell, darling, and when someone has been there, it takes a while to pick up all the shattered pieces. Just like an animal who's been mistreated, you'll learn to trust again and believe in kindness. One day at a time."

"One day at a time," she echoed. "Will it ever get better, Cooper? Will I ever reach that point where I can move past this ugly thing that was part of my life?"

His touch was whisper-soft on her lips, and his body relaxed. "You'll know when the time is right," he said softly. "And when it is, I'll be here."

For a few moments they sat in silence, and then he gave a rough laugh. "If we stay here, I'll finish what I started. Let's go to the inn and play Scrabble. We can rustle up Aimee and Mom. Mom's killer at the game."

"Scrabble sounds perfect."

As they walked to the inn, he told her his suspicions about Jenny taking his mother's cell phone and how he'd questioned her, but Jenny admitted to nothing. Meg wondered. She sensed something about the shy housekeeper that resonated with her.

One of the guests as well could be responsible for her torn sweater, the rose and the nasty card. The cottage lock had been easy to tamper with, and Prescott had many accomplices.

"We should check out the background of all the guests," she told Cooper. Meg explained about the silent photographer. "It might have been one of them."

"Mom keeps records of where they're from because she likes to make them feel welcome. I'll ask for the files and we can look them over."

Hand on the small of her back, making her feel secure, Cooper escorted her into the large downstairs room that had been converted into the family's private living room. A fire crackled on the stone hearth and Fiona sat on an overstuffed leather chair by the fire, reading a paperback. She glanced up with a smile.

"What are you doing here?"

"Thought I'd engage Meg with a good game of Scrabble. First, I need the files of the current guests. I need to know all you know about them." He frowned. "Has Richard Kimball returned yet?"

Fiona shut her paperback, looking troubled. "Not yet. I'll get those files for you right away."

Cooper followed his mother as Meg remained. Her appreciative gaze swept over the flowered wallpaper and the bookcases flanking the fireplace. It was her first time here, and she liked the cozy warmth of the living room. It felt like home.

A large oil painting hung over the mantel.

Fiona and an older man, obviously her husband. Cooper stood behind his mother, looking like a typical rebellious and cocky teenager. A brown-haired girl, flashing a shy smile, stood between him and an older, dark-haired teenager with rugged good looks. Brie and Derek.

There was something about the girl that bothered Meg, but she couldn't figure it out. Not until she saw another photograph on an end table of a woman wearing a police uniform.

Her blood turned to ice. She had seen this particular photo before, in the newspapers. Had memorized each inch of it, the woman's smile frozen in her memory.

Cooper returned, carrying a manila folder. "We can look this over later."

Meg forced herself to speak.

"Was your sister's name Brie Johnson?"

"Brie was her nickname. Her birth name was Sabrina, but she always said it was too prissy, so we called her Brie. She kept her married name of Fletcher even after the divorce, much as we tried to convince her to drop it."

Meg's blood turned to ice. Sabrina Fletcher, the female

police officer killed in the line of duty while wearing body armor manufactured by Combat Gear Inc. Meg's company.

She had killed Cooper's sister.

# Chapter 12

She had to tell them the truth. Cooper's family deserved to know.

Meg swallowed hard. She liked this family, and most of all, she liked Cooper and his quiet air of confidence and how safe she felt with him. And now she stood to blow the fragile relationships she'd forged sky-high with the news that she was responsible for their beloved Brie's death.

But it must be done. Several minutes after seeing the photo, Meg gripped her hands in her lap, facing them on the sofa from her perch on the wing chair.

"I asked you here because I have something I must share with you. Something very important that has to do with Brie's death."

Sometimes it was easier to blurt out the truth instead of waiting. Cooper's expression turned from concerned to guarded, while Fiona merely looked confused.

This was going to hurt them badly.

"Brie, your Sabrina, died from a bullet wound to the chest because the body armor she wore was defective."

"Yes." Cooper's gaze met hers. "It was manufactured, far as I can tell, by Combat Gear Inc."

"Yes. Faulty body armor manufactured by that company." Meg squeezed her hands tighter. "A company that I own, legally, and I founded with my trust fund. I am responsible for Sabrina's death."

For a moment only the sounds of the pretty ormolu clock over the mantel sounded. A muscle ticked wildly in Cooper's tight jaw.

"I don't understand. You own the company that made that vest that killed my daughter?"

Meg nodded.

Nothing prepared her for the stark fury in Cooper's eyes, the way he squeezed his fists together as if he longed to take a swing in her direction...

Punch her hard, like her ex used to.

"I'm so sorry," Meg whispered. "I am so sorry."

*Sorry* was a useless word when facing two stricken, deeply grieving people. Cooper swore softly and then walked over to his mother and squeezed her shoulder. "I'll be back."

He left the room, not looking at Meg. Misery curled through her. She gripped her hands tightly.

"I am so sorry, Fiona. I didn't realize Sabrina—Brie—was your daughter. I wouldn't have hidden this from you, and I told you soon as I found out. I tried to get the vests recalled, and I did call the authorities to alert them, but it was too late for Brie. I'll pack my things and call a cab and be gone from here. I don't wish to upset you or your family any further."

As she started to rise, Fiona called out in a strong, clear voice, "Wait."

Meg waited.

"I want to know one thing. Did you deliberately send out those vests for sale, knowing the material was defective?"

Meg shrugged. "My name is on the corporate documents and I'm ultimately responsible."

"Answer me," Fiona ordered.

Startled, Meg shook her head. "I didn't know. My grand-mother was ill, and I was tending to her. By the time I found out what Prescott had done, it was too late. The vests had already been sold."

"Prescott. Your husband."

"Soon to be ex-husband. But that doesn't make me inno-cent." Meg took a deep breath. "I am responsible for what happens in my company. I am CEO of Combat Gear Inc."

"So stop being a martyr to that fact."

Meg slipped into the icy cadence she used in Palm Beach when dealing with reporters and other busybodies who nosed around for gossip. "Are you suggesting, Fiona, that this is not my responsibility? I am accountable for what happened, and I am prepared to deliver evidence that will send the guilty parties to prison for what they have done. I will turn myself over to authorities, but I can't remain here with all of you. It's impossible, and you really don't want me here after what I told you."

Fiona stared at Meg, her dark gaze intent. "Stop telling me what I want or don't want. If her death is on your con-science, then do the right thing and stay here and let's sort this out together. I know you're frightened, but you must stand strong."

Fiona's voice softened. "You must stay here and stop running. Talk to us and let us know why you are really here, Meg. Are you here to bring justice for my Brie?"

Tears clogged her throat, but she refused to let them fall. "Yes."

Out of the corner of her eye, she saw Cooper hovering in the doorway. "I'll tell you when Cooper joins us. I'll tell you everything."

She had nothing to lose now.

Cooper leaned against the doorjamb. "I'm listening."

His cold blue eyes were so icy. But she gathered all her courage and plunged on.

"I'm here to get evidence that my ex knew the body armor was defective and he sold it anyway."

"Go on," Cooper ordered, his gaze remaining hard.

Meg focused on Fiona. "I founded Combat Gear Inc. to make high-quality, low-cost body armor for military and law enforcement personnel. But I left it to Bert Baxter, the family lawyer, to file the paperwork."

Sweat trickled down her back, gathered in the waistband of the flannel trousers. "Randall Jacobs, a senior partner in the company, warned against shipping the vests because they would fail. But Prescott didn't listen and sold them. Randall told me he had evidence of Prescott's wrongdoing. His conscience bothered him."

"Give him a goddamn medal. What a hero," Cooper muttered.

His mother silenced him with a look that could slice steel.

Ignoring them both, she tightened her hands. "Randall said he would let me know where the documents were to give them to authorities to prove Prescott committed fraud. He also promised to hide money for me until I could get on my feet again. He knew…what Prescott did to me."

She paused, remembering the hard work her grandparents had poured into the company. "That's why I'm here. I'm going to find the documents."

Cooper made a low whistling sound. "I'm so impressed."

The snark in his voice indicated otherwise. She looked directly at Fiona. "I want justice for your daughter. And she will have it. However, I need help. It's why I need Cooper's expertise as a Navy diver."

Now she did turn and face Cooper, whose jaw tensed so much he could have shattered granite.

"Randall gave GPS coordinates to a lake by his home. I need you to dive down there to retrieve the documents."

Cooper glanced at his mother and then scowled at her. "And you expect me to believe you? When you've been lying all along?"

"I didn't deceive you. I didn't know Brie was your sister until I saw the photo tonight!"

Fiona stood. "I'll leave you two to discuss this. Right now I'm going to talk to Aimee and tell her everything—very gently."

As the woman started out the door, she felt a fresh pang of regret. "Fiona, I'm so sorry. I never would have hurt you."

Fiona nodded, but brushed away at tears streaking her face.

Meg didn't know if she could feel any worse. And then Cooper sat on the sofa, facing her. The dark scowl on his face made him look furious. She couldn't blame him.

But she hoped he would see reason and emotions would not overshadow what she must say. Lacey told her SEALs were rock steady and focused, not emotional, and she prayed her friend was correct.

"I'm certain the lake behind Randall's summer home is where he hid the proof that Prescott knew the vests were defective when he sold them to police officers."

Cooer's jaw turned to stone. "Now you're telling me?"

"I didn't want to involve you—" she sighed "—any more than necessary. I had no idea your sister was the officer killed because of this."

He opened his mouth and shut his fists, as if itching to smash something. Or someone. Meg tensed, hoping it wasn't her. Cooper said he'd never hurt a woman. Would he change his mind now with this news?

Finally he released a deep breath. Laser-blue eyes narrowed at her. "I loved Brie. She was my kid sister. I vowed nothing bad would ever happen to her and that damn vest, hell, it killed her."

Misery engulfed her. "I'm sorry," she said again.

The last thing she'd expected was to cause them more grief. Hadn't she caused enough?

"Now what?" she whispered. "Are you going to call the authorities? Turn me in?"

*Please don't do this. Because if you do, your sister will never truly get justice and I'll spend the rest of my life looking over my shoulder.*

"No." He rubbed a hand over his bristled chin. "You and I are going to find those missing documents."

"When?"

Cooper pointed at her. "Tomorrow night."

## *Chapter 13*

The woman he had started to care about was the criminal he'd been searching for all these months.

At midnight the next day, his diving gear in the back of the truck cab, Cooper drove to the location Meg gave him. He'd barely talked to her since her confession, only telling her Mike called to say the car's transmission was shot. It would cost thousands to replace.

The princess was stuck with him for now, without wheels.

She sat in the passenger seat, twisting her hands together and staring out the window.

If this wasn't a cluster, he didn't know what was. He almost laughed at the irony. All these months praying for answers and a means to put the corporate powers at Combat Gear behind bars. And now the answers fell into his lap. Along with a pretty brunette he'd promised to protect, a woman he couldn't help thinking of every other minute.

Or every minute.

She headed the corporation responsible for Brie's death. How could he forgive such a crime?

But that wasn't important right now. Finding that evidence was. He had been a SEAL for eight years and thrived on good intel. And right now the source of all he needed to know sat beside him.

"You've been avoiding me all day," she said softly.

Cooper grunted. He'd been busy trying to coax Betsy into eating. Finally he'd managed to get her to eat a carrot. But she wasn't looking good.

His mother had kept an eye on Meg as she worked in the inn's small office, going over all the guest records to see if any of the men might have worn size 14 shoes.

He glanced at Meg. "I'm here now. Tell me everything about the vests and why they malfunctioned."

At his order, she turned her head slightly. "Where should I start?"

"The beginning's a good place."

Meg pushed at the fall of her long dark hair. The move lifted her breasts and made her seem even more vulnerable. Cooper steeled himself against a surge of sympathy. No emotions.

"The material in the body armor we manufactured is called Liholn. It's a synthetic, extremely durable and tough fiber invented by Randall Jacobs six years ago when he was director of research for Taylor Sporting Goods. It's lighter than Kevlar and resistant to impact."

She recited all this as if by memory, her voice monotone and her gaze fixed on the black ribbon of roadway stretching before them.

"So you used it for athletic equipment?" He tried to loosen his white-knuckled grip on the steering wheel and relax. Hard to do, with everything racing through his mind.

"We used it for everything from tennis rackets to bike spokes. It secured our place in the market and helped us get out of the red. We received orders in such vast amounts, we doubled production of the fibers in our plant. Under

Prescott's business model, Taylor Sporting Goods began to operate in the black again."

"Whose idea was it to manufacture the body armor?"

Looking down, she stared at her hands. "Mine. I was at a Memorial Day function for the charity I helped, talking with a vet about my brother. Caldwell died in combat. I wished that Caldwell hadn't rushed to enlist, prove himself. He was too…eager, and headstrong. I wanted to do something to help vets, since I couldn't help my brother."

Cooper said nothing, steeled himself against another pang of sympathy.

"The man told me he wished someone would invent a bullet-resistant vest that was more flexible, lightweight. And that's when I came up with the idea of using the Li-holn for bulletproof vests, and Combat Gear Inc. came into being. I used the money in the trust fund my parents left for me to start the company."

Suddenly she turned to him with a beseeching look. "I wanted to create a product that would save lives. I couldn't save my brother, but I could help other soldiers. An American-run company, creating products made in America at our Massachusetts plant. Low-cost, high-quality vests that would allow the wearer greater range of motion, flexibility, while still preserving the integrity of the vest's protective elements."

His jaw tightened as he thought of Brie. "Protective elements? Not how I'd describe your product, Meg. Defective is more like it. So why the hell didn't you test them in the lab instead of using living, breathing subjects like my kid sister?"

Her little hitch of breath warned he'd pushed hard. A modicum of guilt filled him. She'd been a victim, too, but his anger needed a target.

But Meg looked him straight in the eye. "I did test them

out on a living subject. I believed in this product to the point where I volunteered as a test subject."

Cooper reeled. "You're joking."

"After we did several tests on crash dummies, I wore one and had Randall fire a .38 caliber bullet at me."

He whistled, deeply impressed despite his anger. Having been shot, he knew the impact. He'd also been hit while in Afghanistan, but body armor saved his hide. The impact of the bullet had left him wheezing, with a nice big bruise as well.

"That had to hurt."

A shadow entered her green eyes. "No worse than what Prescott did to me with his golf club."

And then the dry humor he always admired. "Of course, it was a prestigious custom driver worth around $2000. Nothing but the best for Prescott, even when he was beating me."

The anger inside him battled against the fierce need to pull her into his arms, shelter her from any past hurt she'd suffered. He'd promised to protect her, and he would.

Meg touched her left arm, as if remembering the bruise.

"Prescott started marketing the vests right away, before we even finished testing. He had advance orders for ten thousand vests. I pushed Randall into more tests. And when he exposed the vests to water and then intense heat, the fibers started to degrade, to the point where one of the team fired a bullet into it, and it pierced the vest."

Cooper nearly jerked the truck off the road. "You knew the vests were defective?"

"Yes," she said softly. "Randall was working on a way to correct this, but the first five thousand vests were already waiting in the warehouse, ready to be shipped. And Prescott ordered them sent out."

"You didn't stop him." His tone was more than slightly

accusatory, and he regretted it. The woman's husband had been abusive. Dangerous.

"I didn't know he'd done it. By then Prescott was handling all affairs for Combat Gear. Gran was seriously ill and I was caring for her. In the hospital, out of the hospital, and then the aftercare facility…doctor's appointments, trips to the pharmacy… I had my hands full."

"You trusted that psychopath with the company?"

She gave a tiny sigh. "I trusted Randall, who was in charge, to keep Prescott in check. But then one day I logged onto the company accounts and saw the shipment sent to Boston. Prescott had already shipped vests to an ammo shop there more than six months ago. And to other shops."

He named the Boston shop and she grew pale. "Yes, that's the one."

Coop knew, because he'd purchased the vest for Brie at that shop. The cost was extremely low and the shop's owner assured him the vests were top of the line.

"He was also shipping them to a police district in Boston as a test market. He claimed word of mouth would spread once the cops started wearing the body armor, and we'd get many more orders. But he already sold those vests at a huge loss. The vests should have retailed for $900 each, and Prescott sold them for $200."

That kind of loss filled him with nagging suspicion.

Meg buried her face into her hands. "I tried to get Prescott to recall the vests, warn the consumers who purchased them. He answered with his fists. I could barely move for two days afterward."

The bastard had nearly beaten her to a pulp, Cooper realized. "It's not your fault," he said, all the anger draining out of him. "Your ex set you up."

But she lifted her head, and her expression was fierce.

"A person should always take responsibility and I am the CEO of Combat Gear Inc. I've had nightmares thinking about cops wearing those vests, thinking they were bullet-proof and going into a volatile situation."

Her voice dropped. "And then getting shot and killed, which is what happened to your sister."

Time to tell her the truth as well. "Many cops put their body armor on a dummy and fire bullets at it." Cooper took a deep breath. "Brie did. But the vest was dry."

Meg turned to him, and in the light of the dashboard, he could see the sheen in her eyes. "I'm so sorry, Cooper."

He couldn't talk about Brie anymore without that gut-awful feeling and his throat closing. Instead, he changed the subject. "When you get this proof that you think is in the lake, what are you going to do with it?"

"Give the evidence to the FBI and turn myself over to authorities for arrest."

The words, spoken so calmly, jolted him. "What?"

She sighed. "It's why I couldn't say anything to you. I had to wait to verify the documents. Prescott needs to be imprisoned, too."

Meg was willing to go to jail for what she did. Her sense of integrity staggered him.

"You shouldn't be sent to prison," he muttered, his hands tight on the steering wheel.

She looked at him calmly. "Why not? Surely you, of all people, would love to send me there. You want justice for Brie."

"Justice, not revenge. Big difference." All the anger drained out of him, leaving him weary. "Why Boston? Did Prescott ever say why he chose that as a test market?"

Even though the city was closer to the plant, he thought it mighty peculiar her ex was in such a rush to send out the vests.

"No, but I always thought it was odd he spent much of his time there." Meg looked around as if expecting to find her ex lurking in the back of the cab. "I overheard Prescott on the phone one night. He mentioned the name O'Neary."

Cooper's mouth went dry. O'Neary, the same name Jarrett had brought up. Prescott August was rumored to associate with Miles O'Neary, an Irish mobster. The head of the O'Neary gang controlled part of Boston. If Prescott deliberately sent out the vests to police at an enticing price, and he knew they were defective, his motivation might not have been greed.

What if Meg's husband had been ordered to send the defective vests there because O'Neary planned a hit? It didn't make sense. The conditions would have to be perfect—perfect for the mob—for the vests to fail. Weather wasn't something they could plan.

And it seemed far too complex an operation, even with the reach O'Neary had in Boston. Their gang was one of the most ruthless, more dangerous even than the Winter Hall Gang, who had ruled the city for many years until disbanding.

He didn't know the answers, but it became more important than ever that they find the evidence that would imprison Prescott August.

And protect Meg, because if the vests were manufactured for reasons other than profit, she wasn't merely the target of her ex-husband's obsession.

But of something much more deadly—the Irish mob.

A cold wind rippled across the mirror-smooth surface of Lake Beebersim. Silhouetted by the light of the half-full moon, Cooper moved with the shadows as they made their way through the woods to Randall's summer house.

He hefted a heavy-looking black bag and climbed into the rowboat docked behind the home.

Dressed in black, Meg huddled on the dock. Cooper wore a dry suit to protect him from the icy water. He'd ordered her to remain on the dock, but she wasn't having any of that.

Sending him out onto that water to retrieve hidden documents was one thing. Sending him alone was another.

As he untied the boat, Meg climbed into the boat. Cooper lifted his head.

"No," he whispered.

"Yes," she whispered back. "You need me."

"I work solo on this."

"And if someone chances upon you, and you're with me, you'll have a good excuse. Romantic midnight boat ride. And what if I'm sitting on the dock all alone and someone comes along?"

A frustrated sigh tore from his throat. "You sit down, keep quiet and do exactly as I say."

Cooper picked up the oars. They barely made a sound as he dipped them into the inky blackness of the lake.

Muscles flexed smoothly beneath the form-fitting black scuba suit he wore. The suit covered every delicious inch of his body and had a hood that allowed only his face to show. A pair of black swim fins and a dive mask, along with a large, boxlike apparatus, lay on the boat's bottom.

She kept her voice low, aware sound carried over the water, and pointed to the apparatus. "What is that?"

"Rebreather. Closed-circuit scuba. Recycles my breath and eliminates bubbles, so no one can tell I'm down there."

All the equipment and the grim set of his expression reminded her this was a seasoned warrior. Cooper no longer resembled the laid-back cowboy who enjoyed riding horses and teasing her. Or the angry man who'd lost a beloved sister.

He was rugged and focused.

She peered over the side of the rowboat. "I wish my flashlight were waterproof."

Cooper tapped the dial of his wristwatch. "This is enough. It has a compass."

Incredulous, she studied the watch. "And you can see with that? In this water?"

"All farm boys can."

He eyed his watch, and when they were a good mile out on the water, he set the oars into the boat. Cooper dropped the anchor.

"Stay low," he warned. "If you hear another boat, power up that flashlight so they see you. And if they come close enough to ask questions, use this."

Cooper gestured to a fishing pole and a small bait box.

The inky depths swallowed him as he slid into the water without a single splash. The man was pure stealth.

Meg rubbed her arms, more chilled from the implications of what they were doing than the breeze skidding across the lake. She only hoped whatever Cooper retrieved would contain the documents.

Stars glittered overhead like tiny crystals tossed against black velvet. It was lovely out here, little ambient light to obscure the natural darkness. She settled back and tried to distract herself by hunting through the sky for the constellations.

The houses ringing the lake were dark. Most occupants came here for the summer and seldom stayed past Labor Day. For that she was intensely grateful.

Finally she felt herself list sideways. She turned to see Cooper heft a black box onto the boat. Then he pulled himself out of the water. The equipment he wore must weigh at least thirty pounds, yet he climbed into the boat as if it weighed nothing.

Heart pounding with excitement, she examined the box, about the size of a briefcase.

Cooper removed his rebreather and mask, and pulled the hoodie down. "It was down about twenty feet."

"What if the documents inside are wet?"

He sat the box on the seat and fumbled with the catch. "Doubt it. It's a Pelican case. Watertight. Your man Randall knew what he was doing."

Cooper knelt on the boat seat and pried open the box as Meg shone her flashlight inside it.

Empty, but for two bricks weighting the case.

Hope crashed down. "Prescott got to the documents before we did."

"Doubt it." Cooper ran his hand over the case's interior. In the light of the flashlight, his stunning blue eyes were calm and steady as the lake water. "Did Jacobs like puzzles?"

"Adored them. He had the patience to sit for hours with math equations."

"A man as smart as Jacobs would want to make sure only you got the evidence. By planting all these clues, if someone missed one, their chances of finding the documents would diminish."

His fingers skimmed the box and then a smile touched his handsome face. "Gotcha."

Meg craned her neck and watched him pull out a small piece of paper sandwiched between the box and the lining.

"A coupon?" Weary, she rubbed her eyes. "Was he playing games with me?"

Maybe Randall was trying to lead her on a wild-goose chase, and had planned to abscond with the money he'd accused Prescott of laundering.

Cooper shook his head. "It's another clue. But we're out in the open here. Put it away and we'll study it when we get back to the house."

Back at the cottage, after Cooper changed into warm clothing, they sat in the kitchen. Meg picked up the coupon he'd found and turned it over.

Cooper watched her face pucker into a puzzled frown. He didn't like this, didn't like that her ex could be nearby, watching them. He got up and went to check the window, ensuring the shades were pulled down.

The coupon looked normal. Bold lettering at the top said the user would receive 10 percent off a home Wi-Fi camera. The expiration date was good, too.

And then he caught something off. Next to the standard bar code was a square with symbols.

Meg frowned. "This QR code seems out of place here. I've never seen one like this on a regular coupon."

"You use coupons in Palm Beach?" he asked in a dry tone.

She glared at him. "Yes, I clip them all the time while I'm getting a pedi, so I can save my pennies and purchase more designer shoes. Do you have something to scan bar codes in your bag of secret mission toys?"

He leaned forward, irritated. "Meg..."

"I know your world has been turned upside down with what I told you, Cooper. But mine was turned upside down the day I found out as well. I'm trying to do the right thing."

If only he could believe her, trust she told the truth. Too much anger and grief had built up inside him over the past six months.

"You still have a life," he told her, struggling with his emotions. "My sister is dead."

"And I would have done anything to take that back,

to change the past, if I could. I never meant to hurt anyone. If my gran hadn't been so ill, I would have checked and rechecked all the shipments to make sure a single vest wasn't sent out."

Cooper hesitated.

A light sheen of tears shone in her eyes. "Do you believe me that I never wanted to hurt anyone, especially police officers like your sister? Do you believe me when I tell you I want justice, too?"

She sounded weary. He wanted to believe her, but too much was at stake.

"It doesn't matter what I believe," he said finally. "What matters is keeping you alive and safe, and finding those papers."

On his phone, he switched on the app and then swiped his camera phone over the coupon.

A website popped up. She peered over his shoulder.

"Now it makes sense," she said. "It's the listing for Randall's summer home. He must have hidden the documents inside a camera in his home. But why go through all that trouble to hide the documents and cash for me? Why not leave them in the watertight box?"

Cooper whistled at the listing on the house. "Nice digs. Only $2.5 million."

"It's a huge house. The documents could be anywhere. Why did he do this to me? Why couldn't he have handed over the evidence or put it in the car? What's the point of all this super-secret-agent stuff? It does me no good!"

Her voice rose to hysterics.

He had a bad feeling he knew why Randall Jacobs had been so mysterious, and it had to do with the Irish mob. Cooper set down his cell phone and reached for her hand. "Chill, Meg. Calm down."

She took in a tremulous breath.

"The fact is, Randall went through an awful lot of trouble just for documents proving the body armor was defective."

"He did say he would leave me some cash. Maybe he thought water would get into the case and ruin the money?"

"No. There's something else going on here. Something that he wanted to make sure stayed hidden."

Her shoulders sagged. She seemed exhausted, and this midnight foray onto the lake had sapped her. Not wanting to worry her further, he opted against telling her what Jarrett had told him earlier about her ex's possible involvement with Irish mobsters.

Cooper scanned the listing again. "This says by appointment only. We'll need a real estate agent. My mom's friend can do it for us. Perfect time to study the layout and return later to search more thoroughly."

"What's the use? Prescott probably already found and destroyed everything."

"Stop being so negative. You're tougher than that."

"I'm tired of being tough. I just want to give up. What's the point?" She splayed her hands against the table. "I'm all alone in this."

"No, you're not. You have me. I'm going to help you, Princess. And I never give up."

Her carnation-pink mouth lifted in a ghost of a smile. "You're very tenacious, Cooper Johnson."

"Navy SEALs are. Goes with the job description."

Meg's mouth wobbled. "I should never have come here and put your family in all this trouble."

"I told you I'm involved. I want justice for my sister. And we'll find a way to get that bastard of your ex behind bars for good. You're safe here."

"For now," she whispered. "Until he makes his next move."

Cooper squeezed her hand tight. He worried about her, worried about his family. They were endangered as well.

She looked down at his hand covering hers. The bones in her hand seemed so delicate, yet within Meg was a core of solid steel. His blood boiled as he thought of her ex slamming her against a wall, hurting her. No matter what Meg had done, or not done, she didn't deserve abuse.

No woman did.

*Prescott August, you are a dead man if I ever see you*, he silently promised.

"We'll find what you're looking for. Your ex isn't going to get within ten yards of you, Princess."

He would help her search for the missing documents. After that, he couldn't make any promises. But he'd promised Jarrett he'd look after Meg, and he'd see this assignment through to the end.

He only hoped Prescott August wouldn't get to the documents first.

Wearing a plain navy suit, Karen Harrison was a plump middle-aged woman and so friendly and gracious she immediately put Meg at ease.

The Realtor picked them up at the inn the next morning in her beige SUV. For the agent who had listed the house for sale, they would act the part of an engaged couple looking for a home.

Cooper spoke little to her as Karen drove to the house. He seemed distant, and guarded. Gone was the closeness they had shared in the cottage when he almost kissed her. Cooper would have to be a good actor to convince the listing agent he was madly in love with her.

On the drive to Randall's house, Karen told them the listing agent wasn't cooperative.

"She wanted a proof of funds letter, verifying that you have the means to purchase such a high-end house, Coop."

The slightest tension gripped his broad shoulders. "And?"

"I told her that your family owns a very successful and very historical B and B that's hosted such luminaries as Thomas Edison. She relented."

Cooper grinned. "Karen, you are a naughty girl. The inn didn't open until well after Edison died."

Karen shrugged. "So? You have lightbulbs in the inn, right? Edison invented the lightbulb. It wasn't a complete lie."

Meg liked her.

When they pulled into the driveway before the two-story redbrick mansion with its sweeping columns, the listing agent was standing in the portico. A severe-looking woman with dark hair pulled back into a tight bun, she kept glancing at her watch.

They wouldn't have much time to look over the house.

Pretending to be Cooper's fiancée was an act she wasn't certain she could pull off. A knot of anxiety curled in her stomach. Cooper glanced at her. "You all set, Princess? You can do this."

His encouragement lent her courage. Cooper climbed out of the car and opened her door, ushering her out with old-world courtesy.

As they walked through the expansive home, memories assaulted Meg like bullets. Glad for Cooper's steady grip on her hand, she tried to concentrate on the layout, looking for clues with the security cameras. There were six security cameras inside and six outside, the listing agent told them.

Randall must have hidden the documents and cash around the cameras.

There was a camera in the living room, hidden by the

recessed crown molding. The elegant green living room had a marble fireplace with two flanking Greek stone columns holding leafy plants. An Austrian crystal chandelier gleamed overhead with soft, tasteful lighting.

Matching cream twin sofas faced each other across an antique coffee table tastefully decorated with shiny brass candlesticks holding gold candles, brightening the earthy tones of the room. It was formal and resplendent, yet she preferred the coziness of Fiona's parlor with its faded but welcoming blue sofa and leather easy chair, and the African violet on the side table.

The two agents went into the great room as Meg hung back, studying the security camera. Cooper gazed around the room. "Very opulent."

"I hate it," she whispered. "This room is everything I hated about my marriage, my life. It's a beautiful prison. I'd rather live in a trailer if it meant being happy."

He blinked in apparent surprise. "Really?"

She nodded.

They joined the agents in touring the rest of the house, including the basement. The finished basement had a darkroom, which they looked over carefully.

When they returned upstairs, the listing agent took them into the kitchen at the back of the house.

The spacious chef's kitchen featured wood floors, granite countertops and an island with a sink. A bank of windows overlooked the sweeping lawn marching down the gentle slope to the lake.

"This chef's kitchen is exquisite, perfect for serving caviar and canapés for cocktail parties. The very finest high-end appliances are featured in this dream kitchen, complete with a pantry and plenty of counter space," the agent droned.

Meg tuned her out. How many times had she stood at the

sink, gazing out the window at the lake, wishing to untie the boat at the dock and drift away? Far away, to an island where no one would ever find her, where no one could ever hurt her again.

An island where a handsome prince would be waiting. He would be rugged and strong, and promise she would always come first in his life.

Never again would she be the little girl whose parents were more interested in a rich, lavish life than their daughter.

Or the granddaughter whose grandmother wanted her to carry on the family lineage.

Or the wife who was a means to wealth and prestige.

There was no such island or prince. But there was Cooper Johnson. Strong, rugged and dependable. She'd started to deeply care for this man, who kept her safe and made her laugh and forget her woes. Devoted to his family.

She wished she could be the object of such intense devotion.

Cooper looked around the kitchen, shoving his hands into the pockets of his trousers. Judging from his appreciative gaze, he wasn't studying the appliances or the counters. He was looking at places where Randall could have hidden the cash and documents.

Then his gaze focused on the security camera. Small and compact like the others, it hung from the corner of the ceiling. Unlike the others, it did not blend in. Meg's heart raced. That camera had not been there last time she was here. They needed to see Randall's office, where he kept the monitors. The agent had rushed them through the upstairs rooms.

Meg shot her coolest look at the listing agent, who clearly wanted the showing to be over. "I wish to examine the upstairs office again."

Tapping her feet, the woman shook her head. "I have another appointment…"

"Which can wait. I flew in from LA specifically so my dear Cooper could be with me to see this property. If I'm to move my business from Rodeo Drive and work online, I need a spacious office with wiring already in place for my computer equipment," Meg said in her haughtiest voice.

Karen coughed politely and Cooper, bless him, assumed a poker face.

The listing agent looked taken aback. "I didn't realize… what business are you in?"

"Fashion and design," she shot back, not missing a beat.

Cooper's mouth twitched slightly.

The listing agent's expression smoothed out. "Of course, Miss Conners."

Meg curled her fingers around Cooper's strong left biceps. "It's Ms. Conners. The office must be spacious and have the right lighting because I frequently Skype with my clients in London, Beverly Hills and Rome. Kate Middleton is very particular about seeing my designs before ordering them. She keeps a very tight schedule."

When they were upstairs, Karen made a point of asking the listing agent to show her the basement again. They were left alone in the office.

"Kate Middleton, huh?" he teased. "Good one."

"I know how to handle people like that agent. Name-dropping is only one way to impress them."

"I'm surprised you didn't mention Queen Elizabeth."

She smiled briefly. "I did meet her once, a long time ago. She is a very gracious lady."

A large computer monitor showed a display of five interior security cameras and six exterior cameras.

Meg studied the screen. "Cooper, how many cameras did the agent say were inside the house?"

"Six." He ran a hand over the wall and thumbed it with his knuckles.

"Then why are only five cameras displayed?"

He joined her at the desk. "You're right. The kitchen camera doesn't have a live feed. It's a dud."

Her heart leaped with hope. "And the coupon was for a security camera...and that security camera in the kitchen is new. It wasn't in place when I was here last year."

"Thought the kitchen was an odd place to have a security camera."

She felt a surge of triumph. "Oh, I don't know. Maybe Randall was worried about the chef stealing the caviar."

"Or the very fine high-end appliances," he said, mimicking the snobby agent's high-pitched voice.

They grinned at each other. Then his grin faded. "It must be tough for you being back here."

His insight startled her. "Yes. All those memories."

Cooper nodded. "I felt that way about my sister's cottage. It was her refuge, a place where she could be alone. So many memories in that place."

"Good memories." She ran her hand along the desk surface. "I wish I'd never met Prescott, never married him. Your sister would still be alive if I hadn't founded that company."

Cooper gently circled his fingers around her wrist.

"I've been thinking about what you said about accountability. Maybe there's a part of me that wanted you to take the full blame, so I could have a target. But that's not fair and it's not right. Truth is, Brie was a cop. If Brie hadn't been wearing that vest, yeah, maybe she'd still be alive for a while longer. Or maybe there would have been another time. She chose to work in a dangerous area of the city."

Meg said nothing, let him talk.

"She was my kid sister, but she'd made tough choices before. Bad ones. I wanted to protect her, shield her with all I had. But I couldn't be there for her all the time. And that's a hard reality for me to accept."

"It wasn't your fault," she whispered.

He gave her a steady look. "Any more than her death was yours, Meg."

"Do you believe that I never intended to hurt her, or anyone else?" She had to hear it from his mouth.

Cooper drew in a deep breath. "Yeah, I do. I tease you, Princess, about your designer shoes and clothing, but you don't strike me as the type of woman who cares more about material items than human lives."

She gave him a ghost of a smile. "Thank you."

He turned his attention back to the monitor.

"Let's go back to the kitchen. I want to take another look, see if I can dismantle that camera."

When they returned to the kitchen, Cooper climbed on the polished black granite counter and examined the camera.

If they were caught, how could he explain this?

He checked the housing, rapped on the ceiling. "Got a screwdriver handy?"

Meg's heart pounded hard as she flung open the junk drawer where Randall had kept small tools.

"Hurry," she told him, handing him the screwdriver. "That woman wants us out of here. You don't have much time."

He managed to pull free the camera and peered upward. "Just as I thought. It's not wired into the system. Nothing else up here, though. Have to check further. There may be a hidden compartment."

Footsteps sounded in the hallway. "Cooper," she whispered. "Hurry up, she's coming back!"

He screwed the housing back, pocketed the screwdriver. Then he dropped down and sat on the granite just as the two women started to enter the kitchen. Oh damn, this didn't look good.

Cooper pulled Meg into his arms and kissed her. Deep. She melted into the kiss, wrapping her arms around his neck. His mouth moved over hers, not a subtle claiming, but a bold declaration.

*Mine.*

She was caught in the storm, helpless to do anything but go along. And she didn't want to fight him or these feelings. Swept away on a tidal wave of pleasure and sensation, she kissed him back with everything she felt for this man, everything she'd ever longed for and never dreamed she could have in life after her marriage went south.

Someone cleared their throat. But Cooper kept kissing her. Finally he slowly separated them. Meg felt a flush warm her cheeks as both real estate agents looked at them, Karen with amusement, the other agent with disapproval.

Cooper climbed off the counter and nodded. He rapped on the granite with his knuckles. "Sturdy enough. Meets with my approval."

"Sturdy enough for what?" the listing agent snapped.

"Sex. Table gets boring after a while, so I always make sure the counters are rock solid in case I get in the mood."

Blood drained from the agent's face as Cooper placed a possessive hand on the small of Meg's back and escorted her out of the kitchen.

But she couldn't help the smile on her face as they left the house. That kiss was not playacting.

It was real, and the passion behind it as solid as the man himself.

* * *

The pleasure of Cooper's kiss lasted through most of the day, up until the time he told her he was returning to the house at night.

For a "special" visit.

She insisted on going, and argued with him about being left behind. If Cooper was going to break in and find the documents, she had to be there. What if the documents implicated her?

She had to see them first.

At eleven, they set out for Randall's house. Meg couldn't believe they were breaking inside. As he drove, Cooper assured her they'd leave no trace behind. Black leather gloves covered his big hands. He looked grim in his black trousers, soft-soled black shoes and black long-sleeved T-shirt.

Cooper parked his truck a good distance from the house. "Trust me, Princess. I'm real good at sneaking in and out."

She turned to him with an arch look. "As good as you are at sex in the kitchen?"

His gaze turned intent as he switched off the ignition. "Maybe soon, you'll find out."

The words sent a pleasant tingle rushing down her spine.

Meg hung back in the trees as Cooper dismantled the alarm and then the security cameras, and then joined him at the side door leading into the laundry room. He picked the lock and left the door partly open. The house was cold and unwelcoming. As they walked through the laundry room to the kitchen, she thought of all the times she'd been here for corporate meetings.

While Gran and Prescott talked business with Randall and other company executives, she had kept the liquor and drinks flowing and overseen meals. It was the only reason Prescott wanted her to join them. Randall, who was happily divorced, had readily agreed to her playing hostess.

No one ever asked her what her needs were. She, the granddaughter of the company's founder, was invisible. Taylor Sporting Goods and the Taylor name meant more to Gran than Meg had. Letticia Taylor had been obsessed with following her husband's last wishes to take the company public. She'd had little time for Meg.

When would someone finally put her first? She'd always been shoved to the back, an afterthought. Doing what everyone expected of her, not following her own dreams because pleasing others always came first.

She deserved better.

While she remained downstairs, he went into the upstairs to the attic, using a map he'd obtained of the house plans with the help of Karen.

When he returned, silent as fog, he had a triumphant smile.

"Just as I thought. No wiring connected to that camera, or anything stored near that space. But the attic floor is pretty high. I believe our friend Randall created a storage space to hide things."

"He always bragged about how his family custom-designed this house for storage with secret compartments," Meg told him.

They headed for the kitchen, using the thin beam of the penlight she held out. Cooper gazed at the security camera. "If the camera is a prop, then it's not the camera itself, but what it's pointing to. And it would have to be a place where Randall could easily reach. How tall was he?"

"About your height."

Good.

She turned. Cooper gestured to the kitchen chandelier with its showy ceiling medallion.

He climbed atop the island, and Meg set his bag of tools on the counter and shone the flashlight upward. In a few minutes, the chandelier was on the counter. Cooper pointed the light up.

"Got it," he said with satisfaction. "There's a hidden compartment up here."

He reached up and fished out a shoe box and handed it to Meg.

Then he reattached the chandelier and ceiling medallion and climbed down.

Meg stared at the box. This was it. She'd sweated over this, had nightmares about it. Her trembling hand touched the box.

"I'm almost afraid to open it."

Shadowed by the pencil-thin beam of light, Cooper's expression was grim. "Do you want me to do it?"

He'd asked her. That alone said a lot about him, that he didn't grab it and open it, considering how angry he'd been about his sister's death. "No." She drew in a deep breath. "After I read the documents and we return to the inn, I want you to call the FBI."

He recoiled. "Meg…"

"I suspect Prescott implicated me in this on purpose. He put my name on the corporate papers when the lawyer set up the LLC. Not his. I was too big of a fool to even know what was going on."

"Not a fool." He gently touched her cheek. "You were a victim."

Not anymore. Never again. She took a deep breath and opened the box.

Her heart dropped to her stomach.

"Dear God," she whispered.

Stacks of wrapped hundred-dollar bills met her gaze. Not a few thousand. Cooper thumbed through them. "There has to be at least $250,000 here."

He set the money aside. Beneath the bills was a photocopy of a newspaper article about a man convicted of poisoning his wife by spiking her sports drink with antifreeze. And a receipt from an auto parts store for antifreeze, dated exactly a week before her grandmother first fell ill.

The receipt had Randall's elegant, curved signature on it.

At the top of the newspaper article was a scribbled note also in Randall's handwriting: *Letticia Taylor board meeting, Monday 3 p.m. Sweet tea.*

The clipping dropped from Meg's trembling fingers and clattered to the floor. "It wasn't proof of defective vests, after all," she whispered, suddenly nauseated. "But proof of murder."

Her grandmother had drunk, as she always did, a glass of sweet tea at the annual board of director's meeting at Randall's summer home in New Hampshire a few months ago. Sweet tea Meg herself had served from a pitcher in Randall's refrigerator. Sweet tea only Gran drank, because everyone else hated the pure sugar cane syrup she liked in the drink. Hours later, she'd started throwing up.

And then she got better, only to get worse weeks later. At the time Meg blamed it on her grandmother's age and growing frailty.

Now she could see the truth clearly. Gran rallying, only to fall sick again after drinking the sweet tea, the tea Randall insisted on giving her whenever she came to the office because he knew how much she enjoyed it.

Her grandmother hadn't died from old age after all. She had been poisoned. And Randall, the man who helped Meg escape, the man she trusted, had done it.

## Chapter 14

Meg lost it.

All these days she'd held it together, and he'd watched her face each challenge with chin held high. Even when she confessed her true purpose in coming to New England, she never faltered.

That ramrod spine remained solid steel. Except now.

She slid down to the floor and sat, hugging her knees, and began to cry.

Cooper stared helplessly at her, wanting to gather her close, wipe away her tears and promise things would be all right.

But not here. Not now.

In the distance, he heard the crunch of gravel beneath tires. He raced to the living room doorway, careful to avoid the security camera pointing toward the front door. Through the partly drawn drapes, he saw a car silhouetted by moonlight driving up to the house.

No headlights. Damn!

Cooper returned to the kitchen. Meg sat on the floor, moaning, tears trickling down her cheeks. "He killed her, he killed her... Why wasn't I more careful? I should have known!"

"Meg." He clasped her shoulders. "C'mon, Princess, get it together. We've got to get out of here."

That car pulling into the driveway wasn't a late-night visit from a real estate agent. Someone was coming into the house for the same reason he and Meg had returned.

He stuffed the items they found into his knapsack, slung it over one shoulder. "Now," he ordered. "Let's go."

But she sat there, rocking back and forth, her sobs heart-wrenching. Cooper's own heart twisted. No time for grief.

A car door slammed.

Cooper crouched down, squeezed her shoulders. "Meg, now!"

Taking her hand, he pulled her upward. The front door-knob rattled.

Whoever was outside wasn't being very quiet. Cooper glanced at her. "Go to the laundry room, open the outside door and run for that big oak closest to the house. It'll provide good cover. Can you do that?"

Meg nodded.

He touched her tearstained cheek. "I'll be right there, Princess."

As soon as she left, Cooper turned his attention back to the living room and the front foyer. Withdrawing his pistol, he waited, hidden by the bookcases in the living room. On the stately grandfather clock near the entranceway, the pendulum swung back and forth, its ticking echoing his heartbeat.

He needed to see the intruder.

The front door opened and closed. No light switch turned on. He peered around the corner and his grip tightened on his weapon. That scrunched face and hunched shoulders were immediately recognizable.

Richard Kimball, the nature photographer. What the hell was he doing here? And how did he get a key, or the combination to the lockbox? Doubtful he wanted to photograph the fish in the aquarium upstairs.

Kimball turned toward the kitchen. Coop raced into the pantry and squeezed himself into the back, crouching down by stacked boxes. The pantry door opened, but no light came on. Instead, Kimball reached for the stepladder stored near the front.

Cooper waited, heard the man return to the living room. He sneaked out and looked around the corner.

Using the stepladder, Kimball climbed up and reached for the security camera in the front foyer. He removed it and began to check the housing.

Silent as fog, Coop backed up, headed for the laundry room and fled outside. He stayed around the trees for cover until reaching Meg. She crouched down by the oak, shivering. He knew it wasn't from the cold.

Coop pointed in the direction of the truck. They hugged the trees, staying in the shadows in the woods, until reaching the truck. Once inside, Meg's shoulders slumped in absolute dejection.

Cooper drove back to the farm, careful to watch his rearview mirror in case they were followed. Just to be extra cautious, he took an indirect route.

Finally she looked at him. "Did you see who it was?"

Coop glanced at his mirrors again. "Richard Kimball. The guest at the inn. He was dismantling the living room security camera."

The statement seemed to startle her. "What for?"

It wasn't to check the system and make sure the cameras worked. "I bet he was there for the same reason we were. Maybe he works for your ex, and was looking for the proof Randall left. For all we know, Kimball killed Jacobs and wants to make sure no evidence is left behind."

Meg buried her face in her hands. "I've been such a fool

to trust Randall. He was the only one wanting to help me. And all this time, he was working with Prescott to kill her."

"Maybe," he said carefully. "But if he did, what was his motivation? Randall had money. And why would he take precautions to tell you where the documents were? Why tell you anything?"

She lifted her face and stared out the window. "I don't know."

They didn't return to the cottage. Instead, Coop parked his truck by the barn and they walked to the inn. When Kimball returned, he'd be waiting for him.

The inn was quiet when they entered. Late-night guests had a key to the front door, so he knew he'd hear Kimball return. Coop settled Meg in the kitchen, making her a cup of hot chocolate. She kept shivering, her expression woebegone.

He set the steaming mug on the table before her and pulled up a chair next to hers. Coop wiped away the tearstains on her cold cheeks. "Meg, talk to me," he urged.

Her gaze was dull and listless when she finally looked at him. "It's over, Cooper. There was no evidence, no documents. Randall lied to me. He wanted me to find the proof he helped to murder Gran."

Tears shimmered in her big green eyes once more. "I'm all alone. I always was."

A fierce need to protect her surged. He scooped her into his lap and held her close. "No, you're not alone. I'm here, Princess."

Gently he brushed back a lock of her hair from her face. "I'm not letting go, either. You're safe. I'm sticking to your side. We'll get to the bottom of this."

"Randall killed my grandmother." Fresh tears threatened. "But if that's the case, where are the documents we searched for?"

"We'll find them. And answers."

For a long few moments, he held her close, stroking her back and murmuring reassurances. Meg laced her hands around his neck and rested her head against his chest. Having her this close stirred another feeling in him, but he forced himself to focus on her.

Her needs.

So small and fragile, like glass. She felt good in his arms, soft and perfect. He wanted to keep her there forever, protect her from anyone or anything. She rubbed her cheek against his chin, catlike, and finally stopped trembling. Coop needed to gentle her to his touch. Like a skittish horse, he needed to gain her trust and give her assurance he would not harm her.

But he needed to take action to protect his family as well. With Kimball returning to the inn, he didn't want to place his mom or Aimee near the man.

And kicking him out of the inn meant he'd lose his chance of finding out what the hell Kimball was doing with the security cameras. Changing them out? Or looking for hidden documents?

Kissing her forehead, he came to a decision. "You okay for a while?"

Meg nodded and climbed off his lap. She resumed her seat and began to sip the now-lukewarm hot chocolate. Coop checked the exterior security camera on the app on his cell phone. Kimball's black rental car still hadn't returned.

Restless, he paced the kitchen and punched in a number on his cell.

A sleepy male voice answered, the Southern accent more pronounced than usual. "This had better be important, Coop."

"Nomad," he said, using the other man's SEAL nickname. "You still in Saratoga or did you fly south yet for the winter?"

A wide yawn, and then, "Nope. Moved to Connecticut. Got a job in maintenance on a horse farm. Lots of nice scenery."

*Scenery* to former Chief Petty Officer Nick Anderson meant two-legged scenery in silk hose.

"Need your help."

A rustle of bedcovers and a young female voice saying, "What's wrong, Nick?"

"Go back to sleep." Then to Coop, "What and when?"

Sharp, alert, his former swim buddy was now fully awake. "ASAP here, at the inn. I need eyes on my mom and Aimee. I've got a guy here who could be a murder suspect."

He glanced at Meg, who paled.

"I'll be there by nine a.m. Drive straight through. Need anything else?"

Appreciative of his friend's aid, Coop locked gazes with Meg. "We'll talk when you get here. Oh, and Nomad?"

"Yeah?"

"Take the gun. Leave the cannoli."

A rough laugh and a lowered voice. "Yeah, but she's sooo sweet."

"Too much sugar is bad for you," he deadpanned as Nick laughed again.

He thumbed off the phone and joined her at the table and took her hand. "Nick's my former swim buddy from the teams. We went through BUD/S together. He left the Navy a year ago, and we're tight. Good people."

"Why is he coming here?"

"I need backup, someone to guard my mom and Aimee and watch Kimball. Don't want him to get spooked and leave." Coop stroked a thumb over her hand. "I believe he had something to do with your grandmother's death, and Randall Jacobs."

He didn't want to leave her alone, but now that Kimball was a suspect, it was time to take another look at the plaster cast he'd made of those size 14 shoes. Coop set down his phone. "Give me your burner phone."

When she handed it over, he pocketed it. "Take my cell. Go to our private parlor and lock the door behind you. Keep scanning the outside security camera. Soon as Kimball pulls into the driveway, text me. Do not look out the window, just check the camera feed. Got it?"

She nodded. "Where are you going?"

"Gotta check something out."

After dropping a kiss on the top of her head, he slipped out the kitchen door. Cold air sliced into him, but he was too focused to notice the chill.

In a few minutes, he returned with the plaster cast. Kimball's car was still missing.

He snagged the housekeeper's keys off a peg in the kitchen and headed to the upstairs guest rooms. Inside Kimball's room, Cooper found only one 35 mm camera and no other photography equipment. Interesting. Most photographers carried plenty of lenses and other cameras.

He found a pair of polished black leather loafers and fit the right one into the plaster cast.

Gotcha. Perfect match.

Worry and anger twisted inside him. This bastard had been the one outside the cottage, spying on Meg. When Fiona had asked Kimball about getting to the inn, Kimball failed to mention a little stop at the cottage.

Coop left the room, making sure to leave no trace. He went to the family's living room and let himself in with his key.

Meg sat on the sofa, clutching his cell phone like a life raft. "I've been watching and he's not back yet."

Eyelids closing, she looked exhausted. He didn't want her here where Kimball could see her. But he was loath to leave his mother and sister alone.

Coop tugged her hand. "Upstairs. My room."

He led her to the private family wing of the farmhouse. The door to the hallway was locked as usual. He opened it with the housekeeper's keys, making sure to lock it behind him.

At the last room on the left, he ushered Meg inside and flipped on the light. The room faced east, and one window offered a glimpse of the parking lot below.

She looked around at his worn poster of the Foo Fighters and all his sports heroes, and then at the dresser holding a few trophies. Meg walked over to the dresser.

Despite the shadows in her eyes, her mouth quirked upward. "You were a rodeo cowboy? A cowboy in New Hampshire?"

Coop shrugged. "I lived with relatives in Texas for a year after my dad died, and entered a few competitions in my crazed youthful days."

She touched the gold trophy. "And did well."

The thrill had released the pent-up anger and grief. By the time he transferred to school back in his hometown, Coop knew he had to get his head on straight. Soon after graduation, he enlisted in the Navy and set to his goal of becoming a SEAL.

He hunted through the dresser, found a pair of red flannel pajamas and gave them to her. "Afraid this is all I can offer you to sleep in."

Another tentative smile. "Thanks."

He jerked a thumb toward the hall. "Bathroom's two

doors down on the left. There's a spare toothbrush in the top drawer of the vanity."

He'd undressed and tugged on a pair of gray sweats and a Navy T-shirt by the time Meg returned. She'd rolled up the sleeves on his PJ shirt and held the bottoms in her hand.

"They're a little big." Her cheeks pinkened.

So big his pajama top covered her like a short dress. He liked his clothing on her, liked the idea of his pajamas covering her. Coop eyed the bed with regret.

"You take the bed and I'll sleep on the floor."

Only honorable thing to do, and she looked ready to drop.

"Don't be silly," she said softly, sitting on the mattress. "There's room enough for both of us, and you're just as tired as me."

Right. As if it wasn't tempting enough, having her here in his room. "Be right back."

When he returned from the bathroom, Meg was lying in bed, curled up against the wall. Coop stood in the doorway a moment, a tangle of emotions knotting his gut. So pretty and fragile, yet she was no pushover. Seeing her fall to pieces tonight had shattered him.

It was a delicate situation. They needed to inform the police, but the moment they did, he'd have to admit he broke into the house. Worse, the police would question Meg and perhaps even turn her over to the FBI now that an official investigation had opened into Brie's death.

And that louse of her ex would still wander free.

Coop trusted the local sheriff, but he didn't want him involved. Most of all, he was highly suspicious that the so-called evidence was proof Randall Jacobs killed Meg's grandmother.

Meg's ex had the most to gain from murdering her grandmother. All the family assets and money went to him, and he'd stopped the company from going public. And judging from the price on Jacobs's summer home, Randall hadn't been in a hurry to sell for quick cash. Karen, the real estate agent, told him the property had been on the market for four months. Randall refused to lower the price.

After retrieving his cell phone, he stepped out of the room, partly closing the door. Coop made another call, this time to his older brother Derek, the police detective.

When he hung up, satisfied that he had the backup he needed, he went back into his bedroom. Meg still slept, one hand tucked beneath her chin, her long hair spread over the pillows. Desire shot through him. Yeah, they had an intense sexual chemistry, and it was going to be a long, hard night. He gave a rueful glance downward. Very hard.

Coop turned off the bedside lamp and crawled into bed, sliding far away from Meg. Best to avoid temptation. He longed to pull her into his arms, cover her face with kisses.

Helluva way to sleep, with an erection and his mind restless. Using his SEAL training, he forced himself to fall into a deep sleep.

What seemed like a moment later, he heard a woman's shrill cry.

Eyelids popping open, he snapped on the light.

Beside him, Meg tossed and turned, moaning. Reaching over, he gently jostled her. "Princess, wake up, you're having a nightmare."

But she kept crying out. Coop slid over, gathered her into his arms. "Meg, it's okay," he soothed.

She finally stopped moaning and opened her eyes. Two wet emeralds regarded him, the nightmare still shadowing them. "I dreamed of Gran drinking that poison," she whispered. "I tried to warn her, to grab it, but then Prescott dragged me off. She trusted me all those months she was sick. She relied on me to take her to the doctor, to care for her. And I let her down."

A hollowness compressed his chest. Cooper rested his chin atop her head. "You can't be everything to everyone, Meg. The hospital staff, the doctors, couldn't see she was poisoned, so don't blame yourself."

"I knew her better," she whispered. "She was my only family. And knowing that Randall poisoned her…"

"It's not your fault."

Cooper stepped back, and wiped away a single tear with the edge of one thumb. She was so tiny and fragile, the delicate exterior camouflaging a tough steel core. The heart of a true warrior beat inside Meg, someone dragged to hell by another man's fists.

Any person who tried hurting her again, he'd strip the skin from their bones. This time, he wanted her to know a man's touch could fill her with pleasure, not pain.

With extreme care, he kissed away her tears, kissed the corner of her mouth.

This was all wrong, and yet so very right.

Meg's heart galloped still from the wisps of the fleeting nightmare. It raced once more as Cooper leaned close, gazing into her eyes. Filled with concern, his expression was far different from anything she'd ever seen from a lover.

Pure desire, mixed with tenderness.

His mouth dipped closer to hers, his breath a warm puff of air in the coolness of the room. Cooper brushed his mouth against hers, his movements light and subtle. When she parted her lips, his tongue slipped inside her mouth.

Slow, tantalizing, the kiss was seductive. Heady. Heat built as their mouths moved together, tongues mating and breaths mingling.

Then he leaned back and touched her cheek. Wordlessly, she stared up at him.

Cooper was all she'd dreamed of in a lover—strong, fiercely loyal, courageous and tender. He would not knock her unconscious on a cold tile floor. Instead, he'd pull out his own teeth before hurting her.

The man was dangerous. Oh, not because he was a trained warrior who could snap a man's neck like a brittle twig. He scared her because he was a good man, and she feared falling for him, trusting him and then having him break her heart.

That fragile organ had already been broken once by Prescott. She'd barely begun to repair it. It hurt to know her ex was a bastard, but she sensed it would hurt more to face heartache from Cooper. Because he was honorable and good, and her ideal.

Much easier to put him at a distance, pretend there was nothing between them. Not this sizzling chemistry, this combustive sexual need arcing between them, hot and demanding.

As soon as she found the missing documents and microchip, she'd be gone. No bond, no regrets, as if she'd run away from the one person who could reach past her constant loneliness and pull her free.

But it felt so good to be in his arms. Meg felt his body's wiry, tensile strength. She'd had so little of love in her life. Wasn't it about time she rewarded herself with one night of passion and pleasure?

He bent his head close to her ear, his hot breath a whisper against her skin.

"You okay?"

Meg nodded. "You told me I would know when the time is right." She slid her hand down his chest, feeling his heart beat. "No more doubts."

As she reached up to kiss him, his mouth descended upon hers. Teasing, light kisses once more. He flicked his tongue lightly over her bottom lip.

Meg pulled back, trembling, hot. Needing him.

Satisfaction gleamed in his gaze. Cooper's long, strong fingers curled possessively about hers. An air of natural authority clung to him, and overwhelming power. Yet his grip on her was so gentle.

Tender.

The more she knew him, the more exposed she felt, and the more dangerously she teetered toward something more lasting and permanent. Like that four-letter word she'd lost hope of ever experiencing.

*Love.*

Love was scary. All she'd ever wanted was a family who accepted and loved her for herself, but they all tried shaping her into their image of the perfect Meg. Her parents molding her into a good daughter. Her husband beating her into a meek wife. Letticia making her into an approval-seeking granddaughter.

Tired of being strong, she leaned against him. For once, she just wanted someone else to protect her from all the fears screaming inside.

He slid a palm around the back of her neck. Instead of soothing, it stirred all her senses. Her nerves screamed to life. He leaned close enough for her to count hairs in the dark stubble shadowing his jaw. She felt open, wet and aching. His touch lingered over her neck, featherlight, erotic as he stroked her skin.

Making love with him forged a physical link between them. But she deserved passion.

Deserved love as well, though Cooper did not love her. For tonight, passion would suffice.

She silently unbuttoned the shirt, watching his eyes

darken. Cooper kissed her again and then slid down her body, dropping tiny, melting kisses across her skin. Tremendous heat suffused her. She felt as if her body were on fire and would never be cold again.

Meg watched as he tugged off his own shirt, displaying a muscled chest dark with hair. After he was fully nude, Cooper reached into the nightstand and withdrew a condom, and sheathed himself. As she lay back, he began to stroke her body. Cooper's hands were warm, calloused and gentle. The earlier chill wrought by the terrible dream began to fade beneath his heated caresses. She found herself drifting into a sensual haze, pleasure replacing painful memories.

Cooper kissed the side of her jaw, her neck, blowing little hot breaths on her skin as he stroked her skin. One hand closed over her right breast. He gently squeezed and kneaded, creating an aching throb between her legs. She wanted to shut her eyes, float away on the sensual haze, but Meg kept her eyes open.

Experience in bed taught her to never close her eyes, because she had to anticipate the next move. Had to make certain to satisfy her lover.

Yet he made no sudden moves or sounds of displeasure. Leisurely he kissed his way down her body, his hand still cupping and kneading her breast. Then he crawled down her body and parted her thighs.

Cooper lowered his head and put his mouth between her legs.

He licked and kissed her center in long, expert strokes. Cooper's tongue on the aching flesh made her moan and writhe, the pleasure so strong she couldn't lie still. Every stroke and whorl drew air from her body until she felt herself strained with the need to breathe, to burst out of her skin. He licked, swallowed, the rough bristle from his night beard abrading her thighs. Tension heightened, spiraling her upward and upward until she stiffened and gave a keening wail, her body thrashing as she climaxed. The orgasm exploded out of her so fiercely, she almost blacked out.

When she lifted her head, the hint of untamed lust lurked deep in the depths of his eyes. In silent surrender, Meg lay back, holding out her arms to him. Her body tingled with arousal, hungering for the contact between them.

Cooper leaned back on his haunches, aching with the need to penetrate. Mounting her, he felt the enormous strain of his muscles tensing as he tried to keep himself in check. He kissed her again, his mouth drifting down to nip at her throat. Her breasts were like apples, perfectly shaped with rosy, taut nipples.

He kissed one very gently, then ran his tongue around it. She whimpered, her hips rising and falling off the mattress, driven by instincts of her own.

"Soon," he soothed her. Cooper took her nipple in his mouth and gently sucked. She clutched his shoulders, her body twisting.

He released her nipple with a small popping sound.

"I would never hurt you, Princess. I only want to give you pleasure."

He kissed her, rolled atop her and reached down between them to guide his rigid shaft inside her. He was much larger than Prescott and she winced as he slid into her. Bracing himself on his elbows, Cooper stopped and looked down at her.

"You okay, sweetheart?"

Meg's breath hitched at the wealth of concern and tenderness in his voice. She nodded and wrapped her arms around his neck, then opened her legs wider in silent acceptance.

Cooper took her mouth in a deep kiss and laced his fingers through hers, pinning them to the bed, and began to move.

Meg sucked in a breath and relaxed, opening to him, feeling blunt pressure filling her. Making them one. He pulled back and began to stroke inside her, his shaft rubbing against her sensitive tissues, the friction creating a delicious heat that began from her center. His muscles contracted as he thrust, powerful shoulders flexing and back arching.

Cooper consumed her, chased away the bad memories with pure erotic sensation. Silky chest hair rubbed against her aching breasts, his hard six-pack sliding against her soft abdomen. She arched to meet his rhythm.

Wonder came over her face as she watched him. His mouth parted on a gasp, lips trembling. The bed beneath her soft as down, the male pressing her backward onto it solid muscle. It felt as if he locked her spirit in his, a closeness she'd never experienced.

His thrusts became more urgent, harder. Meg's legs lifted as her hips pummeled upward in need. Close, so close…she writhed and reached for it, the tension growing until she felt ready to explode.

Screaming his name, she climaxed, her sheath squeezing him as she shattered, her back arching. He growled in satisfaction, gave one last thrust and threw his head back with a hoarse shout. Cooper collapsed atop her, his face pillowed beside her, his breathing ragged. She bore his weight, welcoming it, but then he eased out of her and rolled over, pulling her into his arms.

She nuzzled her cheek against his sweat-slicked shoulder. He stroked her hair in a tender caress.

Such strong shoulders, bearing much weight. No complaints, nothing but quiet and staunch resolution to bear the burden.

"I told you before I didn't need anything. Or anyone." Meg let all her feelings flow like water. "It's been a lonely walk for me for years since Caldwell died in combat. My parents ignored me, living only for wealth and pleasure. My grandparents loved me, but loved the business more. And Prescott, he used me to get a solid claim on the company. You were the first man to ever ask what I wanted, what my needs were."

Raising her head, she studied his solemn expression. Meg traced a line along his firm jaw and the slight stubble bearding it.

Cooper's heavy-lidded gaze swept along the curve of her cheek to her mouth, swollen from his passionate kisses. "You're stronger than you think, Princess. You're one of the toughest and sweetest women I've ever known."

Meg made small circles on his chest, tunneling through the curly dark hairs with her fingers. "I feel as if I were fractured, and I'm beginning to heal. This can't last. I won't stay."

"Don't run away, Meg. Whatever problems you face, you can work them out."

Meg listened to his heart thud as she rested her cheek on his muscular chest. A huge step, making that kind of promise. It meant tying herself to him, strengthening the bond already forged in the flesh and...

Her heart. She stirred, troubled by the idea, testing it in her mind. He was so good to her, so gentle and tender. What woman wouldn't want this?

She wanted it, badly.

But it was not meant for her to stay.

# Chapter 15

"How much do you trust the attorney who handled your grandmother's estate?"

The question, asked over breakfast in the dining room the next morning, didn't surprise her. Not after what they had found last night in Randall's house.

Meg paused in sprinkling brown sugar over her oatmeal. Now that she knew her grandmother had been murdered, the circumstances of her will became even more suspicious.

"Baxter and Baxter have represented our family for years. Gran and Pops trusted Bert Sr. implicitly. He was executor of my grandfather's will, but not my grandmother's. But he did prepare both her will and her trust. His son, Bert Jr., updated the will and trust last year."

"We need to talk with Junior," Cooper muttered.

"The firm is in Boston. I could call him..."

"Boston isn't a long drive. Let's pay him a visit. Sometimes it's best to catch people off guard." Coop leaned back, hooking his thumbs through the loops of his jeans.

Good point. "There's something else. After Bert Jr. updated the trust, I couldn't find the copies of my grandmother's original will. Anywhere. Prescott may have hidden them or destroyed them."

Cooper slid his palm over hers, his grip comforting. "I doubt she wanted to leave everything to Prescott. From what you told me, that doesn't sound like her. She wanted to retain control of the company until the very end, and someone like that doesn't simply sign everything over to a son-in-law, carte blanche."

"Should we call the Palm Beach police and tell them what we found about Randall?"

"Not yet. I'm not convinced that evidence wasn't put there to frame Jacobs. Your ex could have found the documents and destroyed them, and put the money and newspaper article there to place the blame for your grandmother's death on Jacobs. That's why we need to go to Boston and talk to Bert Jr."

A road trip to Boston suited her jangled nerves. But there was still the matter of the missing nature photographer.

"What about Kimball?"

Richard Kimball had not returned. Or at least his rental car hadn't. Fiona told them he hadn't called, either. The photographer was due to check out today.

If the photographer was working with Prescott, then Meg knew her ex was close. She was certain she'd seen Prescott that day in the woods. Knowing Kimball had tampered with the security cameras at Randall's home solidified her suspicions that the photographer was aligned with her ex.

"Nick will be here soon. And my brother. Both of them will stay with my mom and Aimee, keep an eye on things. I already called the listing agent and asked her to check over the house. Told her I lost my wallet and I was backtracking all my visits. If something is off with those security cameras, she'll find out."

Footsteps sounded on the stairs. Cooper immediately quieted and began to eat.

Meg smiled at the newcomer. Paula, the gray-haired Georgia widow, took a seat by the window at the large dining table. She greeted them with a warm smile, her left cheek dimpling, her blue eyes bright behind wire-rimmed glasses.

Fiona served the guest a stack of pancakes and brought more fresh coffee.

"Such a pleasure to see young people. I don't have much chance to socialize outside my age group." Paula reached for the syrup and poured it over her pancakes. "Are you two guests or do you live here?"

"I live here," Cooper said. "Megan's visiting. She's with me. Megan, if you're finished, help me clear the table."

Meg felt reluctant to leave. Politeness to elderly people had been grilled into her since childhood. "You go on, please. I'll stay here and chat a while with Paula."

The woman beamed as Cooper shot Meg a warning look. "Thank you, my dear. It's been so lonely since my Wallace died last year. I stay busy with my grandchildren, but sometimes I feel as if I'm in the way. Do you have children, dear?"

"No. I'm not married."

"A pretty young lady like you?"

"I was married. I'm in the process of a divorce."

The woman's gaze sharpened behind those round spectacles. "Oh my. What if you change your mind?"

Meg sipped more coffee. "I won't."

"A person can always change her mind, my dear. 'Til death do you part, is what my Wallace always said, God rest him."

Death was too good for Prescott. Meg changed the subject and asked Paula about her visit. The widow chattered about going to see Mount Washington for the first time.

Excusing herself, Meg left, taking her dishes into the kitchen. She and Cooper worked to stack the dishwasher. When she returned to the dining room to see if Paula needed anything else, the widow was gone.

Through the window, she noticed a sleek red Jeep Wrangler pulling into the inn's parking lot. A tall man with dark blond hair got out. Straight-shouldered and stiff, he had the bearing of military. Another man, this one shorter and brown-haired, climbed out of the passenger side.

They came into the inn and Cooper greeted them in the hallway. "Nomad! Derek."

"Thought we'd shock you by arriving together. Had to cut through the city on my way up, so I figured Derek would like to catch a ride," the blond man said.

Aimee and Fiona joined them, exclaiming over the new arrivals. There was much back-slapping and many hugs, and Aimee was especially thrilled to see her older brother. Even Sophie, who'd accompanied Aimee down the stairs, barked in excitement and circled the group.

Family time. Uncomfortable with being the outsider, Meg stepped back into the dining room. What would it feel like to have family to lean on, to be there for you when you needed them? Familiar loneliness arrowed through her. Maybe she was better off alone. But no, Cooper had been there for her. He wouldn't let her down.

The group entered the dining room. Meg turned from the fireplace as Cooper drew the two strangers forward.

"Meg, this is Nick Anderson, my swim team buddy from BUD/S."

Unsmiling, Nick nodded at her. She became aware of the sharp scrutiny from those dark brown eyes. Her gaze flickered to the large black gun holstered at his hip, and the equally wicked dagger strapped to one muscular thigh.

Wide shoulders, narrow hips, and his entire body shimmered with quiet menace. A cold shiver stroked down her spine. She was glad Nick was Cooper's friend, because she didn't want to be on this man's bad side.

"And my brother, Derek."

"Lieutenant Derek to you, little brother," drawled the good-looking black-haired man who bore a strong resemblance to Fiona. Derek shook her hand.

"You got promoted," Fiona exclaimed. "Honey, you didn't tell us."

"Thought I'd save the news for dinner. You are making your famous pot roast, right, Mom?"

Aimee's arms wrapped around his waist, Sophie trotting by her side, Derek escorted his mother into the kitchen as Cooper and Nick quietly talked.

Meg left the inn, aware he probably wanted to catch up with his friend. Barely had her feet touched the steps when a hand caught her elbow.

"Where do you think you're headed?"

She glanced at the frowning Cooper. "Giving you private time for your friend and your brother."

Cooper sighed. "Meg, the reason my friend and brother are here is to help you. Nick's one of the toughest SEALs I know. And Derek is a top-notch detective. His lab can analyze the handwriting on those newspaper clippings to see if it was Randall Jacobs's writing."

He drew her forward, kissed her forehead. "Where you go, I go. I'm serious, Meg. Either someone is trying to scare you into leaving here and smoke you out with all these strange incidents, or your bastard ex has somehow gained access to my farm and intends to catch you alone. That's not happening on my watch."

Warmth filled her. Cooper sounded so determined and

assured. She wasn't alone in this after all. Reinforcements had arrived.

He kissed her again, this time a deep kiss. The front door slammed and she heard a heavy tread on the porch steps.

Reluctantly, Cooper drew back and turned. "Nomad, what's up?"

"Wanted to know where to stash my gear." The ex-SEAL shot her a curious look.

"Upstairs, in the family wing. There's a spare room there. Derek can show you. I need you near Mom and Aimee, keep an eye on them."

The man nodded. "I'll take care of things at home, Coop."

Her gaze dropped to the gleaming pistol holstered on his hip. Once she hated guns. Now she was grateful his friend was armed, and there was another person watching over Cooper's family.

Cooper didn't release her, nor did he seem flustered that his friend caught them embracing. He acted as if all this was normal.

As if they had a relationship. They were lovers, but could she expect more? Did she want more?

*Yes*, a tiny voice inside her cried out. *You deserve this.*

"Another thing, Nomad. Need you to hack into the Taylor corporation database and get me anything on Combat Gear Inc."

His voice never faltered, but Meg stiffened in his arms. "There's no need for that. I can give you the password."

"Which has changed by now," Cooper pointed out.

Nick's gaze centered on him. "And what exactly am I looking for?"

Releasing her, Cooper took her hand. "Documents that prove Taylor Sporting Goods is connected to Combat Gear Inc. Any emails connecting Meg's ex-husband Prescott August to Miles O'Neary. O'Neary is the Irish mobster who has a hold on Boston's waterfront."

Meg tugged her hand free. "Cooper, why are you telling him all this?"

His steady blue gaze regarded her. "Princess, I trust Nick with my life. I told him everything about you and the vests. If there are documents linking your ex to the defective vests, Nick will find them. He's the best damn hacker on the East Coast."

"And West Coast," Nick added, but his expression remained guarded.

The man might trust Cooper, and vice versa, but she remained an unknown factor. That much was clear. Nick was an important part of Cooper's life, just as his family was. But trusting him was another matter. And if the worst happened, and her heart got crushed again?

*You'll survive.*

She had hopes and dreams. Aspirations of doing something good with her life, something meaningful to help others. Those dreams had been smashed beneath the heel of Preston's cruelty, but he hadn't crushed her spirit.

She would go on. New dreams, for dreams were countless as the stars. Life wasn't an absolute. It was wonderfully gray and purple and blue and pink and all the colors in between.

Cooper had showered her with love last night, leaving her deliciously sore in all the right places. He'd promised to protect her and keep her safe, and her feelings for him had blossomed over the past few days.

Still, she wasn't family and she was the one responsible for his sister's death.

She only hoped Cooper would stand with her when the authorities learned the truth.

\* \* \*

The drive to Boston was lovely, with rolling hillsides and pretty farms set among the thick trees. As they headed east on 113, memories filled her.

Meg pointed to a stretch of rolling farmland. "My grandparents' summer house is south of here. It's a lovely farm, but neglected."

"Is that where you learned to ride?"

"Yes. I had my pony when I was younger, and then when I grew older I competed in equestrian events."

She shot him a shy glance. "Like you, I thrived on the competition. It was good for me."

"So you like cowboys, huh?" He winked.

"Oh yeah. I like cowboys. Even ones who abandoned the Patriots for the Dallas Cowboys for a full football season," she teased.

"Hey, I stayed loyal. Just because I lived in Texas didn't mean I changed my colors."

Meg stared at the rolling countryside, lost in thought about those childhood days at the farm. Innocent times, when she had her grandparents' undivided attention, and they showered her and Caldwell with love and devotion to make up for their parents' divorcing. Not like later when they were too worried about the business.

"Did she leave the farm to Prescott?"

Her fond memories turned sour. "That was the one thing that didn't pass to my ex. Gran deeded it to me as a gift when I graduated from college. Prescott wanted me to sell it. I refused. I'd rather let it rot than sell it because he wanted me to."

Cooper glanced at her. "You stuck to your guns. Good for you."

It hadn't been too terrible, because Prescott had been preoccupied with business. "The last time I was there was more than a year ago. Gran and I went there to pack the antique quilts that had been in her family for generations. The furniture still sits there, all covered. The farmhouse has no running water or electricity now. I hired a guy to mow the fields every three months, but other than that, it's a sad little abandoned place."

His mouth flattened. "If there is a hidden will, I bet she left it in the house."

Meg had considered it. "Maybe. I packed the key when I left Palm Beach, but it's back at the cottage."

"Let's see what this lawyer of your grandmother's has to say."

But when they entered the stately, carpeted offices of Baxter and Baxter, the young receptionist snapped her gum and told them in a cold tone that Mr. Baxter was on extended leave. Meg glanced around the empty waiting area. It was a small firm, but the office had a deserted air to it.

She had been here a few times, and the receptionist always kept a dish filled with butterscotch on the desk and there were stacks of files near the computer. The candy dish was gone now, along with any files. Even the computer had been shut off.

It almost seemed as if the office were empty, and the receptionist was trying to conceal the fact.

"His assistant is taking appointments. She's busy right now. If you call later…"

Meg narrowed her eyes. "We are here now. I need to speak with Mrs. Sandors, Bert's assistant."

"I'm sorry, but that's not possible."

"Then I want to get a copy of my grandmother's original last will and testament. And a copy of her original trust."

The receptionist stood, went to a file cabinet and pulled out a form, handing it to Meg. "Fill this out and leave it and we will mail it. You will receive a copy in about five to six weeks."

"I need it now," Meg insisted.

The woman did not budge. It was clear things had changed from the time Meg had last been here.

Cooper folded his arms. "We aren't leaving until we speak to someone in charge."

A minute later, a beefy security guard arrived and ushered them out of the law office.

In the truck, Cooper drove, his jaw tight.

As he navigated through the busy city traffic, she tried to quell the nervous tension in her stomach.

"I don't know why she was so uncooperative with us. My grandmother was a valued client," she told Cooper.

He stopped at a red light and glanced at her. "They had other problems. Since when does a law firm hire a receptionist who chews gum and wears jeans?"

Meg startled. "I thought she seemed new... She must be a temp."

A temp given orders to keep clients away and give them evasive answers and forms.

No copies of the trust. No copies of her grandmother's original will. And an attorney who was absent and a dragon of a receptionist clearly guarding the front gate.

*What is going on here?*

## Chapter 16

His mother called while they were driving back to the inn. Richard Kimball had returned an hour after they'd left, rushed upstairs and abruptly left.

"He was in such a hurry he left his camera. I'll have to ship it back to him," Fiona said.

"Hold off on that." The camera could prove useful if Kimball had taken photos of the house.

Next he called the listing agent for the Jacobs house. When he finished that conversation, he hung up, even more puzzled.

"She didn't find my wallet."

Meg glanced at his seat. "Probably because you're sitting on it. You have a cute butt, by the way."

He grinned. "Thank you, ma'am. I appreciate you squeezing it so tight last night."

Loving the becoming blush on her face, he wished they'd had more time together. More time, under less stressful circumstances.

"The agent did tell me if I left my wallet there, someone might have taken it. She called the sheriff because someone broke in last night and removed all the security cameras from the house."

A little gasp from Meg. "Did they take anything else?"

"Just the cameras. And the monitors and recording tape."

It was a good thing he'd disabled the cameras before they broke in last night. "Damn," he muttered, remembering.

"What?"

"I disabled the security cameras by spraying them with black paint, but if Kimball took the video recorder, we're on it from our more legitimate visit with the Realtor."

"Is that a problem?"

"Maybe." He didn't like that Kimball now had proof they were there. He didn't like that he didn't know why Kimball was interested in the cameras. If the man worked for Prescott, why would he take all the cameras? Was he looking for the evidence that Randall Jacobs had poisoned Meg's grandmother?

His instincts warned that evidence was too convenient. Why the hell would Jacobs hide evidence that would point to him as the one who killed Letticia Taylor? Why wouldn't Jacobs simply destroy it?

She abruptly changed the subject. "How's Betsy doing?"

Cooper's chest tightened. "Not good. I asked Mom to call the vet while we were gone. She didn't seem interested in food this morning. And she was lying down."

"Oh no." Meg placed her palm on her arm. "I'm sorry, Cooper. I hope she'll be all right."

The light pressure of her touch felt damn good, made him feel less burdened. "I hope so, too, but we have to prepare for the worst. She's thirty years old. Pretty old for a horse."

When they arrived at the inn, the vet's pickup was parked in the drive. Meg climbed out of the truck and headed straight for the barn.

Hanging back for a moment, Cooper studied his lover. Late-afternoon sunlight gleamed in her hair, picking out the honey highlights. All natural. Cooper grinned, shoving his hands into his pockets. He knew this for certain now.

He knew several things about Meg now. Far from a snobby socialite, Meg was warm and caring, and her love of animals equaled his own.

Man, he was getting in deep. What had started out as an assignment had deepened into something real and lasting. But where did Meg fit in with his family? They needed him.

Family came first, always. He felt the familiar rise of grief threaten to swallow him and pushed it back. Hadn't cried once over Brie's death; he refused to do so now. He hung back, admiring the gentle sway of Meg's rounded hips, the confident stride. Every bone in his body raged to take her hand, march her back to the cottage and make fierce love to her. And that was his problem. He wanted her so badly he shook with the need of it. Meg didn't need an out-of-control man who reminded her of her ex. She needed gentle loving. Someone to cherish her, hold her tight, whisper how beautiful she looked with those sleepy green eyes and her kiss-swollen mouth, branded from his touch...

Not for a night or two, but a lifetime.

Sex had always been a relief for him, a way to blow off the pressure-cooker keg that boiled when he was down-range or returned from a grueling op. He wanted right now, here's the bed, plenty of mind-blowing orgasms and then see-ya-later. The women in his life had been like fireflies, sparkling and pretty, but gone the next day.

Settling down for apple pie and soft brown hair spread over his pillow in the morning and a gold band around his finger, no way. He had plenty of apple pie baked by his mom and he disliked wearing rings, thank you very much.

*She's not from your world. She's not going to stay around, and neither are you*, he grimly reminded himself. He needed an icy dose of reality on his ever-throbbing groin, which seemed to think only of how delicious Meg tasted beneath his mouth and how her breasts felt soft and inviting against him.

Once all this was over and Meg was cleared, she would drift back to Palm Beach and five-star hotels and her Jimmy's shoes world. And he'd remain here, wondering what the hell to do with his life once the inn got straightened out and he was no longer needed.

The realization hit him like a kick to the shins. Cooper leaned against the fence. For years, the adrenaline thrills kept his heart pumping, his purpose steady. And then a bullet killed his sister and Cooper's black-and-white view of the world. Family came first.

But Meg was right. Farm life bored him. What the hell was he going to do? He couldn't see packing up and leaving for a security job that would drag his sorry butt out of the country, away from his family. Hadn't he done that enough over the years?

For a few moments, he stared at the sweep of horse pasture and Adela kicking up her heels as she trotted around the fence. It was good to see the rescue finally relaxing and enjoying herself.

Cooper knew he was avoiding the inevitable. Just couldn't face it. Please, not yet.

But he knew if Betsy's time had come, he had to do the right thing. He, Brie and Derek made a promise long ago when they were kids and their parents gave them their first horses.

Never let the animal suffer, even if it means you have to suffer the heartache of losing them.

Meg emerged from the barn and beckoned to him. Cooper stiffened his spine. It never got easier. And this was going to be the most difficult case of all...

Tears shimmered in Meg's eyes when she greeted him at the barn door. Cooper squeezed her shoulder. "I know."

No words needed. He went into the barn to his sister, brother and mother, who looked stricken. Coop hugged his sister and mother.

"Figured you wanted alone time with her. We'll be outside," Derek said, his voice husky. "Don't blame yourself, Coop. You did your best."

He knew what Betsy meant to Brie. Hell, they all did.

Cooper watched his brother escort Fiona and Aimee, and then he stepped into the stall. A dull roar sounded in his ears as the vet droned on. "Old age."

"Not eating."

"She's in pain."

Kneeling down, he stroked Betsy. "It will be easy. Don't worry. I always promised Brie I would take good care of you."

And he'd kept that promise, even to the point of ending Betsy's suffering.

It was over with quickly. When the vet had administered the medicine and taken away the horse for cremation, Cooper sat on the same storage bin where he'd kept Brie's tack. All her riding gear, and her battered straw cowboy hat she'd loved to wear while riding Betsy.

Meg stood by the stall, looking at him.

"I need to be alone a moment," he told her.

She didn't leave. When he finally raised his dull gaze to hers, he saw tears swimming in her green eyes.

"I'm sorry. I'm so sorry, Cooper."

Then there were no words, just her outstretched arms. She sat on the storage box beside him and hugged him, refusing to let go, refusing to leave, even as he tried to pull away from her grip.

Cooper still could not release all he'd felt over the past

six months. Pain at his sister's death and the unfairness of losing her forever.

Pain at failing to keep her safe and keep her favorite horse alive and thriving.

"You did the right thing," Meg whispered, stroking his head. "Maybe she never rallied because she knew Brie was waiting for her, and she longed to be with her. They're together now at last, riding in heaven."

Digging into his jeans, he withdrew the angel pin Brie gave him long ago. Cooper palmed it. "Brie gave this to me before my first deployment. Said it would keep me safe. I've kept it since."

"You loved your sister very much." Meg closed her hand over his. "You don't need a token to remind you of her love, what she meant to you. She's walking beside you, always."

She touched his chest. "She is here with you, in your heart."

Cooper tucked away the little angel. Couldn't let it go, not now, not when he felt brittle, ready to shatter. Meg hugged him, her arms tight around him, her cheek soft against his.

Around another woman, he'd never get this close while feeling so sorrowful. But Meg was safe, like a warm fire on a bitter cold night, a cocoon of warm understanding.

Finally he lifted his head. No tears from him, but Meg's eyes were wet.

Smiling, she dug a blue bandanna out of her jacket. "I brought this. I always brought what Gran said was a 'crying towel' when one of my pets had to be put down. It didn't matter how long we'd had them, how sick they were. It hurt each time, like losing a friend."

He took the bandanna from her and gently mopped away her tears.

They walked outside and paused by the fence, watching the horses. Cooper shoved his hands into his jacket pockets.

"I feel like part of my purpose is gone now."

Adela trotted over and poked her nose over the railing.

Meg stroked the mare's neck. "Here's your purpose, Cooper. She needs you, much as your mom and Aimee do. She needs your devotion and your love. She's had so little of any kind of love."

Despite his intense grief, he managed a smile. "How did you get so smart, Princess?"

Meg looked troubled. "Because I know what it feels like to be loved and love in return, and then be so desperate for it that you'll almost do anything to get it back from someone, even if they are incapable of loving you back."

Cooper framed her heart-shaped face with his big, work-scarred hands. And then he kissed her. Couldn't help it, she looked so lost and sad, he wanted to kiss away all her sorrow, chase away his own grief and replace it with something pure and solid and pleasurable.

His blood surged hot and thick at the touch of her soft mouth, and how pliant it became beneath the hard pressure of his own. Cooper took her into his arms and deepened the kiss, needing more to ease the grief that had held him prisoner for a long time.

He hadn't ever felt this way about a woman, and every bone in his body said she was the kind of woman you kept in your life.

Hell, he wasn't sure what tomorrow would bring, but for now, he wanted her badly. And judging from the way she kissed him back, she wanted him equally.

When he finally broke the kiss, he stroked a thumb down her cheek. "Thanks," he said, his voice husky.

She smiled.

Arm in arm, they went back to the cottage. Meg said

nothing, but led him into the bedroom. He felt the need clawing at him, the desire to take all the sorrow and push it aside for a little while.

And he wasn't certain if she was ready for the kind of passion he intended to show her.

Meg knew what he wanted.

Wildness flashed in his eyes. No tenderness. She didn't want any, either.

This was about forging new bonds of the flesh and forgetting. Not slow, gentle lovemaking.

Buttons snapped off with explosive violence as he tore off his shirt. Breathing heavily, she stared, then her eager hands fumbled with her own clothing. Cooper cupped the back of her head, tunneling his fingers through her thick hair. His mouth devoured hers, tongue dipping past her seeking lips, to claim. The passionate kiss hinted of ownership and desperate need, and she responded with need of her own.

Cooper's hand dropped to his jeans; she heard the rasp of a zipper. Meg wriggled out of her jeans and tore off her panties, arching against him as he lifted her against the bedroom wall.

Nudging her legs open, he stood between them and cupped her naked bottom, breathing deeply and staring into her eyes.

Meg bit back a moan as he positioned himself strategically. He took her with one upward thrust. The hot, hard length of him pushed inside her, nearly to her womb. Meg cried out and arched upward. He rained tiny kisses over her face, her eyelids, her mouth. This was what she'd missed in her life: real undiluted passion, two bodies melding as one, merging together, chasing away the loneliness inside her. Here was where she belonged.

Her arms slid around his neck as she drew him closer, seeking his mouth. He kissed her and began moving again, his naked flesh slapping against hers. Never had she felt anything this primitive, the warm smoothness of his member sliding in and out of her, her leaden limbs trembling as she wrapped them around his moving hips.

Shifting, he angled his thrusts, sliding against the most sensitive part of her. Meg's fingers dug into his shoulders.

Feeling her climax approach, she bent her head and bit him on the shoulder, teeth sinking into the hard muscles past his shirt. Cooper pushed into her so hard she gasped. She flew apart, convulsing around him. Cooper looked at her, veins bulging in his neck, his nostrils flared as ragged breaths filled the air. He groaned as his body convulsed and he pumped deep within her.

Trembling, their breathing ragged, they remained motionless a minute. Then he let her down. She slid down the wall in a boneless, shaking heap. With a hungry look she watched him smooth back his disheveled hair.

And then he glanced down with a look of dismay. "Oh, hell," he said mildly. "I forgot the condom." Darkness flared in his eyes as he swept her with a possessive look.

Faint disappointment filled her. "It's okay. We're safe."

She picked up her jeans with a shaky hand. "I couldn't see bringing a defenseless baby into the world, not when Prescott didn't care about anyone else except himself. He didn't care about making me happy or ask me what I wanted, so I made sure I couldn't get pregnant...at least while I was with him."

Wanting only to forget that bitter memory, she turned. Cooper turned her back to him. He placed a gentle hand on her chin, forcing her to look up at him.

"That's the past, Meg. I care about you. I want to know what makes you happy."

Cupping her face, he kissed her, his mouth sweet and subtle as his lips slid over hers. The jeans dropped to the floor as she kissed him back, wanting to believe him.

Wanting to know that for the first time in her life, someone else truly did care about what she wanted, not what she could give them.

## *Chapter 17*

The next day was a Saturday, and with Aimee off from school, Cooper suggested a picnic to a local waterfall he and Aimee loved. Meg readily agreed.

Cooper had started to incorporate her into his family life, a life she always longed to have. She finally felt as if she belonged to someone and had found a niche in the world.

All these years of ignoring her own needs in favor of what someone else wanted had evaporated beneath the power of his kisses. Cooper had showered her with devout attention. A blush heated her cheeks as she remembered exactly how much attention he'd paid, especially to certain erogenous zones.

Humming, she went into the kitchen and began making chicken salad for the picnic. Chocolate chip cookies sounded perfect as well, a sweet snack as a reward for a long hike.

Meg carefully mixed the ingredients, making sure to not even touch the jar containing snack nuts Fiona had set aside for guests. Aimee was highly allergic to peanuts. Cooper had nicknamed his kid sister Peanut so no one in the family would ever forget it.

Jenny stopped by for a minute and shyly offered to help.

She sent the housekeeper into the pantry to get the oil needed for the batter, instructing her to make certain it was corn oil. Meg wondered about the housekeeper. With her timid manner and look of a frightened rabbit, she couldn't see Jenny as the one who had torn up her sweater. Or done anything else malicious.

The woman's gaze fell upon the healing bruises on Meg's arm. "Can I ask you something?"

Meg studied the recipe. "Sure."

"Did someone…hurt you?"

Startled, she glanced up into the woman's solemn face. "Why do you ask?"

Jenny turned red.

"Hello there!"

One of the guests, Cathy Murphy, poked her head into the kitchen. Jenny glanced at the woman, mumbled about finishing cleaning the upstairs and left.

Cathy glanced at the housekeeper as she walked away. "Sorry to disturb, but I'm looking for Mrs. Johnson. I need to speak with her about us staying one more night."

The woman's twitched. "What are you baking?"

"Chocolate chip cookies for a picnic with Cooper and Aimee." Meg dried her hands on a towel. "I believe Fiona is in her office. Want me to get her?"

"Would you mind terribly?"

She found Fiona, left her with Cathy and returned to baking. Meg finished making the batter and then checked the oven. As she greased the cookie sheet, frantic barking sounded outside.

She looked at the window. The cookie sheet dropped to the counter with a loud clatter.

Racing out the kitchen door, she ran toward the pasture, where Sophie raced alongside the fence, barking at her friend Adela. Aimee was nowhere in sight.

"Sophie!" She clapped her hands three times. "Come!"

The happy dog dashed over and Meg scooped her up. She didn't set her down until they were inside the inn.

Aimee came bounding down the steps. "There you are!"

As Sophie rushed over to Aimee, Meg gave the girl a pointed look. "Aimee, I warned you to never let Sophie outside without a leash."

"I didn't. I thought maybe you or Mom had her. I was on the phone in my room, talking to a boy." Cheeks pink, she picked up the dog. "I'm sorry. I'll keep her in my room."

Meg returned to the kitchen to finish baking.

Shortly before noon she joined Cooper in the truck as Aimee rode in the backseat with their backpacks and the food and blanket Meg had stuffed into hers. They'd invited Fiona, who declined, saying she had the accounts to reconcile.

Freedom Falls wasn't a long drive away, and the hike was "moderate," but Cooper promised the view was worth it. When they arrived at the trailhead, there were no other cars in the parking lot. She dragged in a lungful of clear, crisp autumn air.

Shouldering her pack, Meg followed Cooper and Aimee up the moderately steep trail.

"Slow down, Peanut," Cooper called out. "Trail's slippery."

"Come on, old man," Aimee called back.

"Old man?" he sputtered.

Meg laughed, her legs aching but her heart full. In excellent physical shape, Cooper could easily outrun his sister up the steep trail, but she sensed he slowed down because of her. After months of living in Florida, the altitude made the ascent a bit of a struggle. Leg muscles burned as she climbed up the pathway, skirting rocks and tree roots. It felt wonderful and freeing to be outside with the man she had fallen in love with.

The thought startled her. Did she love Cooper Johnson? Meg stared at the strong curve of his calves as Cooper climbed ahead of her. Unlike her, he wore shorts and a long-sleeved shirt, tying a light jacket around his waist. The man was a furnace.

She'd felt his warmth last night. Meg flushed, remembering exactly how much heat they'd created in his bed.

Cooper was loyal and devoted, and in his arms she felt alive and invigorated and well-loved. She could finally set aside her troubled past and look forward to life because of him. The dark shadow of her past had begun to fade.

All these long months, Meg had steeled herself to be alone. Her family had been overbearing and controlling, and it was better to rely on herself.

And now she finally found someone who broke that resolve.

Smiling, she poked him in his very fine buttocks. "Come on, move it, old man!"

He turned, giving her a mock growl. "You'll pay for that later."

"Promise?" she asked sweetly, and laughed.

Through the thick trees, she spotted glimpses of the mountains and isolated pockets of brilliant fall color. When they reached the falls, Meg stood breathless with wonder.

The waterfall plunged down several hundred feet, spraying the chilly air with lacy mist. Puffs of white clouds brushed the jagged, majestic peaks of the Presidential Range. Sunlight dappled the thick oak and hickory trees as shadows danced along the ledge.

Aimee climbed down to investigate the water.

"Watch the rocks," he warned, a frown denting his forehead.

"She'll be fine," Meg assured him.

"If she falls, she could hurt herself."

"But she won't fall. Let her have fun, Cooper. Your sister has been on this trail dozens of times. You can't hover over her every minute."

He glanced at her, wiped his sweating forehead with the back of one hand. "Yeah, I know. Sometimes I wish I could wrap her in cotton wool, lock her away so nothing bad would ever happen to her. Like what happened to…"

He dragged in a deep breath. "Come here."

She went into his arms, offering what comfort she could, resting her head against his broad shoulder.

"Feels so good to hold you," he said in a husky voice. "You make me forget all the bad stuff in the world."

As Aimee climbed up the rocks from the waterfall, he released her. Cooper removed the sandwiches and cookies from his pack and Meg spread out the blanket on a flat ledge.

Meg sat on a boulder, dangling her feet over the edge, happily munching on a granola bar.

This was peace. This was the life she'd wanted, no one expecting her to play a role as a wife, hostess, perfect daughter.

This was perfection. She stole a sideways glance as Cooper plunked down beside her.

"Courting danger, Ms. Taylor. That's a long drop."

Meg peered down. "Not too bad. There are bushes that would break my fall."

Cooper took the remaining granola bar from her hand, the warmth from his calloused fingers sending sizzling heat shooting through her. Oh, how she remembered the stroke and caress of those fingers against her skin…

He tossed down the bar. It broke into several pieces on the rocks below, before tumbling into the bushes.

At his arch look, she lifted her shoulders. "I'm not a granola bar. I won't break apart."

A lick of fire teased her loins as he brushed a kiss against her neck, his tongue lazily caressing her skin. "You broke apart very nicely last night," he murmured.

He uncapped his water bottle and drank deeply, muscles in his throat working. Fascinated, she watched. Sunlight picked out coppery highlights in his dark brown hair. From the angles and planes of his hard jawline to the bridge of his nose, Cooper Johnson was perfection as well.

He set down the bottle, winked. "Why, Ms. Taylor, I do believe you are staring at me."

Seeing Aimee feeding a squirrel a short distance away, she whispered, "I'd do more than stare if we were alone."

Cooper grinned. "This rock would make an excellent place to get horizontal. I'll have to wait until we're alone and then watch out."

His voice became a deep, rumbling timbre. "I can't wait to get the taste of you under my tongue."

A tingle raced down her spine, filling her loins with delicious anticipation. Last night he'd made her scream and writhe and claw, bringing out feelings she'd thought were long dead. It wasn't only the sheer erotic pleasure. It was a sense of bonding, connection that she'd lost hope of ever attaining. Others had seen her as a pampered doll, or a pretty shell to serve their needs. Cooper served her needs, and last night paid exquisite attention to each one.

They polished off the sandwiches and Cooper opened the plastic bin containing the cookies. He sniffed, a look of anticipation on his face. "Smells great."

"Ladies first." Aimee snatched up a cookie and bit into it. She frowned.

"This tastes weird." Aimee set down the cookie.

Meg studied the bin. "I used fresh chocolate chips. I thought chocolate chip was your favorite."

Cooper bit into the cookie his sister abandoned. His expression turned from curious to horrified.

"There are peanuts in these cookies, Meg. I told you Aimee's highly allergic to peanuts."

Alarm shot through her. "I didn't use any peanuts."

They turned to Aimee, whose lips were beginning to swell.

"Cooper, I don't feel good," Aimee whispered. "My throat feels tight."

As he raced to his backpack and fumbled in it, Meg coaxed Aimee to calm down. The girl's face paled even more and suddenly she climbed onto her knees and doubled over, vomiting. Meg held back her hair, trying not to panic as Cooper rushed back with a preloaded cylinder filled with epinephrine. He stabbed the needle into her thigh.

The girl stopped vomiting but kept gasping for breath. Cooper hunted through his backpack and cursed.

"She's going into anaphylaxis," he snapped. "I have to get her to the hospital. Can't find the second shot of epinephrine."

Cooper pushed her roughly aside and swept his sister into his arms.

Meg's heart raced. She scrambled over to get the packs.

"Screw it," he barked as he started down the trail with her.

She hooked his backpack and her own over both arms and raced with him down the pathway. "Call 911," she screamed at him.

"No time," he yelled back. "I have to get her to the ER."

Loose rocks skidded out from beneath his hiking boots as Cooper raced down the trail like a mountain goat, Aimee in his arms. Meg picked her way down, skidding once and banging her knee on a rock. Wincing, she ignored the pain and followed Cooper.

Finally they reached the parking lot and the truck.

Meg hunted through her backpack as Cooper bundled Aimee into the backseat of the truck. "Stay with her," he snapped.

He tore out of the parking lot, heading down the mountain.

Aimee still wheezed, her face growing paler by the minute. She'd known Aimee was allergic, and just in case something happened, she didn't want anything happening to Cooper's only surviving sister... There!

Her fingers closed around the cylinder. Meg uncapped the pen and injected Aimee. *Please, please, be okay.* "Breathe, honey," she whispered, stroking Aimee's forehead. "Just breathe."

A few minutes later, her breathing became more normal. Cooper thumbed his phone. "Sam, it's Coop. I need a police escort to Mount Darby ER. Aimee's going into anaphylaxis. She ate peanuts that were in a cookie."

Guilt rushed through Meg. She removed her jacket and placed it around the cold, shivering girl. "I'm so sorry, honey. I didn't put peanuts into the batter. I didn't."

Soon, a police car pulled ahead of them, blue lights flashing and siren blaring. Cooper accelerated, following it.

When they finally reached the ER, Cooper shot out of the truck as medical staff rushed outside with a stretcher and a portable oxygen bottle. Meg opened the door as the orderlies loaded Aimee onto the stretcher.

He ran with them into the emergency room. Miserable, Meg climbed into the driver's seat and parked the truck.

Then she hovered in the waiting room, her fingers curled tight in her lap.

A clerk came over to inquire about Aimee's insurance

information and birth date. Meg didn't know. She wasn't permitted in the room with Aimee, either. Feeling helpless and beyond upset, she methodically went over every single ingredient she'd put into the cookies. Could someone have put peanuts into the batter while she was outside? But she'd been gone only a few minutes. And who would know about Aimee's peanut allergy?

Richard Kimball had known. He knew it from the night at the bonfire, when Aimee had refused the peanut butter s'mores the English couple made.

It sounded too fantastic to be true. Kimball had already checked out of the inn. And why would he wish to harm a little girl?

Derek and Fiona, followed by Nick, rushed into the emergency room. Meg went to the desk as Derek inquired about Aimee and hugged Fiona.

"They'll only allow family," Meg told him. "Cooper is with her now."

The nurse behind the desk peered over the top of her spectacles at Cooper's older brother. "Are you all family?"

"I'm her mother," Fiona burst out. "Please, I must see my daughter.

"And I'm her brother." Derek jerked a thumb at Cooper's best friend. "Nick's family, too."

He ignored Meg. Cooper's older brother herded his mother past the security guard as Nick followed. The trio accessed the forbidding doors blocking her from entering the room where doctors treated Aimee.

Nick was family.

She was not.

Meg tried to ignore the little knot of hurt tightening her stomach. Aimee came first, and Nick had been a close family friend for years.

But the part of her that had started to trust again shattered as cleanly as the granola bar Cooper had tossed on the rocks.

She could have killed his sweet baby sister. Just as her corporation had killed Brie.

Flooded with misgiving, Cooper paced Aimee's box-like hospital room. Meg insisted she had blended everything carefully and didn't even touch the jar of peanuts on the counter. Then how the hell had the peanuts gotten into the cookies?

He'd warned her about the allergies. The entire house-keeping staff had it drilled into them to never give Aimee the food that could kill her. And here they were, his worst fears flashing along with the monitor beeping next to Aimee's bed. If he hadn't jabbed her with the epinephrine, and if he hadn't gotten her to the hospital in time…

*Don't go there.*

But the thought played over and over in his mind. Aimee could have died. Meg would have played a role in the deaths of both his sisters.

Maybe it was an accident.

*Or maybe she wants to hurt your family. You can't trust her,* a nagging voice whispered inside him.

His mother, sitting by the sleeping Aimee and stroking her hand, glanced up. "Stop pacing. You're making me nervous."

Standing by the window, Derek turned. "Is that doctor ever going to get here?"

Nick entered the room, the doctor on his heels. "Found him."

The physician checked over Aimee as Cooper drew his friend aside. "Good job, Nomad."

Holding up a slim cell phone, the other man shrugged. "Cakewalk. All I had to do was take this away from him."

Finished with his exam, the doctor turned to them. "She's going to be fine."

Cooper finally released the breath he'd been holding.

"She's a smart little girl, enough to recognize the peanut taste. Good thing she received the second injection," he said. "It helped stabilize her until you arrived. We'll keep her overnight, just to be certain."

Fiona closed her eyes. "Thank God you had the foresight to pack all the pens."

Cooper raked a hand through his mussed hair. "It wasn't me. Meg had an extra in her pack."

Guilt raced through him. Hell, he'd always been prepared when hiking with Aimee. But this time he'd forgotten and packed only one pen.

Meg might have accidentally put peanuts in the cookies, but he was the one who'd failed his baby sis.

The doctor went to Nick, who handed him back the cell phone. Glaring at the other SEAL, the physician left the room.

"Where is Meg?" Fiona asked.

Cooper started. "Aw hell, I left her in the waiting room. I thought she'd come in with all of you."

"They said only family. And this is all her fault." Derek went to Aimee's other side, stroked her forehead. "Coop, stop thinking about her. Your first duty is to family, not that woman."

"Derek," Fiona warned.

"She was the one who made the cookies, but give the lady a break, Derek, until you have the facts," Nick broke in. "Why would she want to hurt Aimee?"

"I'm not saying it's deliberate, but she's not one of us. She's a stranger," Derek argued.

Ignoring them, Cooper headed for the waiting room. Meg sat on a chair by the window, looking small and lost. One leg of her jeans had been cut off and a large white bandage wrapped around her knee.

Cooper sat next to her. He didn't even know she'd been hurt. "What happened?"

"It's nothing." Meg's fingers curled around the edges of her pack. "Just a scrape when I banged my knee going down the mountain. How's Aimee?"

"She's going to be fine."

"Good."

Awkward silence descended between them. Cooper sensed she wanted to see her, but with Derek's hostility, that wasn't a good idea.

"I'll take you home now," he finally said.

She shook her head and dug a set of keys out of her jeans pocket, handing them to him. "I parked your truck. I was going to call for a taxi. I only waited to see how she was, to make sure she was going to be okay."

Her voice cracked. Meg stood, holding on to the pack like a life preserver. "Tell Aimee I'm sorry."

Coop caught her arm with one hand, herding her out of the waiting room to his truck.

Then, while Meg was climbing into his truck, he called Nick.

"I'm driving Meg back to the inn and then returning to spend the night in the hospital," he told Nick. "Need you to stay at the cottage, keep an eye on Meg."

"Sure thing, Coop." A pause. "Keep an eye on her because you don't trust her?"

"Just watch her," he snapped.

In the truck, Meg stared out the window as he pulled out.

Had to know. "Meg, you're absolutely certain you didn't put peanuts in the cookie batter?"

"I told you. I made the batter fresh and didn't use any nuts."

"Is there a chance you could have used something that had peanuts in it? Peanut oil instead of corn oil?"

A heavy sigh eased from her. "I was so careful soon as I found out about Aimee's allergy. I know how to read labels, Cooper. Why can't you believe me that I didn't do it?"

"My baby sis is lying in a hospital bed right now. I could have lost her."

Meg gripped her pack tighter. "I know."

"If not for you. You gave her the second injection, and the doctor said that helped to stabilize her. Thanks."

A jerky nod and she turned away from him, shutting him out. Cooper concentrated on his driving. Torn in two, he tried not to think of Aimee's graying face and how little she appeared in that big hospital bed.

Or how lost and abandoned Meg looked in the waiting room. But Meg was an adult. And Aimee was his only remaining sister.

Maybe Derek was right. Duty to family did come first. He'd already lost one sister, and wasn't about to lose another. Family mattered more than anything else.

Why then, when he thought of Meg leaving, did this tightness in his chest refuse to go away?

# Chapter 18

She didn't sleep in Cooper's bed that night. Instead, she went to the inn, collected Sophie and returned to the cottage. Meg ate a dinner of canned ravioli and was cleaning up when Nick came to spend the night in the cottage.

He'd told her Cooper wanted to remain with Aimee and Fiona in the hospital.

"Coop asked me to keep an eye on you." Nick had looked away, the scar on his face turning white. "He doesn't want you to be alone."

She went to the guest room and changed into her night wear. Then Meg lay on the bed, unchecked tears rolling down her cheeks.

Aimee would be okay, but the episode had terrified her as much as it terrified Cooper. She had grown to love the little girl as if she were her own sister. And the thought that she'd done something to cause this…

Sophie curled up next to her on the bed, licking her cheeks. Meg smiled through her misery.

"You're such a good girl, Sophie. My only real friend I can trust."

She fell asleep, the dog curled up at her feet.

Leaden dawn light peeked past the drawn shades as

Meg stirred the next morning. She'd spent a restless night, tossing and turning. Stretching, she thought of Cooper and Aimee.

How could everything have fallen apart so quickly? She and Cooper had grown so close, and then with Aimee's allergy attack, all that had fallen apart.

She quickly showered and changed into a green cowl-neck sweater and jeans. After studying the sturdy work boots she'd worn for most of her stay, she chose the comfortable sneakers she'd worn hiking yesterday.

Meg went upstairs, but Cooper's room was empty. In the kitchen in Cooper's big, bold handwriting, he'd left a note that he was at the inn, and he'd see her at breakfast.

The terseness of the note echoed the hollow ache inside her. She left the cottage, headed for the inn.

Not wanting to wake anyone after the trauma of yesterday, she quietly opened the front door, using the key Fiona had given her. Hearing voices, Meg headed for the kitchen. And then she stopped short.

"Who's more important to you, Coop? Aimee or this Meg?"

Derek.

Flushing, she started to turn around, but Nick chimed in.

"Meg is on the run from a man who's aligned with a known Irish mobster. Can you trust her? She may have accidentally put the peanut oil in the cookies, but you're getting involved with someone whose ex could hurt your family."

"Or perhaps she changed her mind about the divorce," Derek told him.

Immobilized, she remained in the dining room, her heart in her throat. The two men had aligned against her.

"I bet she's worried you and Mom will launch a lawsuit against her company. That could be the real reason she's here," Derek warned.

Sweat trickled down her back. No...

"You just don't know, Coop, but I know you. Family and team come first," Nick added.

"Your Palm Beach princess is in pretty damn deep, Coop. Best you consult with a lawyer to find a way to cover your ass before all this blows sky high," Derek chimed in.

"You could be right," Cooper agreed.

After all this time, she'd come to trust Cooper. Lean on him. She'd let him into her life and her body, bonded with him as they made love.

And yet he still didn't trust her. He thought she'd poisoned his beloved little sister.

There was only one person she could rely on now—herself.

How many times had she experienced this before? Her ex cutting her off from business, never revealing plans for the company. Her parents and grandfather, trying to control her life, leaving her on the sidelines.

Even patrician and elegant Letticia, too engrossed in the family business, thinking Meg's duties belonged with civic affairs, society galas and eventually, with producing the next generation of Taylor children.

This time, she couldn't pretend everything was all right. It hurt way too much. The man she'd confided in, believed in and made love with was loyal to family. Not her.

She'd thought she'd finally met a man who would put her needs above all else. Cooper, the man she'd come to trust with her body and her heart. The man who'd promised to shield her from all harm.

Meg made a show of stomping her feet and then went to the kitchen doorway. As soon as Derek saw her, he nudged Nick and they both fell silent. Roasted coffee beans percolated in the pot on the counter. She inhaled the smells of home and family. They seeped into her bloodstream like a drug.

A drug she did not need.

"Meg. You're up early. I thought you'd still be sleeping." Cooper didn't smile at her. His expression remained stony.

*I got lonely in bed without you.* "Farm life makes me an early riser. What are you all talking about?"

Derek stood and drained his coffee. "Family business. Coop, I'll be ready and down in ten."

His brother nodded at Meg and left.

She joined them at the table. "How is Aimee?"

Cooper's guarded expression relaxed a little. He stood and fetched a mug for her and filled it with coffee, adding the amount of sugar she liked.

"Good. Mom says she'll probably be released this morning. I got back a while ago. Spent the night with her and Mom at the hospital."

Nick glanced at her, his expression neutral. "I'll move Aimee's things downstairs, Coop. See you in a few."

When the other SEAL left, she went to the pantry and hunted through the shelves, and then found a bottle of oil.

Meg plunked it on the counter. "This is what I used for the cookies."

The label was faded, but readable. Corn oil.

Cooper uncapped it and took a whiff. Then he tasted it. "It's regular oil. No nuts."

For some reason, she was loath to mention Jenny's name. She didn't know why, but there was something about Jenny. Maybe it was her shyness, but Meg didn't want anyone pointing fingers at her.

Jenny hadn't put peanut oil into the cookies any more than Meg had.

His blue gaze was steady as he set the bottle down. "I

believe you. I don't know how the peanuts got into the cookies. I believe you didn't do it deliberately."

Maybe that should have pacified her, but instead she felt even worse because she had made the cookies, just as her company had made the vests that caused the death of his other sister.

Aimee could have died, just as Brie had.

"I need fresh air," she told him, and headed outside.

She'd longed for love, thought she wasn't worthy of such devotion. And then Cooper with his charming smile and fierce loyalty and protective manner had come into her life. He'd stolen her heart and treated it with exquisite tenderness.

But that was before Aimee's attack. Even if Cooper didn't think she did it, others did. Hadn't she already caused enough grief for this family?

Heart heavy, she went outside to sit on a rocking chair on the porch. The air was chilly and echoed of silence. No loud laughter from Cooper, larger-than-life Cooper. No Fiona with her warm, friendly air or Aimee with her giggles.

For a long while she sat in the rocker, struggling with her emotions. And then the front door opened.

Cooper stepped out onto the porch. "Meg." He pulled up the collar of his jacket and tugged down the brim of his Stetson. "It's cold out here. Go back to bed. It's still early."

Sleep, when sleep proved elusive? When he wouldn't be there with her to keep her warm through the night?

"Are you headed back to the hospital now?" she asked.

"We both are." He glanced at the door as Derek came outside. Cooper's brother looked at her and then tugged on his gloves. "I'll meet you at the truck, Coop."

Meg kept rocking, the creak of the wood soothing. "Can I come with you to see Aimee?"

"No. We're stopping there and then I'm driving Derek

back to Boston. I have a meeting there. I'll be back by sun-down. Don't leave the farm." His voice thickened. "I don't know what's going on, but I don't want anything else to happen."

"Are you going to see a lawyer?"

Surprise flared on his face. His gaze flickered away. "Yes. It's for the best to be prepared."

He dropped a quick kiss on her cheek, but she barely felt it for the aching pain in her heart.

As he turned toward the truck, she fled. He had already left, from the moment she'd overheard him talking in the kitchen.

Putting his needs, and those of his family, before her own.

Refusing to surrender to the tears that threatened, Meg went to the cottage and made her own coffee. She spent the next few hours reading over all the correspondence she'd managed to take from Prescott's home office, but found no clues. Nothing to tie him to the missing memos or the authorization to sell the defective vests.

Around lunchtime, she heard the horn honk and rushed outside, heading for the inn. The staff was gathered outside, greeting Aimee as she climbed out of her mother's car. A little pale, she otherwise looked good.

She offered to carry Aimee's bag into the house, but Hank shouldered it instead. Feeling useless, Meg followed the crowd into the house. Nick had set up the downstairs bedroom for Aimee so she didn't have to climb the steps. Aimee collapsed into the wing chair by window.

"Aimee, get into bed, you need rest," her mother chided.

"I'm sick of being in bed." Aimee pouted. "Can't I go outside?"

"You're far too weak." Fiona shook her head. "Stay inside and rest, and in a couple of hours, we'll see how you feel."

The staff wished Aimee well and left. Meg fetched Sophie and deposited her on Aimee's bed. The girl brightened as the dog licked her face, wagging her tail.

Meg sat on the bed. "Aimee, I am so sorry about the cookies."

The girl buried her face into the dog's fur. "It's okay, Meg. It was an accident."

*An accident I didn't do.*

Then she and Fiona left, closing the bedroom door behind them.

Meg felt awkward, and guilty for the lines of strain on the older woman's face. "Fiona, I am dreadfully sorry. I don't know what happened, or how the peanuts got into the cookies. I take full responsibility, and I'd like to pay for the medical bills, once I get settled."

Fiona gave her a steady look and pushed her hand through her graying hair. "Don't blame yourself, Meg. It happens. And we're fine. Thank you, but you have your own needs to worry about. If you'll excuse me, I'm dead tired. I didn't sleep at all last night."

"Can I do anything?"

Fiona squeezed her arm. "We'll be fine."

*We'll be fine.* She was not part of that particular "we." Meg went to the cottage's home office and powered up her laptop at the desk. She spent a couple of hours searching through the company files, but found nothing. All the emails had been deleted.

The only solution now was to contact the FBI and tell them what she knew. Finding the memos seemed to be a lost cause. Randall said they were close to her heart, but that cryptic clue proved useless.

She'd leave Sophie here, although the thought killed her, but it was for the best.

Aimee loved the dog and would take excellent care of

Sophie. With a heavy heart, she clicked onto her personal email account and began surfing through the dozens of emails.

One caught her eye. It was from Bert Baxter, the attorney who had been absent the day she and Cooper went to Boston. He wanted to meet with her at her grandmother's farmhouse to go over something urgent—her grandmother's will.

Trying not to get her hopes up, she read the email. Bert claimed he had duplicates of the memos Prescott had written. Randall had given him the papers for safekeeping. He gave a phone number for her to call.

I can't risk meeting you at the office, Meg. Not after what happened to Randall. I'm sure that Prescott had something to do with his death. I'm in hiding from your ex and I need $50,000.

Meg sat back, ruminating over the idea. The farmhouse was old, run-down and lacked electricity. It made a perfect, isolated spot for a clandestine meeting. Prescott must really be in trouble to threaten the lawyer.

She called the lawyer. The phone went to voice mail.

Meg texted him. Talk to me, Bert! Where is Prescott now?

A message popped up on her screen. Not sure. Have memos.

A minute later, an image appeared on her cell phone. It showed the official company letterhead for Combat Gear Inc. and was a memo from Prescott to Randall with the subject line "Shipment of new body armor, ASAP."

The rest of the memo was missing.

You'll get the documents and flash drive when I get the

money. Please Meg, I'm desperate. Come alone. Can't risk anyone else seeing me, he typed.

She tried responding, but there was no reply.

Meeting him alone wasn't her first choice, as much as she trusted him.

Meg turned off the computer and went searching for Nick.

The fresh scent of hay and horses greeted her as she entered the barn. Cooper's best friend stood by a saddle, oiling the leather. Head bent, face hidden by the brown Stetson he wore, the man didn't even glance up.

"Meg."

Surprised, she stepped back. "How did you know it was me?"

"Light tread, smell of your perfume. And everyone else is at the inn." Nick raised his head. The scar on his cheek flared against his ruddy color. He'd be movie-star handsome but for that scar. "What's up?"

"I need to borrow your truck."

His guarded expression turned blank. "No."

"I have to run an errand."

Nick dropped the cloth he used to oil the saddle leather. "Then I'll take you."

"I can drive myself, but I don't have a car. Mine's dead, Nick."

"No."

"Then drive me to town where I can get a rental."

The man didn't budge. Didn't even blink. Rock steady. "No. Coop asked me to watch over everyone while he's gone. That includes you. When my best bud asks for a favor, I do it. Coop's family is my family. The only real family I've had since my old man kicked me out when I was sixteen. I'd do anything for him."

"You're as stubborn as he is," she snapped.

Nick pushed up the brim of his hat and studied her with his cool, dark gaze. "Yeah, I am. And if Coop wanted me to tie you up and lock you in that cottage to keep you from running off, I would. So stay put."

Meg turned on her heels and stormed out of the barn.

Nick was her keeper. Not to shield her, but to prevent her from going anywhere. Meg thought fast. She needed wheels, and her car was dead. Or so Cooper had told her.

A convenient way of trapping her here on the farm with him? Prevent her from leaving until he could hire a lawyer to protect himself?

It didn't matter. Cooper was out of the equation now. She had to meet Bert, and Nick already stated that his loyalty, and his purpose here, remained with Cooper's family.

Not her.

He wouldn't drive her to Gran's farm.

She walked to the pasture and gazed out at the horses peacefully cropping grass. A hollow ache filled her chest, knowing Betsy wasn't among them. The pasture seemed emptier today without her.

A door slammed. Aimee trudged down the steps of the inn and joined her at the fence, putting one booted heel on the lowest rung.

"I thought you were supposed to be in bed."

"Mom said I could come outside. I was going to watch Nick clean the tack. I'm so tired of being stuck in bed."

Meg felt another tug of guilt. Cooper already lost one sister. He could not lose another. That, more than anything, nudged her into action. She would leave today. Go to her grandmother's farm and meet Bert. No one else could help her clear up this mess.

*You're better off alone than relying on others.*

Aimee and her family deserved justice for Brie's death. Bert had information she needed to prove Prescott knew about the defects in the body armor. That information would lead to her ex's arrest. She had the cash he desperately needed.

Now all she needed was a distraction. And a vehicle.

As if on cue, Adela trotted over to the fence, pushed her nose over the railing. Aimee giggled as the horse playfully butted her.

"She likes you."

"Every day after school I visit with her and feed her carrots." Aimee stroked the mare's nose. "Cooper says she's almost ready to be ridden. He hitched her to the carriage the other day and she did fine. Wish we could do it again."

"Ask Hank to hitch Adela to the carriage."

"Mom won't let me go by myself. And Nick says he doesn't want me or Mom to leave the grounds." Aimee sighed and stroked Adela's nose.

Perfect opportunity. "So take Nick and your mom for a little carriage ride. Test Adela's wings, so to speak. And if you ask nicely, he'd probably let you hold the reins, see how Adela handles. Your mom will be right there if anything happens."

Aimee brightened. "And you can come, too, Meg."

"The carriage would be a little crowded with the four of us, honey," she told her. "And this should be a special time for you and your mom. For family."

"You're our family, Meg."

A lump clogged her throat at the simple declaration. *No, I'm not, and that much is clear.* "Go on, ask your mom."

Thirty minutes later, Nick, Aimee and Fiona headed in the white carriage down to the fields by the river, Adela's hooves clopping on the dirt road. Meg jingled the keys in her hand and headed for the sedan Fiona had told her yesterday to feel free to borrow at any time.

In one hand, she carried the Louis Vuitton dog carrier

filled with half the money Cooper had tucked away in the cottage for safekeeping. Meg stuffed the carrier into the trunk. She would get those memos, no matter what. Too many people had already been hurt.

No one was ever getting hurt because of her again. Ever.

## Chapter 19

At precisely 9:00 a.m. Cooper paid a visit once more to the law firm of Baxter and Baxter in Boston. The dragon receptionist and the overweight security guard would not turn him away again.

This time, he had his brother. Power of the badge, which Derek flashed at the receptionist when he demanded to speak with Bert Baxter's assistant.

She nearly swallowed her gum.

They were escorted into a private conference room. When Mrs. Sandors joined them, her gaze darted back and forth as if she expected demons to crawl out from the bookcases lining the walls.

As he and Derek sat, she went to the window and peered out. Was the woman expecting company? Perhaps company she didn't want?

"We need to talk with Mr. Baxter immediately," Derek told her.

"He's not here."

"Do you have any idea when Mr. Baxter will return to the office?" Cooper asked.

The assistant turned back, pacing the small room. "I

don't know if he's coming back. He hasn't shown up to the office in three days."

Cooper exchanged glances with his brother.

"Has anyone called the police?" Derek asked.

The woman nodded, looking very troubled. "His wife filed a missing persons report."

Derek leaned forward. "Sit down," he said in a voice that brooked no disobedience. "Do you have any idea where Mr. Baxter is?"

She finally sat down, tapping the table with the edge of one well-manicured nail. "No. And neither does the FBI."

Cooper sat up even straighter. "Why are they looking for him?"

The woman's gaze searched the room.

Derek's expression smoothed out. "Mrs. Sandors, I assure you if you cooperate, it will be easier for you."

She lowered her voice. "We're a small firm, and our specialty is estate law and tax planning. The agents said Mr. Baxter had been working with one of our wealthy clients to hide money in offshore shell corporations to avoid taxes. Specifically, the Cayman Islands. They came here with a subpoena for all Mr. Baxter's files."

He exchanged glances with Derek. Could Meg's ex have roped Baxter into something illegal, such as tax fraud or money laundering? In addition to making out a fake will for her grandmother, leaving him the sole trustee and heir?

Cooper patted the woman's trembling hand. He was a calm, reassuring presence, letting Derek play bad cop. "You did the right thing in cooperating with the authorities. What about Mrs. Baxter?"

The assistant shook her head. "She was out of town with the children and is supposed to return this morning."

"Which client files did the agents take?" Derek demanded.

The woman glanced around again, her mouth working like a fish's. "Miles O'Neary."

A chill rushed down Cooper's spine. The same Irish mobster connected to Meg's ex. He only gave her a reassuring smile. "Then you still have access to Letticia Taylor's updated trust agreement and her last will and testament."

No answer.

"I need a copy," Derek told her.

Mrs. Sandors rose. "I'll make you a copy."

But soon the assistant returned, looking more agitated than ever. "It's not there. I don't know where it could be."

"Perhaps the FBI took it?" Cooper suggested.

"No, I saw all the files they took and made notations of each one."

They thanked the woman and left. Cooper's unease grew. Bert Baxter was missing.

"Where do you think he is?" he asked Derek as they reached the truck.

Derek fished out his cell phone. "I have a bad feeling I know. Let me make a couple of calls."

As his brother did, Cooper paced by the truck. Good thing Meg was back at the inn with Nick. Because the more he learned about what her ex had been involved in, the more he was convinced she was in danger.

The sun was high in the clear blue sky as Meg headed north toward her grandmother's farm. She picked up her cell phone from the center console. Still no service.

Meg would feel better if Cooper were with her. But he was more interested in covering his own tracks.

Bert had represented the Taylor family for years. He was loyal. Randall had trusted him as well. Bert was her last resort.

She thumbed the cell again, trying to call Cooper to let him know her plans. No signal. *You're on your own now, kiddo.*

The jagged tips of the White Mountains and the vista of evergreen, hickory, maple and birch trees passed in a blur. Meg scarcely noticed the rolling hills for all the memories churning inside her.

Good memories, before her brother Caldwell died, before her mother and father did nothing but argue. Memories from when she was little, and they spent summers here, driven to the farm by her indulgent parents who wanted them to experience fresh air and clean living before they dashed off to Paris or Rome or London. The cows lowing in the dairy, the frantic chickens scratching the ground for hidden kernels of corn, and the happiness rushing through her as she sat on the rubber tire swing hanging on the thick oak tree by the farmhouse, and Caldwell pushed her so high.

So high she felt like flying, and laughed for the joy of it.

Staying at Cooper's farm had reminded her of those innocent, carefree days when she had been loved and cherished. Meg had fallen in love with the man sworn to protect her life. She'd felt part of his family, something solid and lasting. Woven into the fabric of their lives was a cord of unity nothing could break. She'd desperately wanted to belong to that fabric.

And she'd forgotten she was a stranger, an outsider who owned the company that caused the death of their beloved Sabrina.

Overhearing Cooper, Derek and Nick talking about her only served as a reminder that she wasn't one of them. A Palm Beach princess, a wealthy socialite who couldn't be trusted.

An hour later, she pulled onto the winding dirt road leading to the farm. Her blood raced with anticipation as the two-story weathered farmhouse came into view. The wraparound porch had sagging boards, and the barn was faded and needed repairs, but this was the only real home she'd ever known.

She pulled into the gravel driveway and parked before the house. A deep feeling of peace came over her. This was why she'd fought against selling the property. Prescott would never understand the roots she'd placed here, the importance of having a home that wasn't a glitzy mansion or a polished, opulent showpiece to impress others.

Walking up the rickety steps, she stood with her hand on the tarnished brass doorknob. Prescott cared only about money, not her heritage. He'd thought the one-hundred-year-old farmhouse was nothing more than rotting lumber.

This was the kind of place Cooper would love. Big and rambling, presenting all kinds of challenges to fix.

It would make a perfect retreat center for veterans wounded in the war. She thought of Caldwell, and the familiar knot of grief rose. Instead of the piercing ache, it was a dull toothache kind of throb.

Maybe she'd finally learned to let her brother go, let go of the past.

Meg unlocked the front door and the memories washed over her like a rush of warm air. Ghostly childish laughter echoed in the hallway as she stepped inside. Only this time, not like last year when she and Gran had sadly packed away all the rest of Caldwell's things, the laughter didn't haunt her.

It warmed her inside. This was why she'd refused to let the farm go. Here, her brother and his boisterous, impish nature lived forever.

The house smelled musty and stale. All the windows had been painted shut, except one. Meg went to the kitchen and unlocked the casement window to let in the cool, refreshing air.

She tried her cell phone again and laughed. Dead. Just like when Cooper had found her, she'd forgotten to charge the battery. No matter. Bert said he would be here by five o'clock.

Glancing at her wristwatch, she settled at the kitchen table to wait.


Perfect day for a carriage ride. Sharp blue skies overhead and a cool, crisp breeze. The company was good— Coop's sister and mother, and the horse was eager to trot.

He handled the reins with confidence. Knew horses, had grown up with them at the farm before the old man kicked him out. Since turning sixteen and surviving on the streets, Nick learned to trust his instincts.

Why were they screeching a warning now, as if something had gone totally wrong?

Sitting beside him on the driver's seat, Aimee chattered about horses. He listened with half an ear, pausing now and then to check on Fiona. In the carriage backseat, Coop's mom hung an elbow over the side, enjoying the ride.

Jenny the housekeeper was back at the inn along with Hank and two other hired hands who worked on the farm. They were airing out rooms, making the inn ready for guests again.

Still, he felt uneasy.

Meg was secure in the cottage. He'd checked on her before leaving. She'd been engrossed in her laptop. She didn't like looking at him. Couldn't blame her. Most women didn't, not with his ugly face. Nick knew the violence simmering inside him, knew most could sense it. He'd never hurt a woman, not an innocent one. And definitely not a woman his best friend wanted him to protect.

He handed the reins to Aimee, instructing her to keep them nice and tight. Aimee grinned like crazy. Nick patted her shoulder, glad to see her misery gone.

"I wish Cooper and Meg could see me now," Aimee chortled. "Next Cooper will let me ride Adela."

"Later," he cautioned. "Does Meg ride? You think she'll know how to saddle one of the geldings and join us?"

Maybe that's why he had this nagging feeling tickling his belly. What if Meg took one of the horses out? He didn't like her leaving the farm, though technically the fields by the river were still farmland.

"Oh, she's very good, but she's not going riding. She took Mom's car."

Nick felt like someone punched him hard. "What?"

"I saw her as we were heading down the hill."

"How the hell did she get the keys?"

Now he was shouting, but Aimee wasn't afraid of him. She only gave him a look that clearly said "duh" in kid-speak. "Mom told her she could have the car any time she needed. Keys always hang on a peg in the kitchen pantry."

Ten kinds of swear words in ten different languages rang through his head. He fished out his cell phone.

"What's Meg's phone number?"

Aimee didn't know. Fiona gave it to him. Nick dialed the number, but it kept ringing.

He grabbed the reins from Aimee.

"We have to get back."

"But Meg didn't do anything wrong!"

"No, I did, Peanut. Not your fault." He coaxed Adela to turn and flicked the reins hard. "Giddyap!"

They stopped before the cottage. The door was unlocked, but Meg wasn't there.

Nick tore through the house and found the office with a laptop on the antique desk. Maybe she left a clue on the laptop. He could hack into all kinds of systems, but this time it wasn't necessary. Next to the laptop was a folded note.

He snatched it up and scanned it. And then dug out his cell phone and called Coop.

His friend answered on the first ring. "Coop, Meg's gone. She left you a note that she went to meet Bert the lawyer at her grandmother's farmhouse. She printed the address on the note."

A string of curses followed. "That's impossible."

"She took Fiona's car."

"Whoever she's meeting isn't Bert Baxter, Nomad. Because I'm at Derek's precinct. This morning Bert Baxter's body turned up in the harbor when someone reported a floater. He's been positively ID'd."

Nick's blood turned to ice. "Damn it, I'm sorry I let her go, Coop. I didn't know. I called her cell phone, but it kept ringing."

"Probably no cell service. It's a mountainous area."

"Coop, let me go after her…"

"No. The farm is only forty minutes outside of the city and I'm already headed that way. I need you with Mom and Aimee. Don't let them out of your sight. I'm certain this Kimball guy is involved." Cooper lowered his voice. "Derek found out he's linked to Miles O'Neary. He worked for him. And O'Neary was a client of Baxter's. All three are connected."

After Cooper updated him, Nick glanced out the cottage window at Fiona and Aimee, standing by Adela and petting her. "Kimball is the same guy who stole the security cameras and was a guest at your inn?"

"Right. I need you to go through the inn and make sure it's secure. Search Kimball's room one more time, Nomad. No booby traps. My family comes first."

Thumbing off the phone, Nick hurried out of the cottage.

Coop had instructed him to stay with his mom and Aimee, and he would. Nick only hoped Coop could get to the farmhouse before Meg did.

Because as his instinct aptly warned, Meg was walking straight into a trap.

Always he'd been there for his best bud. Thick and thin. He'd do anything for Coop. Including ignoring his direct orders.

His guts kicked, and he knew this was the right thing to do. Nick went outside, his hand atop one lean hip where his SIG Sauer rested.

Time to call in the cavalry.

Even if the commanding general didn't want the cavalry to respond.

Bert was twenty minutes late. For a man who claimed to be desperate, he certainly didn't care about being punctual.

Restless, Meg glanced at her watch again. Might as well do something instead of pacing the kitchen. Mentally, she inventoried the house. The missing will might be here, so why not the missing microchip? Randall had been here before with Gran, had helped her move a few things when the auction house came to collect the antiques to sell them.

With all its nooks and crannies, the house was full of hiding places. In the smallest bedroom upstairs, the closet had a hidden doorway that led to a secret passage.

Almost all the house had been cleared out, but for the master bedroom and a few pieces of furniture in the living room and kitchen. The closet still contained some of Caldwell's favorite playthings. The baseball mitt he had used to play catch with their grandfather. And the things Meg had loved to play with as a child…

Like her grandmother's heart-shaped jewelry box.

Her breath caught. Could the microchip be in the box? Randall had said the chip was "close to your heart."

Filled with hope, Meg raced up the stairs.

An overpowering sickly sweet scent assaulted her senses as she opened the master bedroom door. Odd. Maybe an animal had climbed in through the chimney and died.

She found the jewelry box in her grandmother's top bureau drawer. But it contained only rhinestone costume jewelry Gran had let Meg use.

Meg opened the closet and the smell got stronger. She reached on tiptoe, but couldn't get the baseball mitt from the top shelf. Switching on the overhead light, she pushed back the hangers holding clothing Gran had meant to donate. The stepladder was back there against the wall. She shoved all the hangers to the side and winced at the stench... It was much worse back here...

The dead face of her ex-husband stared back at her.

Screaming, Meg pinwheeled her arms and fell back, landing hard on her bottom. Panic clogged her veins and made her heart stutter. She gasped for breath, struggling to control herself.

Meg closed her eyes. Opened them.

Prescott was still here, sitting on the closet floor, a bullet hole piercing his forehead.

The killer might still be around. For all she knew it was Bert, and she was in a load of trouble. Meg raced down the stairs, heading for the kitchen to grab a knife.

Barely had she grabbed the old butcher knife when the front door slammed. Her heart thrummed like a war drum. She tucked the knife into her back jeans pocket and remembered what Cooper told her about catching an enemy off guard. Then she pulled out her sweater from her jeans and hid the knife handle by leaving the sweater untucked.

"Meg, sweetie? Are you here? I got worried about you and they sent me to look when you went racing off."

The dulcet tones of Paula Jones, the widow, filled her with relief and confusion. Why would Paula come after her and not Nick?

"Where's Nick?"

The woman came into the kitchen, her expression worried. She carried a big black satchel and peered at Meg with myopic, round blue eyes as big as robin's eggs. "Nick? Who's Nick? Are you all right, dear?"

"Paula, how did you find me? Why are you here?"

Instead of answering, the woman removed her spectacles and tugged off the wig. She plucked out something from her eyes. Contacts, Meg realized with frozen horror.

Wrinkles vanished beneath a swipe of a handkerchief Paula removed from her purse. The widow in her late sixties had turned into a plain-faced brunette who looked to be around thirty.

"I'm Claire. Claire O'Neary." The woman's smile widened as she withdrew a gleaming pistol from her purse and pointed it straight at Meg. "Your husband's lover. Why am I here? Because I'm going to kill you, you little bitch."

# Chapter 20

*Calm. Focus. Don't fall apart, even if everything inside you feels like it's collapsing.*

Meg pulled on every single ounce of poise grilled into her from the time she was old enough to hold a teacup. *Never let them see your emotions,* Gran warned time and again. *Crying is for weak people. Calm and control.*

"You're his mistress. I did recognize that dimple on your left cheek." Meg spoke in the same haughty voice she used to dismiss her ex-husband when he threatened her. "Very clever disguise.

Had to distract her long enough to dodge the gun and get the hell out of there. Sweat dampened her palms, but she didn't dare reach for the blade. Not yet.

"You're a fool, Margaret." Claire waved the gleaming gun back and forth, her eyes wild, her grip on the pistol tight.

Meg blinked, trying to regain a cool grip on an unraveling composure. All this time, Prescott's mistress had been a guest at the inn, watching her. "You're the one who tore up my sweater and left that card."

And then anger flared as she realized the greater crime.

"You put peanut oil in the batter so Aimee would have an allergy attack!"

"It was simple. All I had to do was ask my father's associates, Cathy and Joe Murphy, to spy on you for a week and promise them enough money to make it worth their while. We tracked your every move. Between the Murphys and Richard Kimball, I thought you would finally lead us to the microchip. But you wouldn't leave the farm. You fool! I would have let you live if I'd found it. We had to find a way to get Johnson away from you, kick you out of his home."

Meg felt dizzy with shock. She struggled to keep her balance, focused on the wicked gleam of the gun Prescott's mistress held. A revolver. Six shots. Cooper had taught her that much.

"I don't know where the microchip is!"

"Yes, you do!" Claire screamed. "Randall confessed he left it with you. He told Richard where the hard copies of the memos were, but not the chip!"

Try to buy time. Throw her off guard. "You're lying, just as you set up Randall with evidence he killed my grandmother. They were good friends."

"Friends?" The woman laughed. "Randall agreed to poison Letticia in exchange for cash. We needed her to resign from the board of directors because of sickness so she'd stop this insane idea of taking the company public. But she still held on, stupid bitch. And then Randall got scared he'd be blamed for the old lady's death and changed his mind. He had to go."

Claire held up the gun and said, "Bang!"

A tremor seized her palm. Meg forced herself to remain calm. Had to keep Claire distracted and talking.

"You're very smart, Claire. Was it your idea to do all those things to me?"

In the distance, she heard a truck rumble down the dirt

road. Meg prayed the truck would turn into the farmhouse driveway. But the sound cut off as if the truck stopped.

The woman laughed. "It was my idea to play the merry widow and do all those things to keep you unbalanced, so you'd leave and lead us to the microchip with the memos. Prescott thought it would be great fun to unnerve you that day when you went riding. All he had to do was get the kayak to the right location in the river because everyone knew you went riding at the same time each day. I texted the hired hand to create a distraction. Prescott figured if you saw him, you'd bolt."

Claire's expression turned furious. "We couldn't get that damn bodyguard of yours away from you. He was always nearby. But we knew where you were at all times."

Almost there. Meg resisted touching the knife in her back pocket. "How did you know?"

"Prescott placed a tracking device on all your fancy designer shoes. And then you ended up at that farm, he worried you'd give us the slip. So that pudgy pipsqueak of a clerk was more than happy to bug your new shoes after Prescott gave him $5,000 and told him he was a PI tracking down an unfaithful wife."

The gun wobbled slightly in her hands. "It was easy enough for Richard to plant bugs throughout the inn. He wanted to do that to the cottage the night he arrived, but that bastard Cooper is too sharp."

Meg glanced down at her feet in dumbstruck numbness. The shoes. All this time she'd thought she'd been safe from Prescott.

With every step she took, her ex knew where she headed.

And the steps she needed to take now were out the door, but how could she outrun a bullet? Her only chance was to hurt Claire and grab the gun. Everyone had a weakness, and Prescott's mistress was no exception.

*She likes to brag. Keep her talking.* Meg inched along the wall, toward the doorway.

"What was Randall's involvement? He was a family friend."

"He got scared, gave the money back to Prescott and said he had given you all the information you needed to have Prescott arrested. The stupid old fool. After Prescott threatened him, Jacobs confessed everything and said you had the microchip. Damn you, where is it? I need it!"

"More than you need my husband?"

Claire gave her a quick, startled look.

"I saw the upstairs closet." Meg dragged in a deep breath. "Why did you kill him? If you loved him, why did you kill him?"

"He lied to me!" Wildness flashed in Claire's cold dark eyes. "He swore we'd always be together. He said he was going to leave you and marry me. I'd have everything. Position, power, respectability! But he lied. After I got the missing memos from the security camera, Prescott destroyed them and told me he would never let you go. You were his wife and he'd never divorce you. So he had to die.

"This is all your fault. Prescott loved me, not you! And now you're going to pay for making him stay with you."

The shrill note of the woman's voice rose to hysteria. Claire was unhinged. She had killed the man she loved because he couldn't be faithful…not to his wife or his mistress.

Steely, cold determination shone in the woman's face. Prescott's mistress was crazy. Meg knew Claire would never let her leave alive.

But she knew everything about this house, including the secret passage—leading to an underground tunnel to the barn—in the smallest bedroom upstairs. As a child, Meg had raced through the tunnel with her brother to the barn, until her grandparents closed it off.

They didn't close off the portion leading to the root cellar, however. This would give her a chance.

Her only chance.

Suddenly Claire pivoted her head, still training the gun on Meg. "Outside. Now."

She jabbed the gun in Meg's face, prodding her into the living room. Out of the corner of her eye she saw a shadow slip among the bushes. And then a glimpse of a dear, familiar face.

Cooper! She had to warn him. Claire gestured with the gun. Meg fumbled with the doorknob, pretending it was stuck. "I can't open it."

With a snort of impatience, still training the gun on Meg, Claire sidestepped and reached for the doorknob.

Meg drew out the knife and stabbed Claire, but the woman turned as the knife was raised. The blade sank into her side, not her stomach. A piercing scream tore from her throat, but she didn't drop the gun.

"Cooper, watch out, she has a gun!" she screamed.

Turning, Meg fled up the stairs, zigging and zagging. She heard the gun fire, felt the kiss of the bullet against her cheek. Claire fired again, and the bullet pierced her skin. Stinging pain sliced her side. Fighting shock and the urge to collapse, Meg pushed on.

She had no idea if Cooper was armed or if he heard her. *I'm not going to die here. Not going to let this bitch kill me.*

Meg raced for the last bedroom on the right. Her breath coming in stabbing gasps of pain, she flung open the closet door and fumbled for the hidden access panel in the back. Her shaking fingers found the tiny knob. She pressed against it and the panel popped open.

Instead of a yawning maw of stairs leading into darkness, she was met with a brick wall.

Blocked. No tunnel access. Nearly sobbing with frustration, Meg whipped her gaze around.

She ran into the bathroom and locked the door, hearing Claire's maniacal laugh close behind. She flung open the cabinet door and pawed through the contents. Gran's hairspray.

Uncapping it, she held it out, her finger on the nozzle. Tested it.

Thank God Gran liked aerosol spray cans. If it had been Meg's hair spray, she'd be doomed, because Meg never bought them due to the fact that they ruined the environment. But in this case, what proved devastating to the planet might just save her life.

Footsteps sounded on the stairs, along with a rough, eerie laugh. "You think your puny knife can hurt me? Come out, come out. Or I'll huff and I'll puff and I'll blow your door in!"

The woman was stark-raving insane. Meg prayed this would work in her favor. Prescott's mistress was beyond reason. In her warped perspective, Claire thought killing Meg was justification for all she'd lost.

Even though she, not Meg, had killed Prescott.

Sounds at the doorknob, Claire fumbling with the lock. By the door, Meg squeezed herself into the alcove holding musty towels and bath soap. Waited.

"Ready or not, here I come," Claire sang out.

The door banged open as the woman kicked it. It hit against the cubbyhole where Meg hid. Through the crack in the door, she saw Claire hold out the gun. Saw her turn toward the old-fashioned claw-foot bathtub with the shower curtain. Claire reached for the curtain's edge.

Now!

Meg stepped out and, as Claire turned, sprayed her face. The woman screamed and dropped the gun as she clawed at her burning eyes. Heart pounding, Meg reached down and grabbed the gun, racing out of the bathroom.

She heard Claire behind her and whirled, holding out the pistol. Tears streamed down the other woman's cheeks as she wiped at her face with a towel.

And then Claire threw down the towel and held out the knife Meg used to stab her with. A stray beam of sunlight drifting into the bedroom glinted off the bloodied steel.

"What a useless waste you are, Margaret. Pathetic, sniveling waste. You don't even have the guts to use that on me. You can't shoot me! Prescott told me you're terrified of guns!" Claire laughed and stumbled forward.

Meg's hand shook wildly. She couldn't do this, couldn't fire a gun. And then a deep male voice, a voice she loved, came from the bedroom doorway.

"She can't. But I can."

Cooper! Meg turned, sidestepped, dropped and rolled as Claire rushed at her, screaming. Cooper fired twice.

Screaming, Claire fell onto the floor, blood pouring from the wounds in her shoulder and hip. She struggled to rise and collapsed.

Smoke poured from the muzzle of the pistol he held. Meg hugged herself, the burning pain from her wound making it difficult to breathe.

"So, how was the ride to Boston?" she gasped. "Cut your trip short?"

After checking Claire's pulse, Cooper went over to Meg, still holding his pistol. He gently checked her wound, a deep vee forming between his thick brows.

"Is she…s-still alive?"

He gave a wry smile. "Unfortunately, yes. I didn't kill

her since I'm certain the Feds will want to talk with her about what her father has been doing."

More footsteps sounded on the stairs. Cooper tensed and swung around, then relaxed as Nick, pistol drawn, showed in the doorway. Cooper holstered his gun and tore off his shirt, pressing it against her wound.

"What—" she struggled to catch her breath "—are you doing here?"

"Easy, Princess," Cooper soothed. "You're losing blood. Conserve your strength."

"I told you, Meg. Coop told me to protect his family," Nick said grimly.

"But I'm not family."

Cooper brushed his knuckles against her jawline. "Yes, you are. I called the cops and the paramedics. It's a long distance from town, but they should be here soon."

"How did you know I was in trouble?" she asked.

"Bert Baxter is dead. Whoever you were meeting set you up for a trap," Cooper said.

The scents of clean man, spicy aftershave surrounded her. She focused on Cooper, shutting out the smells of blood and death.

"My husband is dead. My ex." A sob rose in her throat. "I never wanted him dead. All I wanted was to be free to live my life and to get justice, make amends for what my company did. Who will believe me?"

Warm lips brushed against her forehead. "I will. And so will my family, Meg. And the lawyer I hired to defend you."

Her trembling hand reached up to touch his cheek. "You hired a lawyer to protect yourself. I overheard you talking with your brother in the kitchen."

"I hired a lawyer to protect you, Meg. My dime, my lawyer." He brushed another kiss against her chilled skin.

"To protect you, my woman. I told you you'd be safe with me, Princess."

Sirens sounded in the distance. It proved too much effort to keep her eyes open, so Meg closed them. So she wasn't certain if it was her imagination that heard him say softly, "Safe with me, always, and forever."

## Chapter 21

The bullets hadn't struck any of Meg's internal organs. Cooper counted his blessings that she was going to be okay. Today she was leaving the hospital. Everything was ready for her return. Except one small thing he knew he must complete.

Cooper went into Brie's bedroom upstairs at the cottage. He placed the little angel pin into the top drawer. She'd kept all her treasures there, the seashell found on a sandy beach in Maine, a plastic ring given to her by the first boy she'd ever loved and the wooden horse Cooper had carved for her before enlisting.

Cooper stared at the photo on the dresser.

"Stay beside me, Brie, and always be with me. You're free now. You always were."

He closed the drawer, and this time, did not fight the tears brimming in his eyes.

Instead, he hung his head and sobbed for all he had lost.

When he finally finished, he dried his eyes and left the room, closing the door gently behind him.

He loved his sister, would always love her, but at last Cooper felt a sense of peace instead of the terrible emptiness clawing at his chest.

She had died doing what she loved, what fed her purpose. Meg was right. Brie would always walk beside him, in his heart. He didn't need an angel pin to remind him of her love.

It would burn brightly, always inside him.

Meg wasn't looking forward to leaving the hospital, especially with federal authorities waiting in the wings. By now she knew that the police surely must have informed them about her role in all this, especially after Cooper told her about the subpoenaed files from Bert's office. And about Bert, and how he'd been found in Boston Harbor.

Cooper spent many hours with her, brought her flowers, drinks, chocolate and even a video Aimee made of Sophie and Adela.

Jenny came to visit as well.

"I never did anything mean to you, or wanted to hurt you. I only wanted to talk with you," the woman said shyly. "I saw you around the farm, and I saw your bruises. I figured you had been through it, too. And if you could survive and start over, so could I."

Meg studied the woman, understanding at last her timid nature and the fear in her eyes. She touched her hand. "Yes, you can."

And then it was time to leave. Cooper wheeled her outside the hospital and helped her into Fiona's sedan.

When he pulled into the inn's driveway, Meg's jaw dropped.

Everyone stood outside, with balloons and big signs saying Welcome Home. Aimee, Fiona, Nick, Hank, Jenny, Roger and Dan—the two hired hands who worked with the horses—and five people she didn't recognize. Even Derek, Cooper's sullen brother was there, a smile on his face. And Sophie, barking and wagging her tail.

After Cooper helped her out of the car, they all rushed over. There was a flurry of hellos and an enthusiastic hug from Aimee that made her wince, and a gentler one from Fiona.

Cooper introduced the newcomers as his aunt and uncle and their three children. Amid the cacophony, he swung her into his arms and carried her into the inn.

"I can walk," she protested.

"Yeah, but it's more fun like this," he said, winking.

He set her down on the living room sofa. After much talk and greetings, the rest of the family left her alone. Aimee set Sophie down on the sofa beside her.

"She missed you," the girl said, smiling. "She likes sleeping in my bed, but she kept looking for you."

Good smells drifted out, roasted pork and apple pie. The inn smelled like home.

She felt comfortable here, more so than she had in the oceanfront mansion with its horde of servants and gourmet chef. Cooper sat beside her as Derek pulled up a chair, turned it around and straddled it.

Meg stroked Sophie's head, needing to center herself. She had the bad feeling the police detective was going to tell her exactly what was in store for her. And then the authorities would come to question, and probably arrest, her in connection with the scandal rocking through Cooper's small town.

He had harbored not just a battered wife, but a woman whose husband had been murdered by his mistress, and whose lawyer was involved in money laundering and tax fraud for a well-known mobster.

And yet through it all, he'd stuck by her side. Even when his own brother advised him to let her go.

Meg marveled at this as Derek apologized, his dark eyes solemn.

"I've been wrong about you, Meg. I thought you weren't innocent, but now I see you were a victim as much as your grandmother was," Derek told her.

She squeezed Cooper's hand. "Thank you. Did you find out what happened to my grandmother?"

"They exhumed your grandmother and the medical examiner autopsied her body. He found traces of ethylene glycol in her system. It's an ingredient in antifreeze. It tastes sweet, so a small amount wouldn't be detected in a drink that had sugar in it." The detective looked sympathetic. "I'm sorry."

Meg thought back to her grandmother's illness. The first time, when she'd vomited and felt dizzy after consuming sweet tea, Gran had blamed it on an adjustment of her blood pressure pills. A few days later, she felt better. And then she got sick again weeks later.

But she kept getting progressively sicker. The pattern made sense now. Letticia had been slowly poisoned with small doses of antifreeze all the time Prescott had been pressuring Bert Baxter to draft a fake will and trust handing over to him total control of Taylor Sporting Goods so the company could remain private.

The poison had ruined her kidneys, caused her to fall ill. And each time she rallied and seemed to get better enough to take back control of her company, Prescott poisoned her sweet tea again.

Derek told her the rest. In exchange for his testimony against Claire O'Neary and her father, Miles, Kimball broke down and confessed to the murder of Randall Jacobs. He had killed Jacobs on Claire's orders. When she told him police suspected him of the crime, he'd gone in a panic to Randall's summer home to remove the security cameras that recorded him threatening Jacobs when he brought him his cocaine supply.

Kimball had also killed Bert Baxter, after Miles O'Neary worried the lawyer would spill everything to the FBI.

"There was more going on than money laundering, Meg. It had to do with Combat Gear and the vests your company produced."

She clutched Cooper's hand, grateful he seemed rock steady.

"I'm the commander of a drug control unit based at Boston Harbor. Our district in Boston has wanted a way to defend our personnel with military-grade body armor. We got a tip from a confidential informant that a cargo ship from South America arriving in Boston would be smuggling heroin. My unit planned to wear the vests when we raided the ship after it docked in the harbor."

Hah-buh. Cooper's brother had a thick accent.

Cooper spoke up. "Your ex-husband shipped the vests before they were ready."

"Ready for what?" Meg asked.

Derek pulled out a photo from a manila envelope on the coffee table. The color photo showed a small pellet. "This is C-17, a new explosive on the market. Big as a pencil eraser, stable as C-4, but one exception. It reacts to extreme, violent force. Like bullets. Small enough to conceal inside the fabric of a bulletproof vest."

Cooper squeezed her hand. "They didn't want the vests to fail because of the fibers. They wanted to make bulletproof vests like suicide bomber vests."

Her mind spun. "My product would have been made to kill police instead of protecting them?"

Derek nodded. "Many cops, like me, test out the vests with their handguns before wearing them. O'Neary had a man on the inside who would swap out the vests in our lockers before the raid, replacing them with the body armor containing the C-17. Bastard had been dreaming up this plan for a while, but needed the right kind of vest and the right contact."

"But the vests were already defective," Meg realized. "Prescott shipped the defective vests before the explosives could be planted."

"Thanks to you calling the FBI and alerting them about the defective vests, my brother is alive, Meg." Cooper picked up her hand and brushed a kiss against her knuckles. "And maybe, in her own way, Brie helped save the lives of hundreds of officers. If she hadn't died and the defect been discovered, O'Neary's plan might have succeeded."

"Miles O'Neary couldn't risk control of the company going out of your ex-husband's hands. They had him under their thumbs and needed him to stay there. And going public meant tighter federal scrutiny, the last thing they wanted," Derek explained.

Relief swept through her. Some good had been achieved through all this. "What's going to happen to me?"

Cooper stroked his thumb across her trembling hand. "My attorney has arranged for you to turn yourself into the Feds tomorrow. But he's very certain you'll get immunity from any prosecution in exchange for testifying about how Prescott deliberately sent those vests. We're still searching for the microchip. The police have been through every inch of your grandmother's farm."

"Randall said it was close to my heart. Meaning, it wouldn't be at my Palm Beach home, but someplace I treasured. Or someone."

Meg stroked her dog's head. And then she scratched under her chin, her fingers toying with the little gold heart on her collar.

"My heart," she said slowly. "Close to my heart...my best friend."

Cooper and Derek exchanged glances. She unhooked

the dog's collar and examined the heart charm. It seemed too obvious, too simple…

Using the edge of the fingernail file Derek found for her, Meg pried the heart apart. Inside rested a tiny black chip, no larger than her fingernail.

Wonder filled her. After all this time, it was close to her heart—her dog.

Derek took it and they went into Fiona's office. Using an adapter, he inserted it into the desktop computer. Meg's breath hitched as Derek clicked on the files and up popped the documents.

The emails, sent by Prescott, ordered Randall to ship out the vests to the contact he'd made at the Boston PD.

Derek clicked on another icon and brought up a voice recording from Randall addressed to her, confessing his part in her grandmother's death. He had a copy of Letticia Taylor's original will in a safe-deposit box in his bank, a copy Prescott had ordered him to destroy, but he had not.

Randall confessed he'd only meant to sicken Letticia, not kill her, but he was being blackmailed by Prescott, who threatened to tell police about Randall's cocaine habit.

He had introduced Prescott to Claire, the youngest O'Neary daughter, at a party at his summer home while Meg had been home sick. The pair had threatened him and ordered him to ship the vests to the Boston PD. Randall warned Miles O'Neary planned "something big" to permanently take out the drug control unit that had succeeded in several raids seizing heroin shipments.

Hearing the stoic tones of Randall's voice filled Meg with grief. Such a waste. Randall had everything: power, money, prestige. And he threw it all away to gain even more power, a plan that backfired.

Derek closed out the files. "I'll make copies to send to the Feds, Meg."

She nodded, her throat tight. "All I ever wanted was to protect police, protect young, good cops who were on the front lines, in memory of my brother."

Cooper's brother touched her shoulder. "Thanks, Meg."

When he left, she sat for a long while staring at the blank computer screen. They'd had good times once, Gran, Prescott and Randall, so excited about taking the company to the next level. The fibers Randall invented that promised to deliver precision racquetball paddles and tennis balls. She remembered how they sat around the office, cracking open the champagne to toast Randall's new discovery, and how proud and happy the man had been.

She had been a part of that as well. And now they were all gone.

Cooper, sitting beside her, wound a strand of her hair around his index finger.

"You okay, Princess?"

His deep voice jerked her back to the present. Meg smiled and wiped away a stray tear. "I will be. It's truly all over now. Or it will be after I talk with the authorities."

"We'll save that for tomorrow. Today is for you. For us. I have something to show you."

Cooper unfolded his big body from the chair and went to a file cabinet. After unlocking it, he withdrew a small black velvet box. And then he sat next to her, and opened the box.

Upon the black velvet sat a small round diamond, surrounded by diamond baguettes.

"My grandmother's ring. She gave it to the family with the stipulation that the first Johnson child to marry give it to his bride."

Meg's breath caught in her throat.

"It's too much to ask now, and I won't expect you to answer with everything you've been through. But when you are ready, Princess, I want you to consider wearing this.

And being mine for life, just as I know I love you and you're the only one I will ever want as my life partner."

She touched the ring. No huge two-carat stone like Prescott had insisted on giving her. Nothing pretentious, just a simple diamond that was solid and lasting and real, layered with a tradition of love and commitment.

Exactly like the man holding it out.

More tears fell, but this time she made no attempt to check them. "I'm ready now, sailor. I love you, too. And the answer is yes."

He slid the ring on her finger. Perfect fit.

Just like the man.

As he kissed her, Meg let all her past fears evaporate. There would be plenty of stormy weather ahead. She didn't know what the future held, but no longer would she worry.

With Cooper by her side, she would weather whatever storms life tossed her way.

# *Epilogue*

*One year later*

Perfect weather for a grand opening.

A crispness snapped in the air, the cool wind brushing against the lingering color on the thick oak, hickory and birch trees near the restored farmhouse. Fields that once hosted only crops of corn and barley now boasted running tracks, bike paths and tennis courts. The dairy now held rows of mooing cows, and modern machinery to send fresh milk out to a local cheese producer.

On the nearby bike path, amputees rode specially designed bicycles in mock races. The shooting range, which Cooper would personally oversee upon his discharge from the Navy, was farther off, in a secluded cove.

Meg had hired therapists to staff the facility, and with income from the dairy and civilians who wanted to train with a former Navy SEAL, she anticipated the foundation would become solvent in another year.

The farmhouse had been converted into an inn, with additional accessible housing added onto the expanded home. Wheelchair ramps, renovated bathrooms, all fit for disabled veterans. One section of the farmhouse had been converted to offices, where Meg and her team of career counselors would help veterans with job skills, assessments and placement.

And if they needed to talk shop, about how tough it was to adjust to civilian life after the military, there'd be Cooper, because he would soon make the same adjustment.

Lacey and Jarrett flew in for the ceremony. Their daughter, Fleur, had joined Aimee in an impromptu game of soccer with one of the many soccer balls Taylor Sporting Goods donated. Sophie chased the girls and the other children as they raced down the field.

All that was needed to make the day perfect was Derek and Cooper. Derek had begged off because of work, and Cooper wasn't expecting his full discharge from the Navy for at least three weeks.

Meg glanced down at the heirloom engagement ring on her left hand. One year ago, she'd agreed to marry Cooper Johnson, and formally said yes in front of all his assembled family. They'd set a wedding date for December.

She'd always longed to be married at Christmastime.

After being cleared by the FBI, Meg had assumed control of Taylor Sporting Goods as CEO and president of the board of directors, according to the terms of her grandmother's will. And then she'd sold the company for a cool $100 million, along with Combat Gear Inc., and started a new enterprise. The results were standing before them now.

If only Cooper were here.

A red silk ribbon stretched across two poles before the new center. Meg chatted with Lacey. Nearby, Jarrett talked to Nick as he cradled their five-month-old son, Mark, who decided to release a healthy wail like a fire siren. The screams continued until Jarrett popped a bottle into the baby's mouth.

Lacey grinned.

"He takes after his father. Demanding and vocal, until you pay attention to him." Her former sorority sister's face softened as she gazed at her husband and son.

"Thank you," Meg told her. "If not for you and Jarrett, I'd never have met Cooper."

Lacey smiled. "I had thought about introducing you at our wedding, but you still had that millstone of your ex around your neck. I'm so glad things turned out well for you, Meg."

They hugged.

Fiona gave her an expectant look. It was time.

As the crowd assembled near the red silk ribbon, she heard a car pull up behind them. Latecomers.

And then she heard doors slam and Derek call out, "Hey, anyone have room for an old sailor?"

Meg whirled and saw Cooper in blue battle dress uniform striding toward her. He swept her up in a bear hug, whirling around as she laughed and hugged him back.

"I didn't think you could make it!"

"Lacey's dad managed to pull some strings with the brass. Helps to know people in high places." Cooper kissed her, hard and deep. "I needed to get home to my woman. Wouldn't have it any other way."

The possessive note in his voice sent a tingle straight from her head to her toes. Meg hugged him again and thanked Derek, who grinned back at her.

Then the Johnson family assembled before the ribbon. Fiona handed Meg the scissors. Her throat closed up as she gazed at the brass letters on the building.

The Sabrina Fletcher & Caldwell Taylor Veterans Center.

Two people, both young and zealous and dedicated to justice, would be forever remembered after this day.

Cooper placed his warm, calloused hand on hers. In one fluid motion, they cut the ribbon, severing ties to the past. And welcoming a new future—together.

\* \* \* \* \*

*Look for the next thrilling installment in Bonnie Vanak's SOS AGENCY series, coming soon!*

*Don't forget the previous title in the series:*

*NAVY SEAL SEDUCTION*

*Available now from Harlequin.com!*

Allison raised her head with every intention of stepping
away from him. But his arms pulled her closer to him and
his lips crashed down on hers.

The kiss erased all rational thought from her mind.
Instead, all her senses came gloriously alive as Knox's
mouth made love to hers. His tongue swirled with hers as
his scent suffused her, and the heat of his hands on her back
invited her to melt against his broad chest. Their bodies fit
together perfectly, as if they had been made for each other.

He finally left her lips to slide his mouth down the column
of her throat. As her knees weakened with desire, rational
thought slammed back into her. She jerked back from him,
appalled by how quickly, how completely, he could break
down all her defenses.

His eyes radiated a raw hunger as he held her gaze
intently. "Despite everything that has happened between

HRSEXP0217R

us, I still want you. There's always been something strong between us, Allison, and you can't deny that it's still there."

No, she couldn't deny it, but she also wouldn't admit it to him. "It doesn't matter." She took two steps back from him, needing not only to emotionally distance herself but to physically distance herself, as well.

"That kiss was a mistake. I don't feel that way about you anymore." Okay, maybe she could deny it, but she could tell by the look in his eyes that he didn't believe her.

"In any case, anything like that between us would be foolish and it would only complicate things. We aren't going there again, Knox, and now I think it's time we say good-night."

She breathed a sigh of relief when he nodded and turned to walk to the front door. Her legs were still shaky as she accompanied him.

"I'm sorry about my little breakdown," she said.

He turned to face her and before she could read his intentions he grabbed her and once again planted a kiss on her lips.

It was short and searing and when he released her his eyes sparkled with a knowing glint. "The next time you try to tell me you don't feel that way about me anymore, say it like you really mean it," he said, and then he was gone into the night.

*Don't miss*
*COLTON'S SECRET SON by Carla Cassidy,*
*available March 2017 wherever*
*Harlequin® Romantic Suspense books*
*and ebooks are sold.*

www.Harlequin.com